# Dr. Critchlore's
## School for Minions

AMULET BOOKS
NEW YORK

# Dr. Critchlore's School for Minions

## SHEILA GRAU

ILLUSTRATED BY
### JOE SUTPHIN

Library of Congress Cataloging-in-Publication Data

Grau, Sheila.
Dr. Critchlore's School for Minions / by Sheila Grau.
pages cm
Summary: At his boarding school for monsters, a young werewolf learns a devastating truth about his family while uncovering a plot to sabotage the world's finest training program for aspiring minions to evil overlords.
ISBN 978-1-4197-1370-5
[1. Monsters—Fiction. 2. Werewolves—Fiction. 3. Boarding schools—Fiction. 4. Schools—Fiction. 5. Mystery and detective stories.] I. Title.
II. Title: Doctor Critchlore's School for Minions.
PZ7.1.G73Dr 2015
[Fic]—dc23
2014029584

Text copyright © 2015 Sheila Grau
Illustrations copyright © 2015 Joe Sutphin
Book design by Jessie Gang

Printed and bound in U.S.A.
10 9 8 7 6 5 4 3 2 1

Amulet Books are available at special discounts when purchased in quantity for premiums and promotions as well as fundraising or educational use. Special editions can also be created to specification. For details, contact specialsales@abramsbooks.com or the address below.

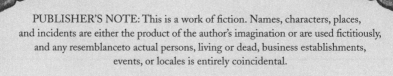

ABRAMS
THE ART OF BOOKS SINCE 1949
115 West 18th Street
New York, NY 10011
www.abramsbooks.com

FOR JUAN

Dr. Critchlore's
School for Minions

A Castle
B Dorms
C Necromancy
D Memorial Courtyard
E Garden
F Tootles's Tree House
G Dead Man's Peak
H Aviary

I   Dragon Stable/
    Animal Pens
J   Boulderball Field
K   Practice Siege Wall

L   Hedge Maze
M   Sports Fields
N   Mount Curiosity

# Dr. Critchlore's

**Dr. Derek Critchlore**
*Headmaster*

**Miss Karen Merrybench**
*School Secretary*

**Dr. Cyril Frankenhammer**
*Professor of Biology*

Frank 25

Pismo Aquova

Runt Higgins

Syke Smith

# School for Minions

Mr. Casper Vodum
*Professor of Necromancy*

Darthin Berg

Janet Desmarais

Mistress Moira
*School Seamstress/Chocolatier*

Eloni Tatupu

Boris Tumblewrecker

# CHAPTER 1

*Give a man a fish, and he eats for a day.*
*Give a man a minion, and the minion will fish for him.*
—ANCIENT MINION PROVERB

The beast in front of me had the body of a lion, a human face with three rows of very sharp teeth, and a scorpion's tail tipped with a barb the size of an ice pick. The manticore was a triple threat of maiming, biting, and poisoning—and she was in my way.

She wasn't the only one. The courtyard was crowded with bodies jostling to get a look at the list posted on the wall. The manticore reared up on her hind legs, and I had to jump back to avoid her barb.

"Can you see anything?" I asked.

"No," she said, plopping back down. "Those ogres are blocking my view."

Most of the students in front of me were first-years, looking for their dorm assignments. I was a third-year, hoping that this time, for once, they had moved me to the right dorm.

"I'll probably be in the Monster Minion Dormitory," the manticore said.

"The Momido." I nodded. "Unless it's full. Sometimes they put monsters in the D-Hum."

1

"The D-Hum?"

"The Dormitory for Human Minions," I said. I should know; I'd been stuck there for two years. Last year I'd missed out on some important events because the notices had only been posted in the Momido. And not just the fun stuff like Night Prowls and games of Capture the Human. I was late signing up for the MMA tournament, and that really stung. I loved Mixed Monster Arts.

"Hey, ogres!" I yelled.

Three warty faces turned to look down at me, their bottom fangs jutting up like boars' tusks. They were kids, barely eight feet tall, but honestly, there was only one option for them.

"Try the Dormitory for Minions of Impressive Size," I suggested, pointing to the list on the right.

They waved their clubs in thanks and moved out of the way. I grabbed the manticore's tail and swung it in front of me like a sword, forcing her to follow me backward. "Excuse me! Third-year, coming through!" We edged past a bunch of kids who looked human, but they could've been anything—werewolves, vampires, shape-shifters, or actual humans (their bad luck). I pushed through a couple of monkey-men, a lizard-boy, and some mummies. At last we reached the wall.

I held my breath, partly because I was nervous, and partly because the mummies smelled like piles of old gym socks with morning breath. I scanned the Momido room assignments. "Runt Higgins," I whispered. "Come on. Where's my name?" My heart beat faster as I scrolled down the list.

It wasn't there.

"This has got to be a mistake," I said, and I started over at the top.

2

"There I am," said the manticore, pointing her barbed tail at the name "Tiffany Smithers-Pendleton." She reached into her backpack with her tail. When she brought it out, a piece of paper was impaled on the end. "Do you know where I turn in my immunization record?"

I pointed in the direction of the infirmary. I couldn't speak. A cold dread filled my body. I didn't have to check the other lists. I knew I was back in the D-Hum.

The D-Hum! Oh, the humanity! (And I mean that literally.)

# CHAPTER 2

*Slow and steady wins the race,*
*if you have minions to sabotage your opponent.*

—ANCIENT MINION PROVERB

The D-Hum was a two-story wood-shingled building with peeling white trim. It looked like an unwanted toolshed next to its neighbor, the Dormitory for Minions of Impressive Size (the D-MIS). That immense stone building had a wide portico, giant Ionic columns, and two stone griffins standing guard at the bottom of the steps. Their motto was engraved above the missing front door: "Anything in Our Way Will Be Destroyed."

By contrast, the motto above the D-Hum read, "Just Do Your Best."

I didn't belong in the D-Hum. I belonged in the Momido with the other werewolves, but it had been full two years ago, when I was a first-year. It was full last year too, because monster minions are always in high demand. Humans, on the other hand, are not.

When I returned to the D-Hum, I found my roommate Darthin standing in front of a mirror as he adjusted some fake horns on his head. He'd also painted himself gray.

"What are you doing?" I asked. Besides the fake horns and gray skin, his blond hair had been slicked flat and he smiled with fake fangs.

"I'm gonna be a gargoyle," he said. "At Mad Scientist Camp, they said gargoyles make the best assistants. Every mad scientist wants one. They're very protective, really scary, and can turn into stone. I'm not sure why that's good, but they can do it. And if they have wings, they can reach things on high shelves."

"Don't they sometimes eat people?" I asked.

"That's actually another plus," Darthin said. "Mad scientists need someone to blame for the, ah, accidental deaths."

"Why don't you be a mad scientist yourself?" I asked. "You're the smartest guy I know."

"Too much pressure," he said. "All those presentations. I hate oral reports, you know that." He turned back to the mirror, pulling on some gloves that had claws built into the fingers. "I'm just testing out the look. If I like it, I think I can concoct a potion to make the changes more permanent."

"Oh . . . kay." Poor Darthin. He probably wanted to look like a monster because they terrified him. He rarely left the dorm if he was alone; he was so frightened of bumping into a mummy or an ogre, or anything else nonhuman.

"I heard you made it into the Junior Henchman Training Program," he said. "Congratulations."

"Thanks."

I stood behind him and checked myself out in the mirror. I felt different, even though I looked the same, wearing the school uniform of black cargo pants, black cross-trainers, and white T-shirt decorated with the school's symbol, a blue griffin. I zipped up my

6

new jacket, in third-year colors: tan with black down the sides. It had the Critchlore family crest embroidered as a pocket logo on one side, my name on the other.

The same old me, but now I was one of the elites: a junior henchman trainee. I was on solid footing for a great career.

As soon as I thought this, the building shook, knocking Darthin and me to the floor.

Fight sounds tumbled in through the open window. I got up and raced over, Darthin right behind me. Next door at the D-MIS, a bunch of ogres jostled one another as they chased a giant through the entryway.

It was no surprise, really, that they didn't have a door.

The floor shook again. Shouts and curses filled the air. A couple of ogres tackled the giant and sat on him, trying to get him to say "Uncle."

"Wally!" I yelled at one of the ogres.

Darthin slugged me on the shoulder. "What are you doing?" he whispered. "He'll see us."

"Darthin, relax. They're nice," I said, for the millionth time. "Wally! What's going on?"

Wally turned around to see who was calling. I was right in front of him. From my second-floor window, I was practically at his eye level.

"Over here, Wally!" I yelled, waving my arms.

He looked to his left. Then his right.

"Wally!"

Finally he spotted me. "Hi, Higgins!" He waved.

"What's going on?" I asked again.

"Knute called ogres sissies," he said. Then he jumped up and landed on Knute's belly.

"Really?" I asked. "Why?"

"'Cause they are!" Knute yelled. Then he lost his breath from another crushing blow. "Didn't you see the video?"

"What video?" I yelled, but nobody answered. A few giants came to Knute's defense, and the ground shook from the giant-ogre scrum.

"We could look it up on the library computer," Darthin said, but I didn't answer. I was watching the size XXXXXXL minions punch and tackle each other, sometimes drawing blood. It was such a tender scene that I felt a pang of loneliness. I missed my pack. I kissed my medallion, the only thing they'd left me. It was the size of a small coin, and it had a wolf's head in the center. I wore it always.

"All that wrestling and chasing and biting reminds me of my family," I said. I remembered feeling safe, snuggled together at night, the soft feel of their fur, and the musty smell of their bodies. The way Dad used to lead the nightly howling. How Mom licked my face clean. "Haven't seen them in eight years."

"My family's being held hostage in Upper Worb," Darthin said.

"What?"

"To make sure I return, after I get my education. Our evil over-lord, the Exalted Irma Trackno, doesn't like defectors."

I'd heard about hostage families. Some people don't enjoy the oppression and despair of their life under an evil overlord, and they would leave if they had a chance. The EOs are in a tough spot—they have to send people to Stull, the country with the best schools, but they also have to make sure they return. One way to do this is to keep the students' family members hostage.

"She imprisoned them?" I asked.

"Nope. They're just watched so they don't leave. They share an apartment with a nice family of yetis. It's cold, but they have cable TV."

"What happens if you don't go back?"

"The Great and Kind Irma will kill my family."

"She doesn't sound very kind, or great," I said. "I wonder where my family is." Upper Worb? Bluetorch? Pinnacles? They could be anywhere. At least I knew they weren't being held hostage. I hadn't been sent to Stull. I'd been left at the school when I wasn't able to keep up with my pack. I was the runt of the litter and I should have died, but my family loved me and left me somewhere I'd be safe.

A giant picked up a chunk of stone that had broken off the facade and threw it. Darthin screamed as it zipped our way. We ducked just as it struck, hitting right above our window and sending splinters of wood on top of us.

We were brushing off the dust when our other roommate, Frank Twenty-five, stumbled into the room. He looked green, which was not his natural color.

"What's the matter, Frankie?" I asked.

He turned to me, a look of fear on his face. "We have to watch a video."

# CHAPTER 3

*Sometimes, monsters are hard to see.*
—FROM THE TEXTBOOK *MINION SPECIES*,
BY DR. D. CRITCHLORE

W hat video?" I asked.

"I don't know," Frankie said. "But everyone's saying it could ruin the school."

Frankie stood in front of me, frantically twisting one of the bolts in his neck, back and forth, back and forth.

Frankie was Dr. Frankenhammer's twenty-fifth attempt to create a superhuman. Even though he was as skinny as a grasshopper, he was faster and stronger than a full-grown man, or even a full-grown ogre. If he'd thrown that chunk of stone, we probably wouldn't have a wall above our window. He had a flattop of black hair, caveman eyebrows, and bolts on the side of his neck that he fiddled with when he was nervous, which was always.

The three of us had been roommates for two years. I felt a little guilty for wanting to move out, but I didn't belong with them. Sometimes I wondered if they'd make it as minions. My foster brother, Pierre, a human, graduated five years ago and wasn't recruited by a single evil overlord. Now he worked in the kitchen with my foster mother, Cook.

Frankie and Darthin were both looking at me. I knew what they wanted, but I had to fix my dorm assignment.

"It's the only place we can watch it," Darthin said.

"I'm sorry, but I have to go see Miss Merrybench," I said.

"What if it does ruin the school?" Frankie said. "What will happen to me? I don't have any other home."

I didn't either, but I thought Frankie was overreacting.

"Everyone's talking about it," Frankie said. "So it's got to be bad, right?" He started pacing. Twisting his bolts and pacing.

"Higgins," Darthin whispered. He nodded at Frankie, and I knew what he meant. Frankie was losing it.

"Daddy's already working on a new model," Frankie went on. He had stopped twisting and was holding the top of his head down, which was a very bad sign. "What if he doesn't want me anymore?"

He let go to hug himself, and when he did—

*Pop!*

His head shot up into the air, landed with a thump, and rolled under his bed. And then, just like a chicken in similar circumstances, Frankie's body began to race around the room, arms outstretched. Blood spurted out: a fountain of red that almost reached the ceiling before his strong neck muscles contracted to slow the gush to a gurgling trickle.

"Quick!" I said, slipping in blood as I reached for him. "I'll grab his body. Darthin, you get his head."

I grabbed the squirming, headless body in a tight bear hug. As blood dribbled over me, I thought it was a good thing Frankie didn't bunk with the vampires. He'd never get his head back on.

Re-heading Frankie was really a four-person operation: one to hold the head, one the body, and two to peel down the neck skin and hook all the tubes back together. It was risky, but I decided to turn off Frankie's blood pump, which stopped his body from squirming, making it easier for Darthin and me to reattach his head. Once we got it all hooked up, I flicked the switch back on and Frankie collapsed in my arms.

"C'mon, buddy," I said. "Wake up."

At last he opened his eyes, blinking a couple of times as he tried to figure out what had happened.

"We'll go watch the video, Frankie," I said, before he could get worked up again.

"Thanks."

The library was located in the West Wing of the castle, on the other side of the foyer from the cafeteria. They were the same size, but where the cafeteria was bright and loud, the library, with its metal bookshelves, heavy carpeting, and thick drapes, was gloomy and quiet. It smelled like neglect: a collection of musty odors that had aged and melded together over decades.

The library was unappealing for a reason. Uncle Ludwig, the librarian, didn't like to be bothered while he worked on his own research. He also kept library operating hours short—and changed them every day, so they were impossible to remember.

I could get us inside, though, even when it was closed.

We approached the double doors, and I peeked in through one of the decorative glass inserts, tapping lightly.

"Uncle Ludwig?" I called. He wasn't really my uncle, but he'd asked me to call him that since forever. "You in there?"

I heard a scuffling of feet, a lot of mumbling, and then the door opened.

"Mumble, mumble . . . Dogsbody Higgins!" Uncle Ludwig peered down his nose and through his glasses at me. He had a habit of mumbling his thoughts out loud, like he was talking to an invisible person standing next to him. He looked to the side. "The Ice Shelves of Dorn, of course." Then he looked back at me. "Have you been assigned to me again? I need help reshelving books."

Before I became a student two years ago, I was an all-around helper at the school. They called me "Dogsbody," probably because of my werewolf-ness. I'd worked in the kitchens, cleaned labs, swept out animal stalls, and done just about any other grunt work you can think of. I knew every living thing, every dark hallway, and every brick of the castle. I'd also spent a lot of time reshelving books for Uncle Ludwig.

"No, Uncle Ludwig. I'm a student now." I pointed to my jacket.

"Of course, of course," he said, turning around and snapping his fingers for me to follow. "The books are over here . . . Or the Etarne Cliffs, mumble, mumble."

I chased after him, my friends following. "I'm not here to reshelve books. I was wondering if I could use a computer."

"Good luck with that." He sat down behind a desk piled so high with papers and books that he nearly disappeared behind it. "The network's been sabotaged three times this week. Can't get any online research done. Not that it matters. As soon as I find a useful site, the EO Council takes it down. *Hmmph.*" He picked up a stack of papers. "Maybe Wickerly's Half Domes. Why didn't I think of them before?"

"Is it okay if my friends come too?"

He looked up at me and ran a hand through his tangled brown hair. "Hagritano, maybe. Hmm? Yes, you can all reshelve books."

"Uncle Ludwig," I said, looking him in the eye, "my friends and I want to use the computer."

"Yes, yes," he said. "You'll help me reshelve books before dinner, then?"

"Sure."

"Fine." He shooed me away. "What are you bothering me for? Honestly. How I get any work done is a mystery. Mumble, mumble."

I waved my friends inside. Frankie had the computer up and going in no time. He found the MonsterTube video site, one of the few sites not blocked by the Evil Overlord Council. Darthin and I stood behind him as he searched for "Critchlore ogres" and scrolled through the list.

"There it is," Frankie said. "'Epic Minion Fail.'"

Oh no! It had gone viral. Suddenly it felt like I had a thousand bats flitting around in my stomach. Frankie clicked on "Play."

Trees framed the opening shot: a group of minions standing at the edge of a cliff in a defensive position. From the camera's point of view, we could only see the minions. Whatever they were facing was out of sight, behind the cameraman, who was hiding at the forest's edge. We could hear his frantic breathing as the camera shook in his unsteady hand.

"Look, there's Reggie Clobberman," Darthin said. He reached over Frankie to point. Reggie had graduated last year. He and the rest of the minions were ogre-men, which meant they were huge, cruel, and hideous, like ogres, but smart, like humans. It was an excellent mix of traits for a minion.

Those ogre-men were everything we strove to be: fearsome, powerful, and vicious. But on-screen they were cowering, frightened, and feeble.

"What's attacking them?" Darthin asked.

"Some kind of monster, I bet," Frankie said, still fiddling with the bolt in his neck. "Something huge."

"Or a pack of werewolves," I said.

As the video played, the minions held up swords and clubs, swinging them at the air. Some glanced behind, looking for an escape. They were terrified, and my heart thumped in frantic sympathy. One ogre-man threw down his club and begged for mercy.

Suddenly the band of minions jumped in fright. The ones in the front accidentally shoved the ones in back off the cliff. We heard screams, and the video shook as the cameraman moved to a safer location.

Five ogre-men remained. Their heads swiveled as they looked down at their fallen comrades, back at their attacker, then back down. At last, they jumped, preferring a painful, deadly plunge to fighting whatever stalked them.

I bit my lip and blinked fast. *Those poor guys.*

Frankie sighed. "That was pitiful."

"What could do that?" Darthin asked.

"Doesn't matter," Frankie said. "It could have been a battalion of vampires riding armored dragons, followed by a pack of werewolves. There's no excuse for cowardice."

That was true. Last year we'd taken a class called There's No Excuse for Cowardice.

"Don't remind me," Darthin said. He'd failed the class. Darthin could find lots of excuses for cowardice.

"Look," Frankie said, pointing back to the screen.

The attackers had come into view. It had been a pack, all right. The video stabilized as they entered the field of vision, moving forward as one, right to the edge of the cliff. They wore matching uniforms: brown shorts, vests covered with small round badges, berets perched jauntily over ponytails.

They were Girl Explorers—little human girls who did crafts projects, sold cookies, and manufactured explosives.

They threw cookies at the fallen minions, and I heard faint screams. I was so relieved the ogre-men weren't dead that it took me a moment to realize what this video meant.

A minion school depended on its reputation more than any-

thing. Those ogre-men were last year's graduates—and they'd just been scared to death (or, rather, scared to injury) by a group of girls in kneesocks. This could ruin the school, no doubt. The guys were quiet, too shocked to breathe.

"It's got to be some sort of trick," I said. "A video mash-up or something."

I looked at Darthin, who knew more about this stuff than any of us. And by "this stuff" I meant "everything." Darthin's hobby was curiosity. He started nearly every sentence with "I wonder . . ." And then he'd find out.

He shook his head. "I don't know. It looks real."

"I can't wait to see what Critchlore does about this," Frankie said. He giggled. "Somebody's gonna pay, and pay big."

Darthin nodded. "Nobody embarrasses Dr. Critchlore and lives to laugh about it."

"True," I said. "He once flooded an entire town when someone there said his banshees wailed too quietly." The evil overlords who ruled the countries around Stull had nothing on Dr. Critchlore.

"Let's go," I said. "I've got to see Miss Merrybench."

"After reshelving!" Uncle Ludwig called.

"Okay, Uncle Ludwig." I turned back to my friends. "You guys go to dinner. I'll catch up later."

I walked over to Uncle Ludwig's desk. He didn't look up, just pointed to the reshelving carts. There were six of them, stuffed full of books. Flea dip, what had I agreed to?

It took me ages to reshelve two carts, and in that time Uncle Ludwig filled two more.

"I've gotta go to dinner," I said. "I'll finish the rest later."

"Right, right," he said.

My stomach rumbled with hunger, or maybe it was worry. Put in the wrong dorm, and now this horrible video. My third year at Dr. Critchlore's School for Minions had gotten off to a terrible start. I told myself it could only get better from here.

# CHAPTER 4

*I love my Critchlore Flying Monkeys!*
—THE WICKED WITCH OF WEST CHAMBOR,
IN AN ADVERTISING TESTIMONIAL

After dinner and more reshelving, it had been too late to catch Miss Merrybench and fix my dorm assignment, so I headed to her office first thing in the morning.

Honestly, I'd rather collect bat dookie in the Caves of Doom than visit our school secretary on the first day of school. Miss Merrybench was a thin woman who wore flowery blouses and a scowl that could make an angry ogre jump back in fear. (I'd seen it happen. Twice.) It only took one glance at her desk to know she was as tough as they came. Perched on the corner was the trophy she'd won in the Iron Woman Triathlon. That's the race where contestants swim through shark-infested water, run from hungry devil hounds, and cycle through the Primeval Forest while imps shout rude things about their bike shorts.

I approached her door, bracing myself for a blast of Merrybench anger. I took a deep breath, just like I had during that cave job, and opened it.

She looked up at me, her famous scowl turned to maximum power. I'd heard that, once, long ago, she'd eaten a piece of face-freezing curse candy that tasted like ogre breath. I wasn't sure if that was true, but she always looked annoyed, so who knew?

Plus it helped to think that maybe she was smiling on the inside.

"Mr. Higgins," she said. Then she made a little puffy sound, sort of a cross between a sigh and a grunt. A quick exhale that told me *This had better be good.* It also told me that she probably wasn't smiling on the inside.

I was about to launch into my plea when a buzz sounded from her desk. She held up a finger for me to wait. "Dr. Critchlore's School for Minions," she said into her headset.

She made shooing motions at me, but I pretended not to notice. I sat down in one of the chairs along the wall, next to an imp named Spanky. The little green guy's hands were bound, which wasn't surprising. Imps had long fingers that itched to steal things.

He nodded at Merrybench's Iron Woman trophy. "Know why the devil hounds don't catch 'em?" I shook my head. "'Cause they can't stop laughing at them ridiculous bike shorts." He snorted with laughter and I shushed him. I did not want to get on Miss Merrybench's bad side this morning.

"What'cha in for?" he asked.

"They put me in the D-Hum," I whispered. He eyed me up and down, and I knew what he was thinking: I looked like a scrawny human boy. But there was a powerful werewolf inside me. Once, when I was seven, a giant swamp creature broke into our house, screaming and smashing furniture. In that moment of terror, I'd morphed into a werewolf and scared him off. So, yeah, I was fierce.

But it hadn't happened since, and even though my foster mother, Cook, kept telling me I needed to wait until puberty, I knew that if I was with my kind in the Momido, I'd morph again. I just had to wait for Miss Merrybench to finish on the phone so she could move me there.

"I told you before," Miss Merrybench said into her headset. "Dr. Critchlore has no comment. That video is a fake." She disconnected and hit the next button on her console. "Good morning, Dr. Critchlore's office." There were four more blinking buttons. *Dog whistles! This is gonna take forever.*

I picked up a brochure from the table next to me. Dr. Critchlore's face filled the cover, along with the words: "In a world run by evil overlords, you're either a minion or you're nothing. Train with the best at Dr. Critchlore's School for Minions!"

Inside were pictures of powerful minions and a map of the Porvian Continent, separated into the seven Greater Realms, the thirteen Lesser Realms, the Dismantled Realm, and the Island Realms. There was no mention of the Forgotten Realm. Red dots indicated where Critchlore minions had been placed. "This could be you!" was written next to an arrow pointing to the capital of Lower Worb, realm of the superpowerful Wexmir Smarvy.

I'd never seen a recruitment brochure before. We were always bursting with minions.

"I'm from Bluetorch," Spanky said, pointing to a country south of Stull, where our school was located. "I miss the food, but not the daily calls to admiration."

"The what?"

"Every hour a gong rings and we have to say something nice

about our EO, Dark Victor. 'Dark Victor is so handsome,' 'Dark Victor is so smart,' 'Dark Victor makes the best cheese soufflé.'"

I was glad, yet again, that the Neutral Region of Stull was not ruled by an evil overlord. The United Nations of Overlords was located here, and the EOs had an agreement not to attack our country. We lived in an oasis of peace in a warring world.

". . . Yes, Your Supremacy," Miss Merrybench said. "He's well aware of your concerns. I assure you, there is absolutely nothing wrong with the minions you recruited last spring. That video is a fake. Our minions have been, and always will be, top-notch."

I looked at Dr. Critchlore's open office door, and a thought popped into my brain—*he* could switch my dorm assignment. Why not? Hadn't he just selected me for the Junior Henchman Training Program, the most exclusive training the school offered? He'd want me in the right dorm.

"Go for it," Spanky said, as if reading my thoughts.

I looked down and saw him unwrapping a piece of my explosive gum. I hadn't even felt him reaching into my pocket. I grabbed it back, then nodded toward Miss Merrybench. She didn't have fangs or claws, but she held a ruler, and I had a feeling she knew how to use it.

Spanky shrugged. "You probably wouldn't want to, anyway. Critchlore scares the fur off my fingers."

Most kids thought he was scary. Most monsters thought he was scary. But Dr. Critchlore was like a father to me. I'd known him as long as I could remember.

"General Nix, you've recruited minions from us before; you know they are first-rate," Miss Merrybench said. "Don't believe that video. Why, if you look at the brochure, the customer testimonials . . ." She spun around in her chair and opened a file cabinet.

This was my chance. I sped past her desk and slipped into Dr. Critchlore's office, stopping as soon as I was out of her view.

I loved Dr. Critchlore's office, with its dark floor-to-ceiling bookshelves on three walls, its fireplace in the alcove, and the rare works kept under glass, like in a museum. A huge desk sat in front of a bay window that looked toward Mount Curiosity. His office had everything an office should have.

Everything except Dr. Critchlore. He was gone.

# CHAPTER 5

*They call him the Minion Whisperer. It's said he can train any species, even mermaids, who are known to be breathtakingly stupid.*
—ARTICLE ON DR. CRITCHLORE IN *MINIONS TODAY*

I heard music coming from the alcove, and when I peeked around the corner I saw him sitting in a wingback chair by the fireplace. He was watching a television that sat in a hidden compartment in the bookshelves.

I gasped. I had never seen Dr. Critchlore looking so . . . so casual. Usually he was as evil overlord-y as they came—tailored suit, pinkie ring, slickly gelled hair, goatee trimmed to a point, and a stare that could melt steel. He wasn't quite so intimidating wearing a bathrobe and fuzzy slippers.

Even worse, he was crying, dabbing his eyes with a handkerchief.

I tried to back away, but he spotted me before I made it to the door.

"Oh, Handley," he said, reaching out to me.

When I said he was

like a father to me, I meant the sort of father who was busy and distant. The kind who couldn't remember his kids' names.

"What have I done with my life?" he said. "What have I accomplished? Look at me, past my prime, with no children of my own."

The TV commercial showed a father tenderly dabbing cream on his smiling daughter's cheek. The voice-over said, "WartGrow, because people trust a witch with warts."

This wasn't the Dr. Critchlore I knew. Just last year he taught us about exploiting an enemy's weakness without mercy. He'd invented tactics such as Shock and Maul, the Monster Wave Attack, and the Hammer and Mace. He was a steel-hearted genius who ran the school with an iron fist, because it prepared us to work for an evil overlord.

He beckoned me over, and I carefully sidestepped the trapdoor in the floor. It was hidden, of course, but I knew exactly where it was. You don't watch someone disappear screaming without it leaving an impression. Dr. Critchlore told me he'd installed it because sometimes people bored him and it was too much effort to call Miss Merrybench to come in and take them away.

"Hickenlooper, my boy." He patted my hand, looking up at me like an eager-to-please puppy. "I have this overwhelming desire to buy a new dragon."

"A dragon, sir?"

"A really mean one. Powerful. It's what the kids are riding these days, right?"

"Well, I have a Domvoy."

He dropped my hand, a look of confusion on his face. "What's that, a griffin? A pegasus?"

"Um, no, it's a bike."

"Hmm. Lacks *pizzazz*, Hollins, if I'm honest. What are you, nine?"

I shrugged, because I didn't know how old I was. Closer to eleven or twelve, though. I thought I'd better change the subject so I could get out of there. I really wanted to get out of there. "Dr. Critchlore? I've been put in the wrong dorm again, and I was wondering, since I'm a junior henchman trainee now, if you could change—"

But I didn't get to finish my sentence, because at that moment a new commercial came on the television—an advertisement for the Pravus Minion Academy.

Dr. Thiago Pravus strolled through his ultramodern campus wearing a black suit and a bright teal tie. He looked like the kind of action hero who wears a tuxedo at night but can kill you twenty different ways with his bare hands. Word had it that he'd personally trained Wexmir Smarvy's dragon militia.

The commercial cut from one impressive building to the next, showing what seemed like thousands of minions in various stages of training. The school looked humongous, and everything in it was so new and shiny—the buildings, the weapons, even the dragon's teeth. (I'd been on dragon tooth-cleaning duty before, and let me tell you, it's not easy. And getting them to floss? Forget about it.)

"Gone are the days when an evil overlord could make do with a posse of weak, servile, untrained minions," Dr. Pravus said. "Today's evil overlord must have the very best: Pravus minions."

I glanced sideways at my bathrobe-wearing headmaster, who was turning the color of cayenne pepper.

"I despise that man," Dr. Critchlore said.

26

"And unlike other minion schools we could name"—Pravus winked at the camera, like he was looking right at Dr. Critchlore—"we guarantee our graduates won't become the embarrassment of the entire minion community."

Dr. Critchlore clenched his fists and pounded the arm of his chair. "Damn that video."

"Yeah," I said. "About that—"

He waved a hand in the air, as if he were shooing the subject matter away. I saw his other hand move toward the "boring person button," so I quickly reached into my pocket.

"Explosive gum, sir," I offered.

He took the gum, chewed it for a few seconds, and then tossed it at the TV. I plugged my ears as the TV disappeared with a bang.

This was terrible. Dr. Critchlore didn't look like he was doing anything about that video. I turned to tiptoe out of the office—and that's when Miss Merrybench caught me. Literally, because she was running into the office to check on the explosion and she knocked me over.

"Did he destroy another TV?" she asked.

I stood up and nodded.

Her face looked different—softer, somehow—as she gazed into the smoke.

"He's fine," I said, and then regretted it, because she turned her angry stare at me full blast.

"What do you think you are doing?" she asked, yanking me out of Dr. Critchlore's office. "He's a very busy man. He mustn't be disturbed."

*Busy watching TV*, I thought, but I didn't say anything. I'd learned long ago that it was a bad idea to cross Miss Merrybench. She could make a kid's life miserable in many ways, and not just by assigning him to the wrong dorm. I'd heard she had a whole arsenal of tiny weapons in her hair bun.

I wasn't sure if that was true. I tried to check, but she was taller than me.

Miss Merrybench let go of my arm and returned to her chair. I knew I had to make my plea before she picked up her headset, so I blurted out, "I think I'm in the wrong dorm."

"Mr. Higgins," she said. "I make all the dorm assignments. Are you suggesting I made a mistake?"

"No! It's just, I thought that maybe, since I've been in the D-Hum for two years already, maybe you didn't think about moving me now that there are vacancies in the Momido."

This year, some of our top monster recruits had gone to other schools, scared off by the freaky outbreak of wyvern flu we'd had last term. And I'd heard a rumor that some Cyclops recruits had just withdrawn. And then I remembered Tiffany. We usually had a whole pride of manticores each year. As far as I'd seen, she'd been the only one.

I gasped.

Was it because of Dr. Pravus's commercial? Because of the video?

"I think you are fine where you are," Miss Merrybench said. She had a pile of file folders on her desk, and she opened one.

"But last year I missed out on—"

"Mr. Higgins," she interrupted. "It's the first day of the new term. I have hundreds of things to attend to, each one of them more important than a room assignment. Ever since that video went viral, the phones won't stop ringing, and Dr. Critchlore won't take any calls."

She took a quick glance toward Dr. Critchlore's open office door, but then her gaze shot my way like a flaming arrow, so searing I almost ducked. "I understand you are starting in the Junior Hench-man Training Program this morning?"

"Yes, ma'am," I said.

"I suggest you concern yourself with that," she said. She returned her attention to her files, muttering under her breath, "As I see it, you'll be lucky to last a day."

The bell rang. I had five minutes to get to my class, which was all the way on the other side of campus, on the sports fields.

"Tardy on the first day," Miss Merrybench said, shaking her head.

# CHAPTER 6

*Be prepared, with explosives.*

—THE GIRL EXPLORERS MOTTO

I raced out of the castle, my feet propelled by panic. Sometimes, when something bad happens, it immediately puts me on edge, because bad things always come in threes. I'm not saying this because I'm superstitious; I'm saying it because it's true. Unless you're cursed, in which case bad things will keep happening until you find whoever cursed you and make amends. This usually involves some groveling, a bag of gold, and maybe your firstborn child.

So far, two solidly bad "bad things" had happened: the video and my dorm assignment. I had to think of another one, and quick, or my third bad thing would be what Miss Merrybench had predicted, and I absolutely could not be tardy on my first day as a junior henchman trainee.

I had a lot of ground to cover: down the main road, past the dorm section of campus, and then around the infirmary to the sports fields. I thought about stubbing my toe, just to get the third bad thing over with, but I hadn't heard the final bell yet, so I sprinted.

My legs were burning as I burst out onto the field. I skidded to a stop next to Coach Foley just as the bell rang. Phew.

Every junior henchman trainee was assigned to a professor for one class period. By helping train the minions in that class, we would learn not only how to be an excellent assistant, but also how to lead a group of minions, two essential traits in a junior henchman.

My mentor was Coach Gunner Foley, a former lineman in the NFL, the Nefarious Forces League, a ruthless band of mercenary fighters. He was six and a half feet of solid muscle, with the disposition of a snapping turtle. As PE teacher he wore tight polyester coach's shorts and a polo shirt with the Critchlore logo on the pocket. A whistle dangled from a chain around his neck. The ragged bunch of first-years stood in a huddle while Coach Foley checked his clipboard. I heard him muttering to himself as I caught my breath.

"He questions *my* training methods? I've trained champion maulers. I trained the Monster Death Squad! I've trained more outstanding minions than anyone in Stull. And he questions me? Because of one little incident with Girl Explorers?"

He was talking about the video. Dr. Critchlore must have blamed him for the disaster.

He gave me a once-over, noting the bloodstains that still covered my jacket. He nodded approvingly and then blew his whistle to get the first-years' attention.

"Line up, over there!"

I listened as he gave the students his usual spiel, the same one I'd heard when I was a first-year. It felt so good to be standing there in front of the other students as a junior henchman trainee. I felt ten feet tall, which would make me a short giant.

"All right," he said. "I don't like to talk, I like to get to work, so I'll be brief. You are here to learn how to be an effective minion. That means maximizing your physical fitness and strength. That means learning to work together as a team. That means training your brain to think quickly when in danger. Dr. Critchlore's School for Minions has a tradition of training the best, and that's what we expect from you. Your best effort.

"Our first order of business is to place you in the proper level for PE. So let's get started." He held out the clipboard for me without taking his eyes off the prospects. "Attack the Cyclops on my whistle!"

Coach Foley blew his whistle and started his stopwatch. The first-years started toward the giant stuffed Cyclops at the end of the field.

"Lift your knees!" Coach yelled. "For goodness' sake, lift your knees for speed! You pathetically slow worms!"

I watched the sixteen first-year minions make their way down the field. It was true, they were slow, but I didn't think calling them names was going to make them any faster.

"Pump your arms! You'll move faster if you swing them, like this." He waved his arms back and forth. The minions looked at him, mouths agape.

"Go on, try it. Go!"

They moved forward again, same as before, with their arms outstretched.

Coach Foley knocked his head with his palm. "They're useless, Higgins, useless."

"Well, Coach," I said, "they *are* zombies."

"Tactical zombies," Coach Foley corrected me, pointing at the clipboard I held. "They're supposed to listen to orders."

I scanned the page. Tactical zombies were engineered to obey simple orders given by the instructors, and to respond to a whistle.

We watched as one of the zombies veered away from the target at the sight of Miss Merrybench. The school secretary had driven up in a golf cart containing two big orange Critchlorade™ coolers. Soon the other trainees noticed her too and followed the first one, all of them moaning and not one of them lifting his knees for speed.

"Brains . . . brains . . . brains," they moaned.

"Why are they going after Miss Merrybench?" I asked.

"She wears too much perfume," Coach said, like that explained things. He shook his head at the sight. "Aw, Higgins, we used to get good minions here. Minions with strength and speed. Trolls and ogres and werewolves, like yourself." He looked at me and chuckled. Then he got serious again. "I'd have killed for more Sasquatches, but we only had the one."

"Bigfoot." I nodded.

"These zombies are worse than the golems!"

"Well, times change, Coach. I guess you gotta make do with what you have." I watched Miss Merrybench swing her ruler at the zombies. She seemed to realize that it wasn't much of a weapon, so she calmly turned around, got into the cart, and sped away at five miles per hour. The zombies followed, stumbling into one another.

"Do you think you could show them a thing or two?" Coach Foley asked.

"I'll try, sir."

"Class! Attention!" He blew his whistle.

The zombies stopped and turned to look at him. "Watch Higgins here. Higgins will take down that Cyclops. Shark-attack style!"

"Sir, that works best with a team. It's hard to have a feeding frenzy by yourself."

"Just go!"

Channeling my inner werewolf, I bounded over to the Cyclops and knocked him down. I pulled at its limbs, trying to rip them off. The minions watched for a minute before turning back to Miss Merrybench, who had just made it to the end of the bleachers in her cart. They lifted their arms and moaned. I returned to Coach Foley.

"Mindless eating machines, ha!" he said, disgusted. "It sounds good on paper, but look at them."

I shrugged. They *were* pretty pathetic.

"Who do I have next period?" Coach asked, pointing to the clipboard I'd dropped on the ground.

I flipped through the pages for the schedule. "The intermediate mummies, sir."

Coach Foley threw down his stopwatch and stormed off. "The board of directors will hear about this."

# CHAPTER 7

*One termite can be squashed, but thousands of termites*
*can raze a toolshed, or maybe a small cottage!*
—DR. CRITCHLORE, IN A COMMENCEMENT ADDRESS

I didn't know what to do with the class after Coach left. I felt like I'd been given a test on a subject I'd never studied. I had to do something, but what?

I noticed that one of the zombies hadn't chased after Miss Merrybench; he'd stayed on the grass. On closer inspection, he didn't look like a zombie at all. He was tan, his long blond hair was clean, and there were no flaps of skin dangling from his body. Rather than wearing tattered clothes like the other zombies, he was dressed like me, only in a first-year jacket (purple with black sides).

As I neared him, he half smiled at me. "Hey," he said.

"Hi . . . um . . . who are you?"

"Pismo," he said.

"You're not a zombie."

"Sharp as a knife, aren't you?" he said, rolling his eyes.

"What are you?" I asked. He looked human, but then so did I.

He shrugged. I could tell this kid had attitude, which was a big no-no in a minion.

"Looks like you lost your master," he said. "What'cha gonna do now?"

"I was hoping to get the zombies to work together." Miss Merrybench had disappeared, and the zombies were now stumbling around the track like blindfolded kids trying to pin the tail on the centaur.

"These mindless mutts?" Pismo said, standing up and brushing grass off his cargo pants. "Good luck."

"Zombies are mindless for a reason," I said, remembering what I'd learned from my first-year Introduction to Minion Species class. "It's so they can be controlled by the person who raised them from the dead. They're usually under a spell of enchantment. That, or they were created by an infection, or an apocalyptic event." I looked up. Nothing but blue sky and a few birds. Not really apocalypse weather.

"I can't do anything if they were created by infection," I went on. "But if they are sorcerer-controllable zombies, all I need to do is give them a potion for mind control."

Pismo looked at me with raised eyebrows. "Well?"

"Well what?"

"Do you *have* a potion for mind control?"

"I might." I began emptying my pockets, handing things to Pismo as I went. "Let's see, here's my class list, my rubber ball (for fetching), my school-issued DPS—"

"DPS?"

"Dungeon Positioning System—it's a labyrinth down there. A pack of explosive gum—"

"Wait," Pismo said. "Did you say 'explosive gum'?"

"Sure, unwrap-chew-spit-*kaboom!*" I pulled a piece of paper out. "Boris's locker combination—he always forgets it. My gargoyle action figure, a cool rock I found in the catacombs. A key, a whistle, some change. No potions."

"Check the other pocket," Pismo suggested.

"Right. A pack of wolf treats, the tooth I lost last week, my Critchlore Pocket Tool™. A package of Firstline flea medicine." I looked at Pismo, my face hot. "It's, ah, required for all minions with fur."

Pismo eyed me up and down with his eyebrows raised, probably because I didn't seem to have any fur.

"I'm a werewolf," I explained. I tried not to smile, because I hated to brag.

"Ah," he said.

I reached back into my pocket. "And my manticore antivenom," I finished. I'd grabbed that from my locker after almost getting jabbed earlier. "No potion," I said, taking my stuff back. Everything was snugly in place, but I felt a gap. I held my hand out to Pismo. "Hand it over," I said.

"What?" He gave me that innocent look that just screams "I'm guilty."

"The gum," I said. "I could get in big trouble if Coach found out I gave explosive gum to a first-year."

He shrugged and gave it to me.

"Let's check those Critchlorade™ coolers," I said. We walked over to the sideline bench where Miss Merrybench had left the coolers. There, nestled between them, was a flask labeled "Zombie Mind Control Drops." Perfect!

I put a couple of drops of the potion in each cup and asked Pismo to swirl in a little Critchlorade™ while I rounded up the zombies. We passed out the potion, and I raised my hands for attention. "Okay, my name is Higgins." I pointed to myself. "Since Coach Foley isn't back, I guess I'm in charge. So . . . um . . . I'm ordering you to take your potion." I tried to sound commanding.

They stood there holding the cups, but they wouldn't drink the potion.

"Drink!" I ordered. I drank my own cup of Critchlorade™, to show them what to do, but they just stared at me mindlessly. I felt like I was teaching a cat to fetch.

"This stuff smells terrible," Pismo said, sniffing a cup of the Critchlorade™. It was supposed to taste like orange juice, but the protein powder and vitamin enhancers added a chalky, medicine-y flavor. It was pretty bad. "Maybe try water?" Pismo pointed to the other cooler.

"Okay." We gathered up the cups, dumped the contents, and re-filled them with potion. I held the first cup under the spigot, but nothing came out. I shook the cooler, and it felt full.

I opened the top and saw why nothing came out. It wasn't filled with water. It was filled with brains. *That Miss Merrybench*, I thought, smiling. *She thinks of everything.*

"I should have known," I said. "A fresh brain provides the electrical impulses a zombie needs to be controlled by the potion." Pismo looked at me funny. "Or something. It's science."

I scooped some brains into each cup. We swirled in the potion again and passed out the cups—but they still wouldn't eat.

"It's brains," I said. "Higgins"—I pointed to me—"brought you zombies"—I pointed to them—"brains"—I pointed to my head. "Zombies eat!"

Their expressions changed from mouth-agape confusion to mouth-agape "aha!" and they gobbled up the brains.

"What now?" Pismo asked.

"It says to wait ten minutes to take effect," I said, reading the bottle. "And then I guess I have to figure out what to do with them." We sat down on the bench. "One thing I learned in my Minion Species class is that you have to know the strengths and weaknesses of each type of minion. So, for the zombies—"

"Weaknesses: They're slow," Pismo interrupted. "And easy to kill."

"I wouldn't say 'easy,'" I said.

"Why not? Who doesn't know how to kill a zombie? Bullet between the eyes, decapitation, fire. *Bam, slice, sizzle*—dead zombie."

"Okay, how about strengths?" I asked. "They lack initiative."

Pismo laughed.

"What? That's a plus in a minion. As it says above the gymnasium: 'Yours Is Not to Question Why, Yours Is but to Do and Die.' Plus," I continued, "they're really scary looking, and I mean gruesome. And they're not afraid of anything, being already dead."

"They *are* somewhat determined," Pismo agreed. The zombies were swiping their fingers along the edges of the cups, getting out every last bit of brain.

"Come to think of it," I said, "what are you doing with the Class 5 minions?"

"Class 5?"

"Also known as 'Bodies, No Brains,'" I explained. "Unlike Class

40

4 minions, 'Brains, No Bodies'—you know, ghosts, wraiths, skeletons. 'Bodies, No Brains' are zombies, mummies, reanimated animals. The mindless types."

"Definitely not me—I'm all brains," he said. "Why would they put me with these guys?"

"Don't worry. It's just a mistake. They happen." Like my dorm assignment. "Someone'll fix it."

I turned my attention to the zombies, who were looking at me so intently that it was like they were challenging me to a staring contest. "Higginsbrains," one muttered.

"How am I gonna turn them into an awesome display of minion power?" I had to do something impressive, with or without Coach Foley's help. My future as a junior henchman depended on it. Everyone knew junior henchmen were rated on the performance of their minions.

I stood up and raised my hands for attention. "Attack the Cyclops!" I said, pointing to the Cyclops at the end of the field.

The zombies didn't move.

"Okay, follow me," I said. I led the way, but they didn't follow. I was getting really frustrated, so I practically whined, "You have to follow me."

And they did.

They followed me to the Cyclops.

"Attack!" I ordered, pointing at the Cyclops.

They stood there.

"Attack!" I said, with more vigorous pointing motions.

Nothing.

"Come *onnnnnn*," I said. "You have to attack."

They moved forward. They pulled the Cyclops apart, tearing and ripping and biting. Pismo laughed and joined them. I felt like crying, I was so proud of them. They were doing it.

The bell rang, ending first period, and there was still no sign of Coach Foley.

"Okay, good work, guys. Um, you're dismissed. I have to go to my second period, History of Henchmen class, so I'll see you tomorrow. Bye, Pismo."

"See ya."

"Bye, zombies," I said.

"Higginsbrains," they moaned, shuffling after me.

"No, zombies. Stay!" I blew my whistle and backed away.

"Higginsbrains," they moaned, a little softer.

"Stay," I said again, both hands raised. They stopped chanting "Higginsbrains." I took a deep breath, turned around, and ran for my next class.

And then I heard Pismo yell, "Bye, Higginsbrains!"—and the chanting started up again.

# CHAPTER 8

*Critchlore minions: They're not just for evil overlords anymore.*
—ADVERTISEMENT IN *MINIONS TODAY*

I headed back to the castle, edging around the fountain in the middle of the circular drive. The water sparkled and the castle itself seemed to glow in the morning light. It was massive, looking much taller than its three stories, castellated as it was with turrets and battlements, and anchored by a tower on each side, one wide and round, the other tall and slim.

I thought about how quickly things had changed for me. I'd always dreamed of being a top-notch minion, like I imagined my brother and sister werewolves were. What could be better? Minions do great things, because they work together to achieve a common goal.

I'd never imagined being anything else, until Dr. Critchlore offered me a spot in the Junior Henchman Training Program. Suddenly it was like a whole new world opened up.

It's hard to describe what I felt, but I guess it was like this: You're at the park, swinging on the swings, happy as a troll with a peanut butter sandwich. Then someone comes up to you and says, "Hey, come with me. On the other side of the hill is an amusement park."

You go on roller coasters and bumper cars. You ride that giant pendulum thing that lifts you so high and fast it makes the swings at the playground seem as thrilling as jumping off a brick.

It's so exciting you can barely breathe.

That's what being a junior henchman trainee felt like to me.

"How did Runt get into this class?"

That was Rufus Spaniel, the alpha werewolf of my grade. He was sitting in the back row of Professor Murphy's History of Henchmen class with two other werewolves, shaggy-haired Lapso and supersmart Jud.

"Hey, dog," Jud said to me, lifting a hand for me to slap as I walked by. I'd spotted an open seat near the front, by the window.

"'Sup, beast," Lapso nodded.

"Hey, guys," I said.

I did a quick check of the students on my way in. Besides the werewolves, there were a couple of monkey-men, a hunchback, a Cyclops named Dusty taking up two chairs, Tim the arachno-human, and some regular humans.

The class was much more crowded than I'd expected. In fact, more kids kept coming in, until all the desks were taken and students had to stand crammed in by the wall.

At last Professor Murphy entered the room. He was a short, round man with thick black-and-gray hair. His glasses rested on a nose that looked like a strawberry, red and spotted with pores.

Professor Murphy took one look around, shook his head, and sighed heavily. "I see our esteemed Dr. Critchlore has offered junior henchman positions to too many kids yet again." He sighed again.

"I told him I could take five students in the program. We have"—he began counting—"twenty-seven. *Oy vey!*"

Nervous whispering spread through the room. I'm sure we all wondered the same thing—were we going to be kicked out of the Junior Henchman Training Program? Would we have to go back to regular minion training?

"Why don't we fight it out for the five spots?" Rufus said. He looked at me and sneered. "I call Higgins."

After the laughter died down, someone pointed out the window. I turned my head and saw that the first-year zombies were crashing through the bushes, heading right for my window. They were moaning, "Higgins, Higgins, brains, Higgins, brains."

"What is going on out there?" Professor Murphy said.

"They want Higgins's brain, sir," Rufus said. "They must be dieting."

More laughter. I chuckled at that one myself. I had to admit, that was pretty funny.

"Higgins, brains, Higgins, brains."

"Higgins? Dogsbody Higgins is in this class?" Professor Murphy said, looking around. Kids snickered at my old nickname, but I ignored it and raised my hand so that Professor Murphy could see me.

"Yes, sir," I said. "I'm sorry, sir, I was assigned to Coach Foley this morning, but he, uh, left. I did my best with them, sir."

"Did you feed them?" he asked.

"Yes," I answered. "It was the only way to get them to take the potion."

"So, they're potion-controlled," he said, raising his eyebrows and

45

nodding, like he was impressed. "Very well, just order them to report to the necromancer."

I opened the window. The zombies seemed excited to see me. They moved a fraction faster as they crashed their bodies into the wall. They moaned a bit faster too. "HigginsbrainsHigginsbrains."

"Report to the necromancer," I said in my most commanding voice.

"HigginsbrainsHigginsbrains," they kept saying.

"Please, report to the necromancer," I said a little quieter. "Please."

"HigginsbrainsHigginsbrains."

I heard some giggles. A few comments, like "Not really henchman material," floated through the air in my direction. My skin felt hot, and I think my lower lip might have trembled. I really, really wanted the zombies to obey.

I practically whispered, "You have to go to the necromancer." It came out squeaky, which almost made me cry from embarrassment.

They stopped moaning, turned around, and left.

I nearly collapsed with relief. But then I wondered: Why did it take so long for them to obey a command?

"All right, then," Professor Murphy said. "If nobody else's first-year minions have followed them to class, we can get to business."

I went back to my seat, but someone had taken it. So I stood by the window.

"As I said, I have only five positions available," Professor Murphy continued. "Dr. Critchlore is, apparently, somewhat distracted at the moment. I'm sorry for the lot of you who will have to return to the regular minion program, but that's the way it is.

"This happened last year, when I had seven candidates for the five openings. We decided who'd stay based on a series of tests. I don't know if I can do that with twenty-seven students. Part of me wants to throw the lot of you out and skip the program this year altogether. But I know that wouldn't be fair.

"So, if any of you would like to volunteer to exit the program now, I'd appreciate it. Any volunteers?"

Nobody raised a hand.

I thought I should probably bow out. There was no way I was as good as any of these guys. I looked at them and they all seemed to scream "junior henchman": smart, resourceful, strong. If I were an evil overlord, I'd take any one of them over me.

I sighed. I felt my arm inch up, but something held it down. I looked over and saw Janet Desmarais, another third-year. Her gaze was on the teacher, but her hand was wrapped around my wrist in a grip so tight I couldn't move my arm.

"Don't you dare raise the other one," she whispered.

As if I could. I was too shocked. Janet Desmarais was holding my hand! My chest felt squeezed and floaty at the same time. She kept her gaze forward, but I couldn't take my eyes off her—those playful brown eyes, the way a smile danced on her lips. She tucked her hair behind her ears and glanced at me, and I had to look away.

Despite my shock, I felt someone's stare on me, probably because of my enhanced werewolf senses. In the back of the room, Rufus sat scowling at me. His gaze traveled down to my hand, clutched in Janet's grip. Then back up to my face. If those eyes could have shot flaming balls of fire, I'd have been nothing but a pile of smoking ashes.

I looked back at Professor Murphy and tried not to think about

Janet holding my hand. *Janet Desmarais is holding my hand!* I felt like howling.

I'd had a few classes with Janet in the past, but I'd never talked to her, not once. She hung around with the other girls, most of them part-sirens like her, able to lure men to their death with their beautiful singing. Their world seemed off-limits and mysterious, like the Forbidden Quarry.

"Right, then," Professor Murphy continued. "Until I can figure out how to pick the five, whether it's a random draw or a contest of some sort, you'll all have to take today's lesson. You've all been assigned to a professor mentor, yes?"

We all nodded.

"Good. Their evaluation of your performance will have an impact on my choice too."


After class I chased after Janet, hypnotized by how perfect her dark hair was—it fell past her shoulders in a shiny wave that shimmered in the sun. She'd taken off her jacket and her arms were smooth and brown, like a perfect mud puddle.

"Hey," I said. "Why'd you do that?"

"I didn't want you to quit, obviously," she answered.

"But why?"

"Runt, you always give up. Remember last year, at field day? Right before your race, Rufus asked you to go to the other side of the track and tell his mom to watch him. And you went! You missed your own race to do that self-absorbed lump a favor."

I remembered. I had a hard time saying no when people asked me to do stuff.

"I thought you liked Rufus."

"Well, he *is* a good-looking self-absorbed lump—those dimples, those blue eyes." She sighed. "But I want you to stay in Professor Murphy's class. And do your best."

"Okay," I said.

I hadn't been paying attention to my surroundings as we walked, but when I looked up I saw that Janet had made it to her territory, and I was still standing next to her. Five girls glared at me with raised eyebrows (or, in the case of Frieda, eye*brow*—she's an ogre). I yelped and ran off, their laughter chasing me.

# CHAPTER 9

*You've Just Been Raised from the Dead. Now What?*
—INTRODUCTORY CLASS FOR ZOMBIES, MUMMIES, AND
SKELETONS, TAUGHT BY PROFESSOR VODUM

I was going to have to compete against twenty-six awesome classmates to get into the Junior Henchman Training Program. This was bad.

Which got me thinking. I'd already had three bad things: the wrong dorm assignment, the "Epic Minion Fail" video, and the embarrassing zombies. If I had another bad thing, that meant I was cursed.

*Buuuuut* . . . maybe "Epic Minion Fail" didn't count, because it wasn't really bad for me, directly. It was bad for the school. So, on my list of bad things, I replaced "Epic Minion Fail" with "Not in Junior Henchman Training Program Yet," and I was still at three bad things. Not cursed.

I had Study Hall for third period, which meant I was supposed to report to the library. Uncle Ludwig made us sign in, but then he pretty much ignored us, so we were free to leave—which was what he wanted. Once, while reshelving books, I'd asked him what he was researching, but he wouldn't tell me. It had to be something important, because he focused every waking minute on it.

I could have finished reshelving, but something was bothering me. I needed to figure out what was wrong with the zombies—why did I have to repeat myself so many times before they obeyed? I didn't stand a chance in the Junior Henchman Training Program if I couldn't keep those zombies under control.

I had a nagging feeling the zombies were defective, and that made me think about the ogre-men from the video. Could something be causing our minions to fail? Critchlore's reputation couldn't take any more defective minions. I really hoped I was wrong.

Necromancers are experts at dead stuff, so I headed to their building, which was out by the cemetery. To get there I had to pass through the Memorial Courtyard, one of my favorite places on campus. The courtyard was a grassy pitch sprinkled with stone statues and benches, and shaded by a variety of trees. A curving wall of polished granite called the Wall of Heroes separated the courtyard from the cemetery. It was about fifty meters long. The Critchlore family had trained a lot of heroes.

Normally, it was a peaceful place, but as I approached I kept hearing the shrill sound of a whistle and a lady screaming. I ran into the courtyard and saw Professor Zaida standing on a stump, trying to teach her Literature class. (We took Literature because most evil overlords enjoy a good bedtime story. Who doesn't?)

Professor Zaida, who is a little person, often teaches her class outside. She can really make stories come alive—and I mean that literally. She does this thing with animated clay that's amazing. She's one of the most popular teachers in the school.

*Tweet!* "Zombie Seven, sit back down!" she commanded. Tim, the arachno-human, was her junior henchman assistant, but he was taking a nap in a web he'd spun in the oak tree. It looked like I wouldn't have to worry about beating Tim into the junior henchman class. He'd already given up.

When Zombie Seven sat down, Professor Zaida continued reading the creation story, "Jolki and the First Monsters."

I loved this story. Jolki, the God of Transmutable Species, was hungry and tired after having spent the day creating the fire-bellied toad. He asked three women to bring him food. Intelligent, brave Laru brought him a steak, cooked to perfection, with a side of mashed potatoes and asparagus. Jolki was pleased, and he rewarded her by giving her the power to turn into a wolf.

The second woman, graceful and observant Eglenta, prepared a hearty chicken stew with vegetables from her garden. It was delicious. Jolki rewarded her with the ability to turn into an eagle.

The third woman was the pretty but dim-witted Marvis. Jolki knew that cooking was beyond her ability, so he asked her to bring him some oysters, since the ocean was just a straight walk down the road, and there was a woman there who would give her the oysters. It was an easy job.

Unfortunately, Marvis got lost, fell into the ocean, and unwittingly insulted the oyster woman. Eventually, she got the oysters, but on the way back she grew hungry and ate half of them. At last, she returned to Jolki and gave him his meal.

Jolki was not pleased. "You bring me half a meal," he raged, "so I will make you half a fish."

And thus the first mermaid was created from a very stupid girl.

The zombies weren't listening. Zombie Seven sat, but then

Zombies Four and Eleven got up. They all had numbers on their backs, like on a sports uniform.

*Tweet! Tweet! Tweeeeeet!*

I wanted to help, but I didn't have time. I waved at Pismo, who, I noticed, was chewing gum.

Hmm. Where'd he get the gum?

Uh-oh. I checked my pocket.

My exploding gum was gone.

Pismo rocked with silent laughter. Then he plucked the gum out of his mouth. I shook my head at him. He smiled wider and wiggled his eyebrows. I shook my head more vigorously. He tossed the gum over his shoulder. I winced. It exploded behind his back.

"Hey! Ouch!" Pismo cried.

Professor Zaida stopped whistling and called the students together.

"*He* did it," Pismo said, pointing at me. "That kid over there. He threw something at me, and it exploded."

Professor Zaida frowned at me. My mouth hung open in shock.

I frowned hard at Pismo, who fell backward, holding his stomach as he rolled on the grass with more silent laughter. When Professor Zaida turned around to see if he was okay, his fake laughs turned into moans.

"I think I need to see the nurse," he said.

"That's fine. Do you know how to find her?"

"Yes, Professor Zaida. *Owwww.*"

Pismo took off, showing absolutely no sign of injury. He didn't run for the infirmary, which was located back by the castle. He sprinted in the opposite direction, the direction I was heading, toward the Necromancy Building.

I took off after him. I was going to pound that little twerp, but Professor Zaida's whistle stopped me cold.

*Tweet!* "Runt Higgins!" I turned around. "As if I'm not having enough trouble! I was supposed to have a class of ogre-men. They love that story. But no, I'm stuck with uncontrollable zombies. It is *not* the day to play pranks."

"It wasn't me, Professor Zaida," I said.

"Enough!" She held up a hand to stop me from talking. "You will report to detention after school."

"Yes, Professor Zaida," I said. *Aw, man.* I'd never gotten a detention. Stupid Pismo.

I kicked a rock and continued on my way, now with a sore toe.

Professor Vodum sat at his desk, beneath a wall covered with diplomas, newspaper clippings, and photographs of him with famous people who looked bored. His wall seemed to be saying, "Look at this man, he's important."

I wondered how long he would last in Necromancy. He'd started at the school teaching Weather Control, but Dr. Critchlore had canceled the class when a freak lightning storm set fire to the stables. Professor Vodum bounced around a bit after that, teaching Stealth Techniques (his students were caught sneaking into the Evil Overlord Council Building), Hand-to-Paw Battle (the paws always won), and Poetry (only one person signed up for the class: Frieda, the ogre).

He would have been fired, but he was married to Dr. Critchlore's cousin, and a major stockholder in the school.

"What do you want?" he said when he noticed me standing in the doorway.

"Um." *What did I want?* My brain always seemed to freeze when someone seemed angry with me.

He sighed with annoyance. "Can't you see I'm busy?"

"Professor Vodum, I'm sorry for the interruption." My hand grasped my medallion without me telling it to. "I was working with the first-year zombies, and they weren't responding to my commands, so I gave them some mind control potion, and . . ."

"Good grief," he said. "Let me get the file." He got up and opened a cabinet along the wall. Like Dr. Critchlore, he was tall, but where Dr. Critchlore was slim and precise in everything—from his perfectly trimmed goatee to his spotless shoes—Professor Vodum was kind of a slob. His greasy brown hair lay flat on his head, and he wore a white lab coat covered with spills. I hoped they were food.

He fingered the tops of the files, muttering, "Ghosts, mummies, skeletons, vampires, wraiths . . . where is it?" He threw up his hands and slammed the file cabinet. "Where is it?"

That last part sounded a bit whiny for a grown-up, which made me feel very uncomfortable, like he was about to blame me for the missing file. It got worse when he called for his secretary. "Marcia, Mar-*shaaaaaaah*," he said, the "*aaaaaaah*" changing pitch as it rolled out of his mouth in search of its target. "Where's the zombie file?" He threw up his hands again. "I can never find anything when I need it."

Marcia came in and walked straight to the professor's desk. "It's right here, Professor," she said, pointing to a stack of files next to his computer.

"Well, why didn't you file it away?" he whined.

"I'm sorry, I thought you were using it." She reached for it, but he swooped it up.

"I am now," he said. "You're dismissed."

I bet it took a lot of self-control for Marcia not to roll her eyes. I was impressed. I smiled at her and she winked back.

"Professor," I said, "when you raise the dead, how do you get them to respond to your commands?"

Professor Vodum looked at me suspiciously. "I'm afraid that's a professional secret," he said. "I share that only with my honor students. Seventh-years."

*Rats.*

He looked at me, tilted his head sideways a bit, and then added, "I guess I can tell you that it takes a bit of chanting, a special cocktail of potions, if you will, and it has to take place during the right phase of the moon."

Hmm. That didn't really help me.

"I raised these zombies myself," he said, opening the file. "Even added a scent adapter so they won't attack anyone here at school. Cook puts a little something in our food, and we're safe from zombies. It's brilliant, really."

"Didn't Dr. Frankenhammer invent that?" We'd had zombies for years and never had a problem with them attacking the humans at school.

"I suppose if you want to be picky, he invented the serum. But I administered it, so . . ."

"But they went after Miss Merrybench."

"She wears too much perfume," Professor Vodum said, closing

the file and dropping it on his desk. "I've warned her many times. Where are my zombies now?"

"With Professor Zaida. But haven't they been here?" I asked. "I sent them to the necromancer after first period."

"Dr. Critchlore has just hired three more necromancers. There are five on staff now," he said. "I share this office with two others. The other two have offices on the other side of the cemetery, next to the lake." He looked out the window and pouted. "I should have gotten the office by the lake."

"But if you raised them, why wouldn't they return to you?" I asked.

He looked hurt. "Yes, why wouldn't they? Why don't my minions ever return to me?" His voice rose higher with each word. "It's so unfair. Graggly's undead return to him. They even got him a card on his birthday. Why can't mine?"

I slowly backed out of the room. I had my answer. There was nothing wrong with the zombies. They just only understood whine.

This was great news: no epidemic of defective minions. Plus I could tell Professor Zaida how to control the zombies, and she'd be so grateful she'd let me out of detention. Then I could show Coach Foley, and my junior henchman status would soar.

"Goodness, look at the time," Professor Vodum said. "I've called a meeting of the necromancers to inform them of my seniority here. Mar-*shaaaaaaah*!"

# CHAPTER 10

*An overlord without a minion is like a toothless shark.*
—DR. CRITCHLORE, IN AN ADVERTISEMENT

I raced back to the Memorial Courtyard, hoping to catch Professor Zaida before class ended. As I passed the organic vegetable garden ("A Healthy Minion Lasts Longer in Battle"), I heard a yelp. I looked over at the strawberry patch and heard it again. Someone had gotten trapped in the Strawberry Snare, one of the most successful plant traps in the school.

"Hello?" I called.

"Help!"

"Where are you? Did the Strawberry Snare catch you?"

"Yes. I just wanted a few strawberries. Help me."

I looked down the path to the Memorial Courtyard. I didn't have much time before third period was over.

"Please hurry," the voice said. "It's getting tighter."

"I'm coming."

The plant only awakened when someone touched a berry, so I carefully sidestepped my way toward the voice. If I hurried, I could free whoever was caught and still catch Professor Zaida.

"Raise a hand or something," I said. "I can't see you." The plants

58

grew atop tall mounds, set off in rows, their vines dripping down the sides.

I saw a little hand pop up just a few meters ahead. An imp, probably. We had a lot of them the year below mine. The textbooks said they were energetic, resourceful, and imaginative. In reality they liked to steal things and play pranks on everyone.

"I think I can pull you out," I said, reaching for him. Most imps don't grow taller than two and a half feet, but they have long, very strong fingers. They are greenish in color, with pointy ears that stick up or out, depending on the imp. Our hands clasped and his head popped up, a wicked grin on his face, the tips of his fangs peeking out over his lower lip.

"Gotcha!" he said. Four more imps rose from behind the mound, wearing the light green jacket that all second-year students wear. Before I knew it, I'd been wrapped tightly in vines. I struggled, but it was no use. They had me good. The imps jumped up and scampered off, laughing. "We trapped a third-year! Bonus points for us!"

Great. Just great. I'd fallen for the oldest trick in the book—the "I'm trapped" trap. I gnawed on the vines, but they were tough and rubbery. I heard the bell sound for the end of third period, and I felt like crying. Not only was I not getting out of detention, I was going to be tardy for my next class. Or worse: If I didn't get free, I'd get an "unexcused absence" mark, and that meant another detention.

I didn't know what to do, so I sat back and howled. I howled at the sky, at the stupid imps, at the Strawberry Snare. I put all my frustration into that howl.

When I paused to take in another breath, I heard a voice say, "Lighten up, will you? Some of them are still sleeping."

I looked over and saw Syke (pronounced "sigh-key") and smiled with relief. I was saved! Strands of the Strawberry Snare circled her legs in a gentle embrace. Syke had a way with plants; it was in her nature. Her mother was a hamadryad, a tree nymph.

Syke's skin was the color of mahogany wood, and in the right light her black hair turned an iridescent green, like a humming-bird's feathers. We had grown up at the school together. She was like a sister to me.

"Higgins, you idiot, what are you doing?" she asked. When I said she was like a sister to me, I meant the kind that calls you a moron and steals your clothes. She was wearing my nicely worn-in combat boots.

"Syke," I said, "thank goodness it's you. I was trapped by imps."

"The 'I'm trapped' trap?"

I nodded.

She rolled her eyes. "You are so lame." She knelt down and stroked the vines. They practically purred as they released me and stretched toward her touch. "There, now, my little darlings," she said to them. "Let Higgins go."

I stood up. "Thanks," I said. "But aren't you supposed to be in class?" Syke wasn't a minion; she was Dr. Critchlore's ward. Her parents had been killed in a fire when she was a baby. What was now our boulderball field used to be a lush, dense forest. Dr. Critchlore had saved Syke, but try as he might, he couldn't find a relative for Syke to live with who wasn't a hamadryad. Tree nymphs live in trees. Literally, inside the trees. Syke, being only part hamadryad, can't do that.

Her hamadryad relatives told Dr. Critchlore that he was responsible for the life he had saved, so he took Syke in as his ward. If he promised to raise and educate her, but not train her as a minion, then they would not curse him with chestnut blight.

"I have Literature," she said.

"Me too. Let's go."

I raced out of the field, Syke following slowly. "Syke, we're gonna be late."

She shrugged. "So what? We'll miss Professor Zaida animate a scene from the *Odyssey of Yarnik*. She does it every year. Yawn."

I was really looking forward to it, but I didn't feel like I could abandon Syke and go on without her. That would have been rude after she'd just saved me. So we walked slowly and were fifteen minutes late for class.

I sighed. Framed by Pismo, trapped by imps, and late for class. Three more bad things. There was no doubt about it.

I was cursed.

After fourth period ended, everyone raced to the cafeteria, located on the first floor of the castle.

"With my luck," I said to Syke, "they'll be serving vegetarian goulash, or seafood tetrazzini." Even so, I felt some drool leak out the sides of my mouth (we canines don't have much control in that department).

We got in line behind the ogre-men. I tried to look around them to get a peek at the meal, but they are just too large.

I shook with hunger, silently willing the ogre-men to move faster. We finally reached the front and I saw that Cook was serving my favorite lunch: hot dogs, fries, corn on the cob, and pizza rolls.

Just as I was thinking that my luck meter had finally swiveled from bad to good, a loud explosion thundered in the distance. The building shook, pizza rolls flew off trays, and my luck meter plummeted back past "bad" and landed firmly on "horrendous."

# CHAPTER 11

*To lead uninstructed minions into battle is to throw them away.*
—WISDOM FROM EASTERN PHILOSOPHERS

In seconds, the whole room flew into a panic. Imps and gremlins and brownies zipped in and out of people's legs, while the humanish minions tripped over them and screamed. Monkey-men screeched, lizard-boys clung to the wall, and werewolves and other shape-shifters transformed into their animal forms. A siren wailed—the pretty girl kind, not the alarm kind.

Syke grabbed a handful of pizza rolls and slid under a table. I joined her, wondering if the table could protect us from ten tons of stone falling on top of it. My guess was no.

The room was complete mayhem, except for the undead section of the cafeteria. Mummies, skeletons, and ghosts don't need to eat, but they came to the cafeteria during meals so they wouldn't feel left out. The explosion didn't faze them at all.

On second glance, I noticed that the zombie table was empty. Where were they?

The sound of an alarm bell pierced the air and I covered my ears (I have very sensitive hearing, especially at the upper registers). I felt claustrophobic, trapped in the cafeteria. Werewolves are made for action, not for hiding, but there was a big jam-up at the cafeteria door as the minions trying to get outside crashed into others trying to get in.

I stood up.

Syke grabbed my arm and pulled me back down. "What are you doing?" she asked. "There might be more explosions."

"I have to find the zombies." I pointed to the empty table. Next to it, Rufus had corralled his mummy first-years into a safe, calm little horde.

Syke let go of my arm and followed me as I ran behind the counter, through the kitchen, and out the back entrance. A huge plume of smoke rose in the distance, near the cemetery.

"Oh no! The last place I saw the zombies, *my* zombies, was over there." I pointed to the smoke.

"Let's go," Syke said. That's what I liked best about Syke: She never shied away from danger. She'd make a great minion, but her hamadryad relatives wanted her to study horticultural science at one of the non-minion universities after she graduated. They'd told Dr. Critchlore to keep her out of any battle classes.

We took off, passing humans and creatures running for the safety of the castle. When we got to the Memorial Courtyard, it was empty, but we heard Professor Zaida's whistle coming from the cemetery.

We followed the sound until we found her at the edge of the smoke-filled graveyard. I couldn't see any zombies through the dust and smoke. It looked like something was on fire—maybe a toolshed or mausoleum.

"Higgins! Syke!" Professor Zaida said. "Get back to the castle. Report to your safe zone."

That was what minions were supposed to do when the alarm sounded. But we hadn't had an alarm drill yet.

"I was worried about the zombies," I said. "They don't know where their safe zone is."

Tootles, the groundskeeper, jogged over. He brushed a strand of white hair out of his face. Most of his hair was pulled back in a ponytail.

"Syke, honey, you can't be out here," he said. "Go home. Riga will be so worried." Even though she was Dr. Critchlore's ward, Syke lived with Tootles and his wife, Riga, in their expansive tree house. It was an arrangement that worked for everyone: Syke got to live in the trees, Tootles and Riga got the child they never thought they'd have, and Dr. Critchlore was spared having to raise her himself. He's not really the nurturing type.

"As soon as I help Runt with the zombies," she said.

"If I don't have any first-years to help train," I said, "Coach Foley won't need me as a mentee, and I won't be able to prove I'd be a good junior henchman."

Tootles pointed to the cemetery. "They're probably attracted to the freshly unearthed bodies," he said. "The explosion happened right in the middle."

"But they're supposed to respond to my command when I use the whistle," Professor Zaida said.

"Try again," I said. Professor Zaida blew the whistle.

I yelled, in the whiniest voice I could, "Zom-*beeeeees*! You *haaaave* to return to the *cassssstle. Nowwwwww.*"

Professor Zaida and Tootles looked at me like I was nuts. Then Professor Zaida's face lit up with understanding. "Did Professor Vodum raise these zombies?"

I nodded. And then I smiled, because the zombies were emerging from the smoke. "Well done, Mr. Higgins," Professor Zaida said.

"Thanks. Now, about that detention . . ."

"Four o'clock. In the dungeon," she answered.

*Rats.*

Syke and I headed back to the castle. Students, professors, and support staff stood in groups, waiting for the okay to go back inside. We sidestepped around Professor Vodum and the other necromancers, who were huddled around a tablet computer watching Channel 2's news feed. Professor Vodum was lecturing them on the possible cause of the explosion.

"Of course, an uneducated person might suggest this was an underground gas leak that ignited," he said. "But the disbursement of debris would contraindicate that supposition. Furthermore—"

The other necromancers were ignoring him, and I couldn't blame them. Professor Vodum obviously enjoyed the sound of his own voice. Everyone else? Not so much.

"'Disbursement of debris?'" I asked Syke. "Does he mean how far stuff was blown away?"

She shrugged. "Sounds like he's disbursing his own debris."

The necromancers looked worried, and I could guess why. With the cemetery destroyed, they'd just lost their raw materials, and most likely their jobs. Even worse, that meant no more undead minions for the school.

Syke grabbed my arm, stopping me in my tracks. She nodded toward the castle. Working his way through the crowd was Dr. Frankenhammer. I held my breath, but couldn't look away. He was the most frightening teacher in the school. People stepped out of his path as he strode in our direction.

He looked like a pale phantom, but he was pure human. Frizzy white hair framed a narrow face. His eyebrows wisped straight up, as if something had just exploded in his face. Dark circles cradled eyes that barely opened past "squint." Wearing a white lab coat, he looked like he'd be perfectly camouflaged in a glass of milk.

And in his hand, as always, was a bloody scalpel.

His gaze stopped at Professor Vodum, and half his face twisted into a smile, which did nothing to change his creepy, scary vibe. "Bad luck, Vodum," he called. "Now you'll have to get a real job. Ha!" He strode off without waiting for a reply. Professor Vodum gave Dr. Frankenhammer's back a serious death stare.

"We're lucky, I guess," one of the new necromancers said. "If Vodum hadn't called that ridiculous meeting, we would have become our own raw materials."

Professor Vodum looked ready to explode himself.

Back in the cafeteria, things had calmed down and most kids had returned to more important work: eating. The teachers were back in their private room. It had a glass partition separating it from the rest of us, so they could see us but eat in peace. They'd pulled the shades down, which didn't help lessen the worry that filled the room.

"Someone attacked us," I heard a kid say. "Probably another minion school."

"Minion schools can't attack each other," a red-jacketed sixth-year replied. "It's in the Code. The overlords want as many minion providers as possible. It keeps prices down. No, this was probably Evil Overlord Dark Wendix, paying us back for training those defective ogre-men."

"Nobody's gonna come here for school," a fourth-year werewolf said. "We're done for."

My hunger vanished as worry took over my stomach.

# CHAPTER 12

*With great power comes the responsibility to have great minions.*
—DR. CRITCHLORE

I'd lost my appetite, but I grabbed a tray and headed for my usual table, a six-seater crammed in the corner, near the sealed-off teachers' room. Syke left to sit with the girls. I passed some upperclassmen who were comparing this explosion to ones in the past. The consensus seemed to be that it was bigger than Dr. Frankenhammer's failed "explosive minions" experiment (once one blew, they all did), but not as bad as when Professor Vodum taught Using Care Around Explosives and blew up the gymnasium.

I sat down next to Frankie. Across from us were a couple of other D-Hummers, Eloni and Boris, who were staring at the ogre-man table, where the cool kids sat.

Eloni Tatupu was an islander, brown from the sun, with close-cropped black hair. He was as big as a refrigerator and a fierce fighter when he was serious, which he never was. I had a feeling most of the crazy rumors around school started with Eloni. He could hear someone say "Higgins got a flat tire on his bike," and he'd turn it into "Higgins ran over a nest of snakes, was bitten seventy-three times, and barely escaped with his life."

69

And Boris would believe him.

Boris Tumblewrecker was an ogre-man, but he'd gotten the weaker brew of that genetic mixture: He looked like a human, was weak like a human, but had the intelligence of an ogre. I'm not saying ogres are stupid, but scrawny little Boris didn't realize he was any different from the other ogre-men, who were bigger than Eloni.

Actually, Boris and I looked so much alike that we could almost pass for twins. Same build (I was still waiting for that growth spurt), same brown hair, hazel eyes, pale skin. Looking at us from behind, the only way someone could tell us apart was that I had my pants on the right way.

Propped up in the seat next to Eloni was a giant club. I nodded at it and Eloni said, "That's Little Eloni." He patted it on the top. "Little Eloni, meet Higgins," he said.

"Nice to meet you," I said to his club.

Most of the ogre-men carried clubs. Eloni wouldn't admit it, but he really wanted to hang out with them. I couldn't blame him. The ogre-men had a sort of confidence that drew everyone's attention, even now, post–"Epic Minion Fail" video.

"Crazy explosion, huh?" I said.

"I heard someone say they thought a propane line blew," Frankie said.

"I heard that the disbursement of debris was contradictive of that suppository." The guys looked at me funny, so I added, "Vodum thinks not."

"Vodum," Frankie said, shaking his head. "What does he know? Did you see the plume of fire? Definitely a gas explosion."

"Nope," Eloni said. "It was Explosive Eric, the dude who died last year. He wanted to be buried with his explosives so he could go out with a bang. But his partner messed up the timer. By a year."

I didn't think that was true, but then, who knew?

Frankie shrugged. "As long as it's over, who cares? I've got bigger things to worry about."

"Did you get some replacement blood?" I asked him.

"Not yet," he said. "I had to stay after Biology class because . . ." He sniffed. "Because Daddy, er, Dr. Frankenhammer, said he wanted to do something about my lisp." His voice cracked a little when he said that. "I didn't even know I had a lithp." He blinked fast, like he was trying not to cry.

"You don't," I said. "Er, you didn't."

Darn that Dr. Frankenhammer! No matter how hard Frankie worked, Dr. Frankenhammer always seemed disappointed in him. If Frankie ran a mile in three minutes, Dr. Frankenhammer would sigh and shake his head, saying, "I was hoping for two minutes."

"He said I shouldn't call him 'Daddy,' either," Frankie continued. "It's unprofessional."

"Frankie, don't worry about him," I said. "You're amazing. I mean, look at you. First of your kind—"

"Twenty-fifth," he corrected.

"First of your kind to make it past infancy. And look what you've accomplished. You breeze through all your classes, you're our best third bagman/offensive tackle in tackle three-ball, and I think Bianca's been checking you out."

"She asked me if my arms detach." He sniffed. "Then she giggled and asked if I'd lend her a hand."

Eloni spit out some of his milk, and then pretended to cough. Boris looked confused, so Eloni leaned toward him to explain the joke. "Because his head pops off, see—"

"You've got a lot going for you," I said to Frankie. "Don't let that nitpicky scientist or one snooty girl make you feel bad."

He shrugged. He couldn't help but feel bad; he was a sensitive guy.

Darthin squeezed his way through the tables and sat next to me. His dirty-blond hair had puffed up a bit from its earlier flatness, and he had a huge smile on his face.

"Wow, Darthin," I said, "you look happy." Lunch was usually kind of stressful for him, because of the monsters.

"I just had Biology," he said. "It . . . was . . . awesome."

"Who do you have?" I asked.

"Frankenhammer," Darthin said.

"Me too," Boris said. "I was late, and he made me the Test Subject of the Day." He scratched his head. "We're studying head lice. I have to go back after school." He leaned forward and whispered, "I don't want to go back."

"Sorry, guys," I said, leaning away from Boris. "Frankenhammer is scary."

"Are you kidding?" Darthin smiled. "Frankenhammer's awesome. He's a genius. And he likes me. Me!"

I shushed him, because that was the sort of thing that would send Frankie's head flying. Fortunately, Frankie had fallen asleep, his head propped against the wall.

"Sorry," Darthin said. "I bet it's because of my horns." He stroked a fake horn, like he was thanking it. "I'm thinking of adding a bony hump. Young gargoyles have them. Eventually, they sprout wings. But listen. I'm helping him in his lab during my free period, and I'm learning so much. Did you know he invented the Slime-Spewing Lizards?"

"No," I said. "That was Dr. Critchlore. It's in his autobiography."

"No, Critchlore just took the credit," Darthin said. "Frankenhammer showed me his lab books on them. How he sketched them out and plotted different spewing methods and everything."

"Why did he let Dr. Critchlore take his idea?"

Darthin shrugged. "He said it's in his contract. Anything he invents while working here becomes the property of Dr. Critchlore. He's inventing something new now, but he's very hush-hush about it. I think he doesn't want it to get stolen too. How's the junior henchman thing going?"

"I probably won't last long," I said. "Dr. Critchlore posted twenty-seven kids to the program and there are only five slots. Plus I'm cursed."

"Bummer."

I saw Pismo eating with some first-years. I almost waved at him until I remembered that I was still mad about his prank. He nodded at me. His hair looked a little singed. I wondered if he was near the cemetery when it exploded, since he'd run off in that direction.

The bell rang three times, signaling an announcement. The teachers' room unshuttered and the door opened as everyone looked to the flat screen mounted high on the wall at the end of the cafeteria. Dr. Critchlore's face filled it, his beaky nose seeming to stab at us with its sharp point.

"Good afternoon, students, faculty, and staff. I know you must all be concerned about the explosion, and I want to assure you that the school is in no further danger. Our security team is investigating, and Mrs. Gomes tells me that it was an isolated incident.

"Due to the explosion, we are canceling classes for the rest of the day. Students will report to their halls to review safety drills. We had quite a few mix-ups this morning, and this vital area needs to be addressed first. Please be assured that the safety of our minions is a priority for us. Maybe not the highest priority, but it's definitely in the top five.

"What else?" He looked up, as if the answer was floating in the air above him. "Oh yes. Students in the Junior Henchman Training Program will report to the base of Mount Curiosity for their first test tomorrow morning at seven."

The screen went black, but we could still hear Dr. Critchlore's voice. "That's it, right? I'm a very busy man. Now, where's my remote? My soap opera comes on at one."

There were a few giggles from the students. The teachers frowned. A few of them muttered something about the board of directors hearing about this.

I felt ill. Junior henchman test tomorrow morning? Outside? What could they be testing us on? What if it was fighting skills? I tried to imagine something else, but nothing came to mind. I was doomed.

# CHAPTER 13

*Just as you cannot teach a crab to walk straight,*
*you cannot teach a Critchlore minion to be unfaithful.*
—DR. CRITCHLORE, IN AN ADVERTISEMENT

The afternoon crawled by like an explosive minion. (Did I mention they were slow?)

Professor Twilk, the weapons teacher in charge of the third-year students, showed us where to report during safety drills and emergencies. Our meeting spot was the ballroom located at the end of one arm of the castle. Decorated with mirrors and chandeliers, the huge room was where we had Dance class once a week. Evil overlords liked to party, and they liked to fill their parties with excellent dancers. Our bad luck.

Detention was in the dungeon, so I headed there after school. The dungeon's central hub, located beneath the castle foyer, was a busy place. Phones rang, printers hummed, people darted between cubicles. Brownies (the small, hairy creatures, not the delectable dessert) dashed about, cleaning up spills and delivering coffee. There were doors leading off the chamber on every wall of the room. The dungeon spread out in all directions.

I signed in at the sign-in desk (they kept track of who came and went because people tended to get lost in the dungeon). Then it was off to the fifth-years' practice laboratory, located on the main dungeon level, past the blood bank (for the vampires), the spare-parts freezer room (for the biological engineers), and the day-care center (for the children of school employees). Mr. Griphold, the dean of Class 3 minions (human-size), stood at the door with his tablet computer, having downloaded his list of detainees.

"Higgins," he said, "go on in and take a seat. When everyone's here, I'll hand out assignments."

The room was brightly lit with fluorescent lights. Out of four rows of lab tables, only three chairs were occupied: Hector, a hob-goblin wearing the blue jacket of a seventh-year; Drangulus, a fourth-year lizard-boy (light blue jacket); and Fiona, a third-year siren. I tried not to stare, but she was really cute. Her blond hair looked so silky that I wanted to run my fingers through it. She was drawing a picture of a unicorn on her binder. Drangulus tried to show her his picture of a two-headed swamp cat, but she just shivered and looked away. We had quite a few two-headed swamp cats on the school grounds, but not one unicorn.

I sat down and pulled out a brochure I'd picked up at the library: *What to Do if You're Cursed.* I read:

*Section One: Who Gets Cursed?*

*Those who wish ill on others, either consciously or unconsciously, make themselves vulnerable to curses, because they fill themselves with nega-tive cursing energy.*

Hmm. Had I wished someone ill? I didn't think so. Maybe I had unconsciously cursed Pismo. Or the imps.

*The first step to remove a curse is to cleanse oneself of the resonant en-*

*ergy of cursing. Think happy thoughts about the people you would curse.*

Okay. I closed my eyes and thought, *Pismo is a nice kid. He was just trying to be funny. Same with the imps. I do not wish them harm. Pismo is a friendly, funny guy.*

"Boo!" Someone yelled in my ear.

I jumped, knocking over my chair. Half the contents of my backpack jumbled out onto the floor. I turned, ready for attack, and saw Pismo's smiling face.

"Hey," he said.

Most people know you should never, ever sneak up on a werewolf. I straightened my chair and stuffed everything back into my backpack. I opened my curse brochure again. There had to be another way to get rid of curses, because I couldn't stop my negative thoughts about Pismo.

The little pest sat down behind me and leaned forward, whispering in my ear, "You're not mad, are you?"

I decided to let him figure out the answer to that question.

"C'mon, it was a great prank. Don't be a poor sport."

"It may come as a surprise to you," I said, turning around, "but some of us don't think it's cool to get detention."

"Hey, I'm sorry. I just didn't want to be here alone, okay?" He flipped his long bangs out of his eyes. "This place gives me the creeps."

Mr. Griphold came in and shut the door. "Five students who couldn't make it one day into the new term without getting into trouble." He shook his head and tsked us. Then he smiled. "Well, more workers for me. Let's see." He tapped the screen of his tablet. "Tootles needs someone to pull weeds in the gar—"

"I'll take it," Hector said. He got up to leave and muttered, "Too slow, suckers," as he went.

Of course, that was a good job—outside with Tootles, who was a pushover.

"Next," Griphold went on. "Mistress Moira—"

"I'll take it," the lizard-boy said. I smacked my head. Any job with Moira would be easy. She was the school seamstress and chocolatier. Everyone said she was crazy because she claimed to be the Fourth Fate from mythology, but she was really nice.

"Okay," Griphold said. "Next, I have a job in the kitchen."

"I'll take it," I said. It was a job I'd probably do anyway, when I went to check in with Cook like I always did after school. She'd give me a hug and a snack, ask me how my day went, and then put me to work.

"Aw, I wanted to work in the kitchen," Fiona said. She pouted her lips and blinked at me.

"Oh, you can have it," I said. She smiled, smacked her gum, and skipped out of the room.

"That leaves you two," Griphold said. "Dr. Frankenhammer had an accident in his lab. Report there for cleanup."

Of course. Hey, I was cursed, what did I expect? A job testing Professor Dunkirk's off-road vehicles?

We turned to leave, but Griphold grabbed my arm. "You might want to pick up a hazardous materials suit in the Supply Station first. Just to be safe."

"Yes, Mr. Griphold," I said. Then, in a whisper, I added, "What's Pismo in for?"

"Tried to swipe a book from Dr. Critchlore's office," he said.

I looked at Pismo, who had dumped his books out of his back-pack and was looking for something at the bottom.

"He doesn't strike me as the reading type," I muttered.

"It was the *Top Secret Book of Minions*," Griphold said. "He was probably after the jewels."

Leash laws! Pismo had tried to steal the most valuable book in the whole school. But how? It was locked in a display case. The *Top Secret Book of Minions* was an ancient, leather-bound book with pages edged in gold. Inlaid with jewels, the cover was held closed by metal gears attached to a wide band. It had taken Dr. Critchlore months to figure out how to open it.

It was supposed to hold the secret of creating an undefeatable minion, but it was written in some ancient code.

And Pismo had just tried to steal it. What was that boy up to?

# CHAPTER 14

*Discipline, Duty, Determination, and On–Time Delivery.*
—DR. CRITCHLORE'S FOUR PILLARS OF BUSINESS SUCCESS

F rankenhammer," Pismo said. "That's the creepy dude, right?"
"Yep."

I led Pismo to a stone staircase that descended to a lower dungeon level. Mr. Griphold had given Pismo a DPS (Dungeon Positioning System), so I pulled out mine and showed him how to plug in the Supply Station as our destination. Something told me he'd be back in detention again, and I wasn't planning on joining him. The least I could do was make sure he didn't get lost.

We watched the route light up on the device. "Please proceed straight down the amber hall until you reach the Column of On–Time Delivery," it said.

"'Column of On–Time Delivery'?" Pismo asked.

"Dr. Critchlore inscribed his four pillars of business success onto the four columns that support the school," I explained. "The four Ds."

"What are they?"

"Discipline, Duty, Determination, and On–Time Delivery."

Pismo looked back to his DPS.

"I hardly ever use the DPS," I told him. "The routes are always longer than they need to be. Plus I know the shortcuts." I probably knew the school better than anybody, but I didn't want to brag.

"Still, always check one out," I cautioned, "because, as it says above the Strategy Room, 'A Minion Prepared Is a Minion Not Snared.' You'll get your own when you're a third-year."

"Right," Pismo said. "Does this have any weapons capabilities?"

"No, it's just a map," I said.

We walked to the Column of On-Time Delivery, which was as wide around as an old-growth redwood tree. Each column stood in its own circular room, the column in the center like a tent pole. The curving walls were decorated with tapestries, photographs, and testimonials to honor the great minion battles of the past.

Once past the Column of On-Time Delivery, my DPS said, "Left turn in five meters." *Yeah, right, if you want to go past the Poison Development Center. I don't think so.* I led Pismo to the right, going down a staircase and into a tunnel with unfinished rock walls, dim lighting, and bats.

"Hey, Victor," I said as we passed him hanging upside down from the ceiling.

"Hi, Higgins," the bat said.

Once we were out of earshot, Pismo whispered, "Isn't that kind of dangerous? I mean—he's a vampire, right?"

"Nah, they're well fed. Harmless. If you really want to be safe, just eat a batch of Cook's garlic fries once a week, and the vampires won't come near you."

We plunged into the darkness, my DPS providing a dim glow

that only reached about a foot in front of us, like a flashlight about to run out of juice.

"How scary is this guy Frankenhammer?" Pismo asked.

"Have you heard of the Festering Boil Spitters?" I asked.

"Of course. Catlike creatures. They spit a blackish tar that makes their victims break out in pus-oozing boils. Gross."

"Dr. Frankenhammer invented them. Unfortunately, they were uncontrollable and had a tendency to run off and hide in dark spaces."

Pismo shrugged. "Nobody's perfect."

"A few escaped down here."

It was hard to tell in the dim light, but I think Pismo might have paled a little. I felt bad. I shouldn't have told him about the Spitters. I knew that we wouldn't see one, but he was just so smug, I couldn't help myself.

We reached the Supply Station, which was like one of those giant warehouse stores, only less bright and more dungeony (think *waaaaay* fewer people and *waaaaay* more spiders).

A long counter blocked access to the shelves. Behind the counter, workers darted around the stacks, collecting goods off the shelves to fill orders. They were mole people (MPs), who enjoyed working deep underground. I'd always thought they were creepy, with their large red eyes and bumpy green skin. They had huge hands with long, thick claws.

I walked up to the counter and rang the bell, but I couldn't hear it, the room was so noisy. Forklifts beeped, workers shouted to one another, and machinery clanked as products came in on moving conveyor belts.

I rang it again. And again. I tried to catch the eye of a worker darting by. Finally a guy printing out orders from the computer hollered, "Felix, help those kids at the counter!"

"You do it!" Felix yelled. "I just got five orders for the chemistry department."

"Fine." The MP walked over and put both hands on the counter, his claws pointing at us like a threat. "What?"

"Two hazmat suits, size small, for cleanup in Dr. Frankenhammer's lab, please," I said. These mole people weren't much for small talk. You had to state your business and get out of there as fast as you could or they'd "accidentally" scratch you.

"Wow, this place is huge," Pismo said. Behind the counter, row after row of two-story-high shelves stretched away as far as we could see. In addition to training minions, Dr. Critchlore ran a successful minion supply company, selling all sorts of useful products he'd invented.

The MP frowned at Pismo as he typed into his computer. We heard the whir of a motor. To the right, a long row of hazmat suits started moving on their conveyor belt, like clothes at the dry cleaner. Green, fireproof ones for dragon stable cleanup; blue for the Necromancy labs; orange for really, really toxic stuff; and, finally, yellow for basic lab spills.

"Can I get one in magenta?" Pismo said. "It highlights my eyes."

I shook my head at him, hoping he'd get the clue that talking here was *not* okay.

"I'm joking," he said.

I ran my hand across my throat, telling him to cut it.

"You're very uptight, Higgins," he said. "Why is everyone here so grim?"

The MP returned and handed me my suit. I honestly couldn't tell the MPs apart, so I wasn't sure of his name. However, I'd figured out that they all responded well to a generic title, such as "Exalted Wise One."

"Thank you, Preeminent Efficiency Maker."

He nodded at me. Then he handed Pismo a much older suit that had a tear in the sleeve. That looked dangerous.

"You want magenta," he said in his raspy voice. "This one will turn you magenta."

Then he disappeared.

Pismo took the suit, his eyes wide. I grabbed his arm and got us out of there.

"What is with that guy?" Pismo said once we were back in the hallway.

"U-MAD," I explained.

"A little. This suit looks dangerous."

"No, U-M-A-D: Underground Mole-person Affective Disorder. Have you ever heard of seasonal affective disorder?"

"No."

"SAD—people get depressed in winter, from a lack of sun. Mole people get a version of that, but instead of depressed, they become extremely rude and impatient. Plus they love to find excuses to hurt people—that's just their nature."

Pismo shrugged. "I don't think this suit will fit me. Wanna trade?"

I looked at my suit, which was shiny and new. I looked at his—the plastic was wrinkled, the viewing port was cracked and cloudy with age, and there was that cut in the sleeve.

"Sorry, no." I said.

"C'mon, Higgs. I'm a first-year. Help me out here." He pouted. "I won't know what to stay away from. You've been here forever; you probably don't even need the suit."

"I can't get sick," I said. "I have my junior henchman test in the morning."

"You'll ace it," he said. "I know you will. Please?"

"No. You earned that suit."

"I didn't know about the mole people! This is so unfair." He started crying. "I hate this stupid school. I can't wait to get thrown out of here so I can get sent to a decent school where they don't try to kill their students."

"Don't say that," I said. "This is a great school. Here, I'll take it." I took the broken suit, telling myself it was just a precaution anyway. We probably wouldn't even need them.

Pismo immediately stopped crying and grabbed my suit. "Sweet," he said, smiling.

*Pismo is a nice kid,* I thought to myself while trying to unclench my teeth. Then I pulled out my medallion and kissed it. I was going to need all the luck I could get.


I opened the door to Dr. Frankenhammer's lab and we entered. The room was lit by a flickering overhead light. Dark shadows cowered in the corners, as if they were afraid of Dr. Frankenhammer too. A crackling electric buzz filled the air, and it smelled like chemicals.

Behind the table, Dr. Frankenhammer stood beneath the light, his face in shadow. He held a very large syringe filled with blood. Strapped to the table was my ogre-man friend, Boris.

# CHAPTER 15

*Take six hairs of werewolf, extract of valerian root,*
*tooth of sloth. A sloth's tooth? Do they even have teeth?*
*This one looks like a four, or it could be the moon.*
—DR. CRITCHLORE, TRYING TO DECIPHER THE

*TOP SECRET BOOK OF MINIONS*

I cleared my throat, and Dr. Frankenhammer's head jerked up.

"Sorry to interrupt, Dr. Frankenhammer," I said. "I . . . um . . . we . . . the two of us . . . are here for detention . . . and . . . Is Boris okay?"

"Borisss forgot his lab kit," Dr. Frankenhammer said, lowering his surgical mask. "He graciously offered to supply a few . . . ssssamples for class." He unstrapped the pale-looking Boris, who now sported a buzz cut.

"Cookie?" Dr. Frankenhammer said. Boris took the cookie and stumbled for the exit. I grabbed him as he passed.

"You okay?" I whispered.

He nodded, swayed on his feet, and then left. I looked over at Dr. Frankenhammer, who was putting Boris's blood and hair into sample dishes. He turned and looked at me, then down at a pile of surgical instruments on the counter. He picked up his scalpel and smiled.

87

I reflexively backed up and bumped into Pismo. He felt rubbery. I glanced back and saw he was already in his suit.

"Mr. Higginssss," Dr. Frankenhammer said. I hated the way he said my name, like he was drawing it out on his lab table, preparing it for dissection. I tried not to shiver, I really did, but I couldn't help it. Dr. Frankenhammer walked over to me and put a hand on my shoulder. He was either trying to make me feel comfortable or keeping a tight grip on me so I couldn't escape, I wasn't sure which.

"Um, Mr. Griphold sent us to help clean up."

"Ssssuper." Dr. Frankenhammer ushered us out of his lab with outstretched arms, as if he were afraid we would try to duck around him to see his research. "The messsss is in the testing lab next door." When we exited his lab, he turned and locked it behind us. "Follow."

We walked down the hall to another door. I would have passed right by without seeing it, because the door was perfectly camouflaged into the rough wall. Even the PIN pad seemed to blend right in. Dr. Frankenhammer entered the code and turned to me. "Better put on your suit, Higginssss."

I jumped into my suit, closing it up as best I could. The inside smelled like sour milk mixed with puke, and I could feel a draft on my arm. Pismo smiled at me through his clean view port. His probably still had that "New Hazmat Suit" smell: fresh and plasticky, like a new rubber ball.

"This way," Dr. Frankenhammer held the door open. Pismo again let me go in first.

Dr. Frankenhammer grabbed a filter mask that was hanging just inside the door and covered his mouth and nose. The room looked like a duplicate of his regular lab—an impeccably clean space with lab tables and equipment, lots of stainless steel cabinets, and shelves filled with neatly lined-up specimen jars. One held a small being with a line of horny bumps on his skull. His small, razor-toothed mouth was frozen in a silent scream, like he was terrified of the fate awaiting him. *You and me both, little buddy.*

"This is my testing lab," he said. "I use it for my prototypes, and ssssometimes, when I'm feeling ssssilly, I do a bit of, shall we say, genetic brewing to ssssee what I can come up with. Just for fun." He held a finger to his lips, like it was a ssssecret.

The room was dim, only safety lighting was on, so of course I noticed our target: a glowing greenish goop dripping off the table on the right.

"What *is* that?" I asked.

"I spilled my ssssoup," he said. "I'll clean that up myself. You boys need to focus on the ssssupply closet." He pointed to the left.

"The closet with the sign that says, 'Danger: Infectious Disease Storage'?"

Dr. Frankenhammer waved a hand. "Not to worry, I only put the sign up to scare off nosy looky-loosss." *Phew.* "The infectious diseases are stored in that cabinet next to you."

I jumped away from the cabinet and hustled over to the closet. It was closed, but something brown was leaking out the bottom. It looked like it was sprouting hair.

"Better hurry," he said. "I gave it a shot of evolution acceleration, which means it will grow and mutate very quickly. If it reaches full stasis, it's likely to sprout very sharp barbs."

"What is it?" Pismo asked.

"I haven't named it. It's a rapidly growing organism that has no bonessss. My mistake." He shrugged. "It's like a muscle-blob, with quills. Sometimessss, the best creations come out of simply letting yourself go and not thinking about what you are doing," he went on. "But that method leads to a lot of garbage as well."

I walked over to the closet door and rested my hand on the handle. "It doesn't spew anything, does it?" I asked, remembering Dr. Frankenhammer's fondness for creatures that spew.

"Why, yes, Higginssss, it does," he said. "It spews toxic bile that blinds its victim. You know, I think there may be a use for this . . . this Thing yet."

I pulled my hand off the handle.

"Don't worry," Dr. Frankenhammer said. "It only becomes bile-spewing in its final evolutionary stage. This one is harmlessss. Just scoop it up and put it in that bin." He pointed to a large, metallic garbage can. "Make sure to put the lid on tight."

Pismo grabbed a broom that was propped next to the closet door. It was a pretty feeble tool for this job, but we didn't have anything else. Dr. Frankenhammer turned and very quickly left the room.

"Ready?" I asked. A smoky fog emanated from the part of the blob escaping beneath the door. It smelled like gym socks. And the reason I could smell it was because my hazmat suit was completely ineffective.

Pismo nodded. I took a deep breath, held it, and opened the door.

The Thing plopped out. It looked soft, like brown jelly with hair, but when I touched it with my rubber-gloved hand, it hardened, like a muscle tensing.

And then it lunged at me, knocking me onto my back and sliding on my legs, pinning them down.

"Pismo!" I screamed. "Hit it now!"

No matter how hard I pushed, I couldn't budge it. The Thing was a gigantic muscle, as big as a beanbag chair, so of course it was incredibly strong. And it was oozing up my body.

"Pismo!"

Where was he? I looked back and saw the broom on the floor next to my head. Pismo was across the room, sitting at Dr. Frankenhammer's workstation, staring at the computer screen while his fingers typed frantically.

"Pismo! Get over here!"

"Just . . . a . . . sec," he said calmly.

*Are you kidding me?* The Thing pressed on my hips. I tried to hold it back, but it was too strong. And heavy. My toes had gone numb. I stretched my fingers for the broom, but it was just out of reach.

"Pismo! Now!"

He held up his pointer finger without taking his gaze off the screen. I didn't think I had one more minute, or even one more second. The Thing was mashing me. No amount of effort did the slightest bit of harm or slowed it down. It covered my chest, and I couldn't breathe. "Pismo," I managed to yelp.

It plopped up my neck, then my chin.

"Yelp," I yelped. This was it. I was going to suffocate underneath a gigantic hairy muscle that smelled like armpit while Pismo read Dr. Frankenhammer's files. *At least it hadn't sprouted quills,* I thought, trying to find a bright side. Then I felt my hazmat suit shred as thousands of tiny barbs scraped my skin. Tears leaked out of the sides of my eyes and were quickly covered by blob.

Good-bye, world.

And then, suddenly, the Thing turned back into jelly.

I heaved with all my might, and the heavy muscle just plopped right off me. I collapsed on my back and breathed in deeply. Pismo stood above me with a syringe in his hand.

"Extra-strength muscle relaxant," he said.

I closed my eyes. "Great Danes, that was close."

We got the Thing into the bin and shut the lid tightly just as Dr. Frankenhammer returned with a mop and a bucket to clean up his soup. He put them down and picked up a couple of metal helmets with lots of wires and pokey things running in and out of them.

"Well done, boysssss," he said. "Now, if you would help me with an experiment—"

"We've gotta go," I said. I grabbed Pismo and we ran out of there as fast as we could.

Returning to the Supply Station, I asked Pismo what he was doing on Dr. Frankenhammer's computer when he should have been rescuing me.

"I *was* rescuing you," he said, eating one of the snickerdoodles he'd snatched from Dr. Frankenhammer's lab. "Had to find his supply list to see if he had the muscle relaxant. Found it in a file labeled 'Inventory and Where It's Stored.'"

We turned in our hazmat suits. The MP scowled at me as I handed him the shredded remains of mine.

"Sorry, Most Esteemed Realm Master," I said.

He grunted at me.

"Here you go, um, Super Amazing Guy," Pismo said. I think the MP actually smiled at him.

In the tunnels I contemplated ditching Pismo. *Let him find his own way out, the little pest.*

"You want to ditch me, don't you?" Pismo said.

I sighed. I wanted to say, "Nothing went the way it was supposed to today. I was so excited this morning, but then I found out there are five times as many junior henchman trainees as there are spots in the program, the zombie minions I'm supposed to help train are impossible, a bomb exploded in the cemetery, some imps trapped me in the garden, I got a tardy and then detention, and I was attacked by a hairy muscle Thing."

But instead of saying all that, I punched him on the shoulder.

"Bad day?" he asked, laughing. "C'mon, it could have been worse." I scowled at him. I wasn't in the mood to talk. "No, you're right, that was pretty gross."

We reached the final hallway before the dungeon exit. Everyone was heading home for the day, or to the cafeteria for dinner, and we joined the exodus.

"I know what you did," I said.

"What?" Pismo asked. "The book?"

"Yes, the book. What were you thinking?"

"That it was pretty, and mysterious, and I wanted to see what was inside."

I pictured the book, sitting in its display case with the gentle overhead lighting that made its gears shine like gold. "That book is always locked up in Dr. Critchlore's office. How'd you get your hands on it?"

"It was just sitting on his sour-faced secretary's desk," he said, and then he took off without saying good-bye, joining the first-year skeletons on their way to dinner.

I had only taken two steps into the cafeteria when a hand grabbed me from behind.

# CHAPTER 16

*Have a problem with encroaching neighbors?*
*We have the minion for you!*
—ADVERTISEMENT FOR CRITCHLORE'S MINIONS

I spun around and looked up at the face of my foster brother, Pierre. He wore an apron and held a ladle in the hand that wasn't holding me.

"Hey, squirt. Mom wants you." He nodded to the kitchen.

We walked over together. He took his spot behind the serving counter, and I went through the swinging door into the kitchen.

This was Cook's resting time. She ate while the meal was being served. Once it was over she'd get to work cleaning up and preparing for the next meal. I found her sitting at a table in the nook, eating a salad.

"Hi, Mom," I said.

"Good heavens, Runt, look at you," she said. She got up, wiped her hands on her apron, and walked over to the broom closet. "I will not have a son of mine showing up to the dining hall looking like that." She waved a hand in my direction.

"What? I look fine."

She came out with a new third-year uniform on a hanger, shaking her head. "Sweetie, is that blood?"

"Frankie's," I said.

She lifted one of my jacket sleeves. It tore off in her grasp, having been shredded by thousands of tiny barbs. She raised an eyebrow at me.

"Here," she said, handing me the clothes. "You can change in the closet."

"Fine." The closet was large, mostly filled with shelves of canned goods, but there was also a row of uniforms hanging along one side. "Do you keep spare uniforms for everyone in here?"

"Just you," she muttered. "What happened?"

I told her about Frankie's head, and about the Thing in Dr. Frankenhammer's lab.

"That man," Cook said, shaking her head. "He's too reckless."

"But, Mom?"

"What, dear?"

"I didn't change." I came out in my new uniform. Cook was back at her table. "I was under attack, and I didn't change. You said it would happen when I needed it to, but it hasn't."

"You've got to be patient, honey," she said. "And it did happen, that one time, remember?"

Of course I remembered. I was about seven. I'd been sitting on the bleachers with Pierre, who was a seventh-year at the time. We were watching the werewolves work out. They were so powerful and sleek. The way they moved and smelled reminded me of my real family. They all seemed to know what the others were going to do. I howled. They stopped what they were doing and howled back.

That night I transformed into a werewolf and fought off a massive swamp creature that had gotten into our house.

Cook stood up and gave me a hug. She was soft and warm and smelled like fresh-cooked bread. "Don't worry, honey," she said.

"It probably didn't happen because the Thing was crushing me," I said.

"That's probably why."

"Mom, *you're* crushing me," I said. She released me from the hug, smiling. "If I get into the MMA tournament, I'll change for sure."

"Not if you don't eat," she said. "Go on now."

I got my food and plopped down at my usual table with Frankie and Darthin. Eloni and Boris were over with the ogre-men. Eloni waved his club at me and smiled. I gave him a thumbs-up sign in reply.

"What's up with Eloni and Boris?" I asked.

"This morning, Ranko forgot his lab kit," Darthin explained. "While the other ogre-men were teasing him for having a mermaid moment, Eloni convinced Boris to let Ranko use his. Boris took the blame with Frankenhammer."

"I saw him in the lab," I said. "That was nice of him."

Darthin shrugged. "The ogre-men were going to let only Boris sit with them because he has the same DNA, and they're kind of picky that way. But Eloni convinced them to let him go too. He was the one who convinced Boris to give up his lab kit, and he's almost as big as they are."

Eloni looked elated. He was smiling and talking, and everyone was laughing.

The whole cafeteria was filled with excited chatter. Even the skeletons seemed happy, which was weird, since they don't have faces.

*And look who's sitting with them.*

"Something about that new guy really bugs me," I told my friends.

"Who?" Darthin said.

"That guy, sitting with the skeletons," I said. "His name is Pismo. And get this, he tried to steal the *Top Secret Book of Minions*."

"Mommy?" Frankie said.

Dr. Frankenhammer had told Frankie that the *Top Secret Book of Minions* helped him find the solution to why his Frankenminions never made it out of infancy. Since Frankie was created by Dr. Frankenhammer and the *Top Secret Book of Minions*, he called them Daddy and Mommy.

"No way," Darthin said.

"It's true. He also set me up so I'd get detention with him. And he stole my exploding gum and threw it at himself so he could get out of class—but he didn't go to the nurse, he went off to the cemetery, right before it exploded.

"And then in detention, while I was pinned by this Thing in Dr. Frankenhammer's lab, instead of helping me, Pismo was reading all of his files."

"What thing in Dr. Frankenhammer's lab?" Darthin asked.

"Some sort of giant hairy muscle," I said. "But that's not important. I just don't think Pismo is minion material."

"By hairy, do you mean 'shaggy dog' hairy, or 'Otto's back' hairy?" Darthin persisted. The guy was obsessed with Dr. Frankenhammer's work.

"Otto's back," I said. Otto was a human groundskeeper who went shirtless in hot weather. It wasn't pretty.

"Did it spew?" Darthin asked.

"He said it would spew in its final evolutionary form. And he'd given it some sort of accelerator to speed up its growth. It seemed to grow right over me."

"Fascinating," Darthin said. He had a dreamy, far-off look on his face.

"Darthin, you be careful down there," I said. "That Thing could have killed me. And Dr. Frankenhammer just left us there with it."

"He tried to paint me green once," Frankie said, stirring his mashed potatoes in an absentminded way. "He told me he didn't like how my color came out. I don't look gruesome enough."

"Sorry, Frankie," I said. He looked miserable. I needed to distract him from thinking about Dr. Frankenhammer. "But listen, this thing sprouted quills right before Pismo shot it. Ripped my suit to shreds!"

"Pismo shot it? With a gun?" Darthin asked.

"No, he gave it a shot of muscle relaxant."

"That's brilliant."

"No, he's rude and selfish," I said. "And he seems older than eleven. He makes me feel like I'm the little kid. I tell you, there's something not right about him."

"Why would he want me to be green?" Frankie said. His face was screwing up in that way we all knew meant trouble. What made it worse was that Frankie was absolutely petrified of having his head come off in front of other people. So it became one of those self-fulfilling-prophecy type of things. He worried about his head coming off in the cafeteria, and that worry caused his head to come off in the cafeteria.

I stood up, pretending to stretch, while signaling Boris and Eloni at the ogre-men's table. It had worked once before, in the library. But there was too much going on in the cafeteria, so they didn't notice me. I really didn't want to turn off Frankie's blood flow again. That wouldn't be good for his brain.

I stretched again, this time adding a loud yawn. Still nothing. Their attention was completely focused on the ogre-men.

Frankie's hands pressed down on the top of his head. He bit his lower lip.

I was desperate. I didn't want to call attention to Frankie by running over there and dragging the guys back. But if Frankie's head blew, we would need Boris and Eloni. I thought about yelling, but that would be as bad as running over there. So instead, I threw a dinner roll across the room at Eloni.

That was a mistake.

I was thinking that I could get Eloni's attention and they'd come over and assume their positions for re-heading Frankie, should he blow, which looked likely at that point. Unfortunately, everyone else in the cafeteria interpreted my actions in a different way. They thought I was starting a food fight, and as everyone knew, as long as you weren't the one to start the food fight, you could join in without repercussions. For some reason, only the person who started it got into trouble.

On the plus side, Eloni looked up and saw me, so he grabbed Boris and they raced over, ducking under flying cheeseburger macaroni as they ran. Cook made a mean cheeseburger macaroni, and I mean that literally. The stuff would punch you in the gut and then insult your mother.

"I did everything right today," Frankie went on, oblivious to the mounting food war taking place around him. An overcooked corn on the cob flew right by his head and squished off the wall, leaving a mushy yellow splotch. "And at the end of class he said, 'Why can't you be more like Darthin?'" He gulped, barely able to swallow. "'Darthin will create a fully functional homunculus by his sixth year.' I don't even know what a homunculus is!"

"It's a small human," Darthin said. He couldn't help smiling at the compliment. "About a foot tall. Dr. Frankenhammer really said that?"

Frankie moaned. I admired how brave he was. It was obvious he wanted to cry, but he wouldn't let himself.

We were getting pelted by flying food: baked potatoes and cheese-filled pizza sticks covered in tomato sauce, mashed peas and Salisbury steaks. I dumped my food and used my tray as a shield.

"What do I have to *dooooo*?" Frankie whined.

He slammed his fists on the table, and his head went *pop*.

"Positions!" I screamed, dropping my tray. Frankie was still sitting, so I bear-hugged him from behind. His legs kicked and it was tough keeping him still.

Darthin caught Frankie's head right out of the air and held it over his blood-spewing neck. Eloni peeled down the neck skin, and then he and Boris reattached the head while I held Frankie still. In all, it took about fifteen seconds, and there'd been very little blood spurting. It sort of mixed in with the tomato sauce we were already wearing.

"Great job, guys," I said. Frankie collapsed in my arms. "You okay?"

Frankie nodded, so I let him go. He fell to the floor.

"Frankie, I'm taking you to the infirmary for a blood boost," I said. "Two times in twenty-four hours. That's not good."

"Okay," he said from the floor. "Just give me a second."

"Eloni? Can you give me a hand?" I asked. Eloni pulled Frankie up, draping one of Frankie's arms over his shoulder. I did the same on Frankie's other side. We headed for the door, stepping over huge piles of mashed food and whatever it was the monkey-men were throwing.

Oh, *ew*.

We hadn't gotten far when the bell sounded. The dean of students walked in and blew his whistle. The combination of noises sent the entire student body scurrying back to their seats. Mr. Everest scanned the room, which looked like a herd of trolls had just projectile-vomited up their last five meals. He raised his eyebrows and put his hands on his hips. He didn't have to say anything. All the kids were pointing at me.

# CHAPTER 17

*To Live Is to Conquer.*

—ENGRAVED ABOVE THE MONSTER MINION DORMITORY

Curse, 9; Higgins, 0.

The curse was kicking my butt.

Eloni and Boris took Frankie to the infirmary. Darthin wanted to stay and help me, but I knew he had to study for a test that would allow him to skip regular Biology and get into Advanced Monster Biology, so I told him to go. I wasn't allowed to leave until the cafeteria was clean.

It was too much. I sat at my table and pulled out my curse brochure.

*Another successful way to break a curse is to not believe in it*, I read. *The power of a positive attitude has been well documented.*

All right, I'd give that a try. I put on my cafeteria helper outfit of rubber boots, gloves, and an apron, and got to work. *I am not cursed, I am not cursed, I am not cursed,* I chanted in my head. Then I slipped on some tomato sauce and landed in monkey-man dookie.

I tossed food scraps into a giant compost bin on wheels, and when it filled up I took it out to the compost heap by the vegetable garden. Back and forth I went, pushing the bin over the cobblestone road. My arms rattled as I tried to keep it steady. I was alone with my thoughts, which weren't helping my positive attitude. I couldn't help replaying everything that had happened that day.

What could I have done differently? If I hadn't tried to train the zombies, they wouldn't have embarrassed me in class. If I hadn't listened to that cry for help, then I wouldn't have gotten trapped by imps and gotten a tardy. And if I'd kept a closer eye on Pismo, he wouldn't have stolen my gum.

I emptied the bin into the compost pile. A couple of two-headed swamp cats watched me from the bushes, waiting to feast on the scraps. I had to reach in and scoop out all the mushy stuff that stuck to the sides and the bottom. *Yuck.*

I told myself that it was stupid to wonder what I could have done differently, because it wasn't like I could go back in time and change anything. So on the way back to the cafeteria, I worried about the future instead.

What was happening to my school? It had started with the outbreak of wyvern flu last year. The whole school was quarantined for a month, and most of our recruits opted to go to other minion schools. Then came the video. Even if the video had been faked, the image of Dr. Critchlore's ogre-men cowering in fear would remain in people's heads.

And now the cemetery explosion. Without the recruits, our first-year class was almost entirely cemetery-created—the zombies, mummies, and skeletons. And Pismo, the delinquent. There were a few other humanish, non-undead first-years, but not as many as in years past. My dorm room could hold eight kids and it only had three.

And all this was happening while Dr. Critchlore was depressed. The timing couldn't have been worse.

I entered the cafeteria and saw that I'd barely made a dent in the job. Load and dump, load and dump. I was on my third bin when I realized I was going to be there all night. And I had my junior henchman test the next morning. This was a disaster.

My breathing came in short gasps as I started to panic. What if I didn't get enough sleep? What if I woke up exhausted? I *had* to be a junior henchman. How else was I going to find my family? It was my dream that I'd become a junior henchman to a powerful evil overlord. I'd save his life or something, and he'd be so grateful he'd do anything to pay me back. I'd tell him, "I don't want riches, I just want to find my family." And then he'd send out his best minions to track them down for me.

My hands shook as I scooped up food, and I bit my lower lip to keep from crying. I was about to lose it when the swinging double doors burst open and Frankie strode in with his arms in the air.

"I . . . feel . . . great!"

I smiled at him. Blood boosts always lifted his mood. He looked good too—his skin tone was back to his normal beige, his brown eyes were sparkling with happiness, and it looked like the nurses in the infirmary had cleaned up the jagged mess of his neck, where the skin had ripped apart. He pirouetted around the cafeteria, jumping on tables and dancing around chairs.

Eloni and Boris came in behind him. "We thought you might need some help," Eloni said.

"That's awesome," I said. "Thanks, guys."

"Woo-hoo!" Frankie came over and hugged me, lifting me in

the air like I was a baby imp. Frankie was incredibly strong. I'd once heard Dr. Frankenhammer say that Frankie could lift ten times the amount of a normal human. Then he'd shaken his head and mumbled, "I was going for twenty timessss as strong."

"I'll take this bin to the compost heap," I said. "You sweep up the rest into a neat pile, okay? I'm guessing twenty more trips and we'll be done."

"Sure thing!" Frankie grabbed a table, the big rectangular kind that seats six humans, turned it on its side, and pushed it across the floor like a giant broom, sweeping up the scraps. "Woo-hoo!"

I was unloading the bin in the garden when I heard Frankie's "Woo-hoo!"s coming closer. I turned and saw him carrying the table over his head. It was piled high with food. Boris hung from the

front end, Eloni from the back. They were swinging their legs, but Frankie held the table steady and didn't spill a drop. As he walked up next to me, Eloni and Boris dropped off and Frankie dumped the food.

"We're done!" he said.

"Woo-hoo!" I yelled.

Frankie picked me up and threw me in the air. Fortunately, he caught me this time. (I still have a scar under my eyebrow from the time that he didn't.) Then he bounded off toward the lake. "I'm going for a before-bed jog. Twenty or thirty miles. See you!"

Thanks to the guys (mostly Frankie), the job I had thought would take me all night took only an hour. The sun had just disappeared, and the school lights had come on, holding back the dusky darkness. Pushing the garbage bin down the road back to the castle, I had to steer around potholes. I looked up and saw a broken window in the gymnasium that still hadn't been fixed.

"This place is falling apart," I said.

"Are you kidding me?" Eloni said. "Back home, as soon as anything is built, someone blows it up. This place has a few broken windows, big deal. Only in Stull would someone complain about that."

Boris picked up a rock and threw it at the broken window. He just missed the last jagged piece of glass.

"You throw like a mermaid," Eloni said. He threw a rock and knocked out the piece. Boris slugged him on the shoulder, which only made Eloni laugh. He lifted Boris up and pretended to throw him into my empty trash bin. I laughed. Eloni always cheered me up.

As we approached the back door of the cafeteria, I saw Cook waiting for me outside. She was holding another new uniform and shaking her head.

Boris and Eloni went back to the dorm. I returned the garbage bin, cleaned myself up, and headed for Dr. Critchlore's office. I'd noticed that his light was on, and I really wanted to know if he'd gotten himself together. The school needed him.

I found Miss Merrybench in her anteroom, staring at the portrait of Dr. Critchlore that hung behind her desk. It was a nice portrait; he seemed to smile with his eyes, like he knew something you didn't. Miss Merrybench held a tissue. "Oh, Derek," she sighed.

I'd never seen Miss Merrybench cry. Or laugh, or smile, or show fear. She was like a robot that had been programmed to be angry and annoyed at all times.

"Miss Merrybench?" I said. "Are you okay?"

She spun around, sniffed, and busied herself with the papers on her desk. "Mr. Higgins." She said that like I was a piece of gum under her shoe. "What do you want?"

"I wanted to see Dr. Critchlore," I said. "Is he available?"

"Definitely not available." She blinked rapidly, then turned around in her seat to face the portrait. "Go on in." She waved me through.

Dr. Critchlore wasn't at his desk, but I noticed that the *Top Secret Book of Minions* was back in its museum-quality protective case near the window. Propped up on a stand and gently lit by an overhead light, it seemed to glow. There was something about that book; I felt its power just looking at it. No wonder Pismo had snatched it.

A new TV was nestled in the bookcase, and there was no sign

of the explosion that had destroyed the original. Miss Merrybench was very efficient.

Dr. Critchlore was again sitting in his wingback chair, a cup of tea in one hand and the saucer in the other. At his feet was a chocolate Labrador retriever puppy, looking up at him with the cutest face I'd ever seen. All brown fluff, with enormous ears and a little button nose.

"Excuse me, Dr. Critchlore?"

"Hagerty," he said, "what do you think of my new dog?"

"He's adorable," I said. "Can I pet him?"

Dr. Critchlore nodded me over. I squatted next to the puppy, which he took as an invitation to jump on me. I laughed as he licked my face.

"Miss Happyseat gave him to me. She said she thought I needed a companion."

Aw, that was nice of her. I was glad someone was looking out for our leader.

"What's his name?"

"I haven't named him yet," he said. "I'm not really good with names, Haversheim."

"How about something easy to remember? When you look at him, what's the first thing that pops into your head?"

"Pizza."

"What?"

"The dog threw up on my rug. It looked like pizza."

"Okay," I said, "Pizza it is. Why don't you try it out?"

Dr. Critchlore finished his tea and placed the cup and saucer on his little table. He patted his hands on his thighs and said, "Pizza?"

Pizza jumped out of my arms and bounded over to Dr. Critchlore, putting his front paws on Dr. Critchlore's leg. "Hello, Pizza." Dr. Critchlore rubbed the dog's head. The dog wagged his tail enthusiastically, his tongue hanging out. "Look at that! He likes me."

"He really does," I said.

Dr. Critchlore looked down at the dog, and the dog licked his hand. Dr. Critchlore giggled, which was really strange. I'd never seen him smile, and here he was giggling. It was almost as strange as seeing him cry. What was happening to our leader?

"Pizza," he cooed at the dog. "Thank you, Higgins. You've made me very happy."

I heard a little yelp and turned to see Miss Merrybench standing in the door, her fist by her mouth, her face twisted in sadness.

"It's a great gift, Miss Merrybench," I said to her.

"I love this dog!" Dr. Critchlore said, lifting the puppy to his lap. "I really love this dog."

Miss Merrybench left, and I turned to Dr. Critchlore. "She's worried about you," I said.

"I *have* been a little down lately. But that's not why you came. What can I do for you?"

"Well . . ." I didn't really know how to start. My face got warm. How could I, a lowly third-year, tell this great man that he wasn't doing his job? "I'm . . . I'm concerned about some things happening at the school. The video, the explosion . . ."

"Oh, not you too," he said. "I just spent an hour on a conference call with the board of directors. Seems they've gotten some complaints." Then he added, in a very sassy voice, "'We need more students.' 'You aren't keeping them safe.' 'It's time for someone new to take over.' Blah, blah, blah."

They wanted someone else to run the school? And he didn't care? Never in my life had I imagined this school without Dr. Critchlore. The school bore his name! Without Dr. Critchlore, there was no Dr. Critchlore's School for Minions.

I'd come here for reassurance, but now I felt worse than ever.

"That's terrible," I said. I wondered what could bring my headmaster back on track. "What if you found out who staged that video?"

"Funny thing," he said. He put Pizza back on the floor. "I did get a call from Dark Wendix's henchman, a former student of mine. He said the Girl Explorers aren't what they seem. Says they've been terrorizing the villages in the Sathrim Plateau."

"'Terrorizing'? That doesn't sound like Girl Explorers."

"Dark Wendix has tried to hunt them down, but they keep evading capture," he said. "And eating all his livestock."

"Are you sure he said that?" I asked. "We *are* talking about little girls, right?"

"Yes." He slapped the arm of his chair. "What I wouldn't give for minions with that kind of cunning! Which is why I'm devoting tomorrow to finding new recruits. I have some leads. It'll be a busy day."

"That's fantastic!" I said. I realized a little late that I sounded too relieved, because Dr. Critchlore looked startled.

As I left, Miss Merrybench scowled at me. She was probably embarrassed that I'd seen her cry. Poor Miss Merrybench.

I felt a little better about my situation. Dr. Critchlore was back on the job, and I would be getting a good night's sleep before my test the next morning. Yes, things were turning around.

As I entered the castle foyer on my way back to my dorm, a voice stopped me cold. "Mr. Higgins?"

I turned. Uncle Ludwig stood in the opposite hallway, motioning with a bent finger for me to follow him.

# CHAPTER 18

*Never walk underneath a flying dragon without an umbrella.*

—GOOD ADVICE

Despite spending a late night at the library reshelving books, I got up early the next morning and headed out to the base of Mount Curiosity for the test. Too early, because the grounds were quiet, the rest of the school still sleeping. I noticed a light on in Tootles's tree house, so I went to see if Syke was awake.

The house stretched between and around a whole bunch of trees. Syke had her own room in the top level, about three stories up. I threw pebbles at her window until I got her attention. She came to the window in her pajamas and waved. Then she disappeared, but a moment later her door opened. Now dressed, Syke grabbed a rope hooked to her porch and swung down.

"Is it time for your test?" she asked.

"Almost," I said. "I was too nervous to sleep, and I wanted to ask you something."

We walked down the path toward the meeting place for the test, which was under a giant oak. Tree branches seemed to wave as Syke walked by them.

"So ask," she said.

"Have you talked with Dr. Critchlore lately?"

"Yesterday," she said. "I always check in with him on the first day of school to show him my class list."

"Did he seem . . . different?"

"Yes. Last year when I checked in with him, he was plotting new siege techniques using little models of minions on a topographical map of Ixtup. Yesterday he was still in his pajamas at ten, watching a soap opera and sobbing like a siren who'd been told she wasn't pretty."

I shook my head. "What is going on with him?"

"Midlife crisis," she said. "Tootles told me he had one himself forty years ago. He said it passed pretty quickly. Riga told him if he wanted to live dangerously, she was more than happy to help. So she sabotaged his tools, put unpleasant surprises in his veggie loaf, and staged surprise attacks on him when he got home."

I laughed. "Too bad Dr. Critchlore doesn't have a Riga of his own." Or did he? Could Miss Merrybench be his Riga?

"He doesn't need anybody's help," Syke said. "Don't worry, it will pass."

We reached the tree and sat down on a boulder. Talking to Syke helped calm me down. She never worried about anything.

The other junior henchman trainees drifted over, and at last I saw Coach Foley and Professor Murphy approach.

"Line up over there," Coach Foley said, pointing to an area marked off with a white chalk line.

He and Professor Murphy conferred over a tablet computer. Coach Foley, big as a tree, had to crouch down to be at the same level as the stumpy Professor Murphy.

"I'm going to watch from a better spot," Syke said. "Don't be an idiot." She turned and climbed the tallest tree. She could climb any tree, whether it had branches or not. With her brown skin and iridescent green hair, she practically disappeared as soon as she touched a branch.

Coach Foley blew his whistle. "Listen up," he said. Then he nodded to Professor Murphy, who took a step forward.

"Thank you, Coach Foley," Professor Murphy said. He rubbed his big, bulbous nose and continued, "Let me just say that selecting the five of you most worthy to be junior henchmen is going to be very difficult. There are many factors to consider: intelligence, physical strength, the ability to think under pressure, and other skills an evil overlord would find useful.

"We have designed a series of tests that will help us rank your skills, but we will also consider reports from your mentors.

"This first exercise will test your physical strength, your ability to perform under pressure, and your bravery. It's called 'Save the Master.' It re-creates a situation where you have to risk your life to save your master, an essential trait in a henchman. Coach Foley will now explain the test."

Professor Murphy stepped back into Coach Foley's shadow. Coach Foley cleared his throat and said, "Right. This test is a re-creation of Evil Overlord Stefano's death, when his top henchman botched the rescue. A rival overlord had captured Stefano and dangled him above a volcano by a giant crane. Over two days he was gradually lowered into the volcano. The eruptions of lava slowly burned him to death. Very sad, but also brilliantly evil.

"We don't have a volcano, obviously," he continued. "So we're using a simulation. Our dragon keeper, Jake, has put our best fire-breathing dragon, Ferocious Flame of Fury, in a pit on the flat ledge on the other side of Mount Curiosity."

"Puddles!" a bunch of kids called out, because that was the beast's nickname. He had a habit of flying around the castle and leaving his mark, so to speak.

"Puddles will be spitting fire at intervals," Coach Foley continued. "Your task is to climb up to the ledge and free the master before he becomes charred.

"You won't be rescuing an actual master, of course. Just a life-size dummy."

"We're going to rescue Runt?" Rufus said. Everyone laughed and then he added, "Oh, wait, he's not life-size."

"Coach Foley, tell Jake to ready the dragon," Professor Murphy said. Coach Foley called the stable master on his walkie-talkie. We all looked up at the mountain. The flat ledge was around the right side, near the valley between Mount Curiosity and Dead Man's Peak, a sheer wall of granite.

We couldn't see the ledge, but a blast of flame rose from that side. Puddles was ready.

"First up," Professor Murphy said, looking at his clipboard, "Rufus Spaniel."

Rufus strutted forward, rolling his shoulders and cracking his knuckles. He stripped down to his Critchlore Shape-Shifter Snap-Free Sweatpants™ and said, "I'm ready." When he morphed into wolf form, the pants snapped off, ready to be used again when he morphed back into human form. Dr. Critchlore had invented them after he got tired of seeing the shape-shifters ruin so many clothes.

"Go!" Professor Murphy said. He and Coach Foley started their stopwatches. Rufus bounded up the slope and disappeared into the forest.

Professor Murphy watched his tablet computer, which had a live video feed of the suspended dummy. I leaned over to sneak a look at it swaying above the pit. A burst of flames came about a meter short of the dummy's feet.

Professor Murphy noticed me watching and turned the tablet away. "This is for judges only, Higgins. We don't want you kids copying successful maneuvers."

"Sorry," I said. I backed away and sat on a rock. Everyone seemed to be watching the mountain, even though there was nothing to see. I looked back at the castle and saw Dr. Critchlore by the side of the building. He was dressed in shorts and a T-shirt that read "Go Climb a Rock." He walked beneath a row of oak trees, and suddenly a rainstorm of acorns fell down on him. Everyone knew Dr. Critchlore had a bad case of dendrophobia, the fear of trees. I could see why. He held his backpack over his head and hopped on his new motorcycle.

*That's just great.* He was supposed to be finding new recruits! I picked up a rock and threw it as far as I could into the distant trees. Then I threw another.

I heard cheers behind me. Rufus had burst out of the forest carrying the master in his jaws.

"Excellent," Coach Foley said after checking the time on his stopwatch. He pulled his walkie-talkie from his belt. "Jake, set up a new master."

Professor Murphy held up a towel so Rufus could turn back into a human without everyone seeing him naked. Behind the towel Rufus put his shirt and Snap-Frees back on.

I waited for my name to be called. And waited. Nearly everyone went before I got a turn, and they all returned with the master. Even Janet, who somehow convinced everyone that Jake doing the task for her wasn't cheating. Which I guess it wasn't, because . . . because . . . um . . . what was I talking about?

"Runt Higgins," Coach Foley said at last.

I jumped up. "I'm ready," I said. I kissed my medallion for luck, and then lined up at the start.

"Go!"

I raced up the hill and into the forest. I tried to pace myself. The trail was clear, and it felt so good to be moving instead of waiting in a pool of worry.

Once I reached the right side of the mountain, I saw the ledge just above me.

And then I heard a scream—a man's scream, low and urgent.

Could the dummy scream? Did they add sound effects to make it seem more real? I sprinted up the hill, a new sense of urgency propelling me forward.

Another scream, and it wasn't coming from the dummy. It was coming from Dead Man's Peak. I looked up and saw a body dangling off the side of that sheer wall of granite. His legs were bicycling in the air as he tried to pull himself back up to the small ledge he held on to.

It was Dr. Critchlore.

# CHAPTER 19

*The difference between the impossible and
the possible is a team of minions.*

—DR. CRITCHLORE, IN A COMMENCEMENT ADDRESS

I couldn't see Coach Foley or Professor Murphy from my position on the mountain. I thought about going back to get help, but I didn't think Dr. Critchlore could hold on that long. He had a couple of minutes, tops.

Jake, the stable master, stood by a pile of mostly charred dummies. He was wearing his silver fireproof suit, and burns scarred part of his face. He was missing a few teeth too. I'd heard he'd taken a few too many blows to the head and wasn't all there mentally. Being a dragon keeper was not a very safe occupation. Dragons are temperamental and territorial and unpredictable.

Jake had taken off his hood, but he still wore his protective headphones. A dragon's screech can make your ears bleed if you're too close.

He smiled at me. "Hi, Higgins," he said, raising a hand.

"Jake! Look, it's Dr. Critchlore!" I pointed to the cliff wall.

He kept staring at me, smiling.

"Jake!"

He raised his hand again. "Hi, Higgins."

*Great.*

*What to do?* My heart pounded furiously. Then an idea burst through my panic. An idea sitting right in front of me. In the pit.

I edged over to the side between bursts of flames. "Puddles!" I called. "Good dragon. Come here, boy! Out of the pit." I waved my arms in an upward motion. "We have to save Dr. Critchlore!"

He answered with a blast of fire directed at the dummy. Dragons are so competitive.

"Jake, can you get him out?"

Jake raised his hand and said, "Hi, Higgins."

*Okay, fine.* I ran over to the crane and released the rope that held up the dummy. The dummy fell right into the pit. I heard the sounds of it being torn to shreds. Bits of stuffing flew into the air.

"Higgins, what are you doing?" Jake said.

"I'm saving the master," I said.

I leaned over the side again. "Good job, Puddles," I said. "You win. Now, c'mon out."

Puddles hopped out of the pit. I stroked his side and he wagged his tail. Dragons are always in a good mood after winning a game. I knew this from when I worked in the stables cleaning out the muck. Puddles's favorite game was checkers, and he was such a cheater. He'd light stuff on fire to distract you, then switch around his pieces while you extinguished the flames.

I climbed on his back, grabbing the harness that he always wore. "C'mon, Puddles, Dr. Critchlore needs us." I gently tugged the harness, moving Puddles's head sideways so he could see Dr. Critchlore.

Oh no! Dr. Critchlore had lost his grip with one arm and was very close to falling to his death. I gave Puddles a "fly" command with my legs, and we lifted into the air.

"Good boy, Puddles!" I screamed. "Get Dr. Critchlore! Big treats if you get him before he falls. Big treats! I'll bring you a goat."

Puddles heard "goat" and whinnied. Goat was his favorite. He lowered his head and we zoomed straight for Dr. Critchlore, who looked like he only had seconds left.

"Hang on, Dr. Critchlore!" I yelled. "We're almost there!"

"Me too!" A voice from above yelled. It was Miss Merrybench. Tied to a rope, she jumped off the cliff, spinning around in midair so that her outstretched feet hit the side of the mountain as she swung back. She rappelled down like a pro, kicking off the moun-

tain and falling a great distance before she reined in. "I'll save you, Dr. Critchlore!"

Dr. Critchlore swiveled his head around—to look at me and Puddles, then back up at Miss Merrybench. Suddenly he lost his grip. He seemed to fall in slow motion, his body floating down, down, down.

Miss Merrybench screamed.

Puddles zoomed in on his target. He stretched out his neck and swooped underneath Dr. Critchlore, catching him just before he would have hit the trees. I grabbed hold of his arms as Puddles flapped upward.

"Got you," I said with relief. "Dr. Critchlore, I thought you were a goner."

"Hankbert, my boy, what a rescue!" Dr. Critchlore righted himself so he was sitting in front of me. He grabbed the harness, and I grabbed him. Puddles rose slowly, maneuvering up and away from the cliff's edge.

"Are you okay?" Miss Merrybench called.

"Yes, fine, Miss Honeychair! Can you climb back up and get my gear? And I left my motorcycle at the foot of the trail. Thanks, you're a dear."

Miss Merrybench didn't look too pleased, but she began the slow climb back up the mountain. That was going to take a lot longer than rappelling down.

"Dr. Critchlore," I said as we swooped away, "I hope this will teach you to be more careful."

He laughed. "You must be joking. That was the most excitement I've had in years!"

"But you could have died."

"But I didn't."

Puddles flew us down to Coach Foley and Professor Murphy. Syke cheered as we passed her in the tree. The rest of the students stood there watching, mouths open in shock. I felt like a hero. Janet was smiling at me, and I had to look away, I was so embarrassed.

Puddles, true to his name, relieved himself in the air before landing. Dragons are a fun mode of travel, but they are definitely *not* zero-emission vehicles.

Dr. Critchlore jumped off, breathed in deeply, and spread his arms. "Fantastic!"

I slid off and stood next to him in my best henchman pose—feet apart, hands on hips, look adoringly at the master.

"Professor Murphy, Coach Foley," Dr. Critchlore said, "Hollins and I just had an amazing ride!" Then he went on his way, back to the castle, dodging tree branches that seemed to swipe at him as he passed.

I felt myself blushing, and I dropped my gaze down. When nobody said anything, I looked up at my teachers. They were frowning at me. That didn't seem right. Professor Murphy looked like he'd just eaten one of Cook's mystery stews. Coach Foley's arms were crossed in front of his massive chest like angry snakes.

"You *threw* the master to the dragon," Professor Murphy said, tapping his tablet, where a video showed Jake cleaning up the stuffing around the hole. Coach Foley shook his head.

"I needed Puddles to—"

"I'm sorry, Higgins," he continued. "But that's the worst henchman failure I have seen in all my years at this school."

123

"Dropped him right to the dragon," Coach Foley muttered, throwing his hands in the air in exasperation. He couldn't look at me. "And that boy is my junior henchman. I'm going to have to talk to someone in administration about assignments."

# CHAPTER 20

*Opinions are unique, so don't have them.*
*Your evil overlord will tell you what to think.*
—DR. CRITCHLORE, IN A COMMENCEMENT ADDRESS

I was reassigned to Mistress Moira, as fate would have it. Get it? 'Cause she's the Fourth Fate? Or was. I wasn't sure if her Fate job was still active. I did know that she was the school seamstress and chocolatier, and that she lived and worked in the top room of the castle's tall tower.

I climbed the circular staircase that wound up the inside of the tower. The climb was long, but it was worth it because Mistress Moira had the most amazing rooms in the castle. Walking into her parlor was like walking into a grassy meadow. The room was alive with nature—lush green everywhere, from the grass and wildflower carpet to the willow tree in the corner and the bushes all around. There was a pond at the base of a fountain. Birds sang, crickets chirped, and frogs croaked. Oh, they didn't die; they made that croaking sound.

I looked out wide windows thrown open to let in the birds and the breeze. I felt like I was floating in a meadow in the sky. I imagined this was how the gods lived.

Mistress Moira sat on her couch in the middle of this splendor, wearing a billowy white robe that looked brilliant next to her dark-chocolate skin. She was sewing a button on a shirt.

"Hello, dear Higgins," she said. "Come. Sit." She patted the couch.

"Hi," I said. "I'm in the Junior Henchman Training Program. They've assigned me to you."

"That's wonderful. I've never been assigned a junior henchman before, but I had a feeling it would happen. Nothing surprises me, as you know."

"So, what would you like me to do?"

"Hmm," she said. "I don't really have anything for you to do. The sports uniforms are done. Since the term just started, the shape-shifters haven't torn up all their clothes yet with accidental morphings. I can't start a new batch of chocolate until the next delivery of cocoa arrives. Why don't you help me with the yarn while I mend this shirt?"

So I did. I sat next to her, winding yarn into balls, listening to the sounds of the meadow. It relaxed me. So what if I failed my junior henchman test? I'd saved Dr. Critchlore, and that was more important. Things were going to get better; they had to. I just needed to stay positive.

"You and I have something in common," she told me. "We were both cast aside by our families."

Well, that didn't help.

I didn't believe my family had cast me aside. They'd left me with someone who could take better care of me. Because they loved me.

"My sisters were jealous of me."

126

"Are they seamstresses too?" I asked.

"You could say that," she said. "We used to work together as a team. One spun the thread, another measured it, and a third cut it. I was the weaver. My sisters were jealous of my job. After all, I had all the fun, putting this thread with that one. Making some threads jealous, keeping some threads apart."

"Are we talking about string?" I asked.

"The threads of life, dear heart."

"Can you still do that? Because Dr. Critchlore could use a new thread in his life."

"Alas, no. They took my power when they threw me out."

They took her power? Interesting. Maybe that was what happened to me. Maybe I'd lost some of my werewolf power when my family left me here, and that was why I had trouble morphing.

"You and I will have the final laugh, though," she said, standing. All at once her cheerful demeanor turned dark as she lowered her head and glared out the window. "Oh yes. We shall have our revenge." I swear I heard thunder rumble in the distance.

A breeze rushed in and ruffled her robe. I shivered.

She turned to look at me; her expression changing from crazed determination back to warm and friendly. "But first, how about a cup of cocoa?"

I left Moira to go to my History of Henchmen class. I wasn't looking forward to it, after this morning's failure at the test. But I wasn't going to give up, and not just because Janet told me not to.

Okay, maybe that was one of the reasons I wasn't giving up. But who could blame me? She was so cute.

I began the long climb down from Mistress Moira's room. When I was a quarter of the way down, I heard a cry.

"Help!"

I stopped and tried to figure out where it was coming from.

"Help. I'm stuck outside the window. On the ledge. Some imps tricked me."

I could relate to that. I went over to the window and leaned out. The ledge was about a meter below the window, but I didn't see anyone on it.

"Where are you?" I asked. I leaned out farther to see around the edge, but the ledge was empty as far as I could tell.

"I'm on the ledge." The voice came from around the side of the round tower wall. "Can you help me get back in? I'm too scared to move."

I swung my legs out the window and lowered myself down feet-first. The ledge wasn't wide, and I felt a little dizzy when I looked down. I gripped the rough edge of the wall and inched my way sideways.

And then I saw the poor guy. A little imp named Fingers. He looked petrified. I held out my hand to him and he grabbed it.

"Gotcha!" he said, climbing up my back and my shoulders and through the window.

I looked up. Five imp faces leaned out the window, laughing at me. They closed the shutter, and I heard a bolt lock.

Stupid imps.

I heard laughter coming from inside. I edged around the tower, checking other windows, but they were all locked. I was stuck. The nearest thing to jump to was the roof of the castle, but that was three stories away, and I was sure I'd break every bone in my body if I tried to drop down.

I was going to miss my History of Henchmen class if I didn't get down soon. Not only that, but I'd get an unexcused absence, another detention, and probably a sunburn. Cat's paws!

I felt like punching something, but any movement might send me to my death, so instead I howled in frustration.

As I paused for breath, I heard scurrying sounds from inside the tower. Then the window opened, and Moira peeped out.

"I knew this would happen," she said, reaching out for me.

"Because you saw it in my fate?" I asked.

"No, because those imps have been hanging around my tower for the past two days. It was only a matter of time before they pulled the 'I'm stuck on the ledge' trick."

She helped me in, and I gave her a hug. She was so warm and friendly; I just loved her. "Thank you, Mistress Moira."

"You'll be late for class," she said. She said that like it was a fact, but I hoped it was just a warning.

I was late for class. As I opened the door, I saw twenty-seven faces turn my way, and I'm sure I turned an embarrassing shade of puce. I tried to squeeze in along the wall, but the bodies were packed tightly in the back, and I had to walk all the way to the front. Professor Murphy stopped his lecture as he waited for me to find a spot. For the first time in my life I wished I were smaller, so I could disappear.

"Thank you for taking time out of your busy schedule to join us, Mr. Higgins," Professor Murphy said.

"Sorry," I said.

I glanced at the board. Our names were listed there in the order in which we had finished. Rufus was at the top, of course—he's such a beast at physical tasks. His werewolf buddy Lapso was just below. And there, at the bottom was me, Runt Higgins, with a big red DQ: Disqualified.

I was going to have to kill the next two tests.

Oh, who was I kidding? It was hopeless.

"As a henchman, blatant insubordination is of course punishable by death," Professor Murphy said, glaring right at me. "But there are other, seemingly less egregious mistakes a henchman can make that could cost him or her dearly. For instance, when Lord Vengecrypt came to power three decades ago, he decided to rename the months of the year after his family members—Edithary, Paulary, Madge, Bobary, . . . etc. A few months later he overheard a henchman misname a month, and he ordered him hung upside down from a flagpole for everyone to see. Evil overlords love making an example of people. It makes for an effective lesson in obedience.

"Another instance: When Elvira Cutter came to power, she decreed that everyone endure the Seven Labors of Loyalty . . ."

I zoned out. I knew all about Elvira Cutter. We all did.

"Where's your necklace?" I turned and saw Janet looking at me. I wasn't sure she was talking to me, so I pointed at myself. "Yes, you, Higgins. Where's the necklace you always wear?"

My hand felt for it, but it was gone.

I gasped.

My wolf's head medallion was gone. It was the only thing I had from my life before I'd come to Dr. Critchlore's. I'd worn it every day for as long as I could remember. I never took it off. It was a part of me.

And now it was gone.

"I hope you didn't lose it," Janet whispered. "It's a nice necklace."

Okay, my body was overloading with a strange combination of emotions. The stress and panic about my lost medallion combined with a wave of fluttery hope and happiness after hearing that Janet liked my necklace. I was stunned she'd even noticed it. Noticed me.

Rufus was on her other side, listening in. He scowled at me. "Necklaces are girly," he said.

"No, Runt's is really cool," Janet said. "With all those mysterious symbols on it and that wolf's head in the center. Very manly." She blinked her eyes at me, and I nearly fell out of my chair.

"I think Fingers took it," I said, remembering my time on the ledge and the way the imp crawled up my back.

Rufus laughed. "Then you'll never get it back. Fingers is psycho. Nobody knows where he stashes all the stuff he steals."

"Quiet down," Professor Murphy said.

"I have to get it back," I said. "It's all I have from . . . from my before time."

Janet pouted in sympathy.

# CHAPTER 21

*One evil overlord shall be my master, until such time as I am laid off*
*or downsized to a foreign evil overlord.*
—FROM THE MINION'S OATH

I'd failed my test, gotten another tardy, and lost my necklace. Thinking positively was doing nothing to help my cursedness.

At lunch I looked for the imps, but there was no sign of them anywhere. I decided to try to find Coach Foley. Sure, he'd gotten rid of me as his junior henchman trainee, but I wanted to tell him that the zombies only responded to whining. I was hoping to impress him and get back on his good side, if that was possible.

I couldn't find him either, but I did see Pismo. Most kids relaxed out in the quad after lunch. It was right outside the cafeteria, and there were benches and trees and a long, low wall next to a grassy ledge where the cool kids sat. As I came back from the sports fields, I saw Pismo running toward the cemetery, his backpack flopping against his back.

I decided to follow him. I would have to be stealthy, because I didn't want him to know I was following him. This may sound mean, but the kid was kind of a twerp. He'd probably make fun of me if he caught me.

I ran up the path and then hid behind some bushes. I peeked out and saw that Pismo had slowed to a walk. And then something else caught my eye. Directly across from me, fifteen zombies swayed my way.

"Higginsbrains, Higginsbrains," they chanted.

*Oh, great.*

They crossed to my side. "Sorry, no brains," I said. I sprinted away from them and hid farther up the path.

Pismo veered to the right when the path split. Yep, definitely heading for the cemetery. Again. But why?

"Higginsbrains, Higginsbrains." The zombies chased after me.

When they got close, I ran away again, this time whining, "I don't *have* any brains." We continued like that—the zombies slowly chasing me, me racing away when they caught up, and the zombies following, chanting. They weren't listening to me, not even when I whined.

Soon I lost track of Pismo. I leaned against a tree and the zombies surrounded me.

"Higginsbrains."

They looked really determined. I checked my watch. I still had thirty minutes left in my break. Maybe I could sneak down to the dungeon and snatch a tray of brains for them. I knew there was a secret entrance to the dungeon over by the lake.

"C'mon," I said. "Let's get you some brains."

"Higginsbrainshigginsbrainshigginsbrains," they chanted excitedly. They had a bit more spring in their steps as they followed me.

You'd think, being surrounded by zombies as I was, that nothing would startle me. But you'd be wrong, because I nearly leaped out of my skin when Pismo jumped in front of me from behind a tree.

"What'cha doing?" he said.

"Pismo, jeez," I said. "You scared me half to death."

"That takes you one step closer to your friends, then," he said, laughing at his joke. All at once he turned serious. "Were you following me?"

"What?" I said. "Me? Following a twerpy first-year? I don't think so." He gave me a look that said he didn't believe me, so I added, "Somebody thinks an awful lot of himself."

"Yeah, you're about as subtle as a punch in the face. Then, what are you doing?"

"I'm—I'm going to get some brains," I said. "For the zombies."

"Isn't the lab that way?" He pointed to the castle.

"Shows what you know," I said. "There happens to be an entrance closer to Dr. Frankenhammer's lab over here. But it's a secret, so run along, first-year."

"Yeah, right," he said. "Like I'm not gonna follow you now. Secret entrance, you say?"

Oops.

"No—uh—actually, I *was* following you."

"I know," Pismo said, smirking, "but I still want to see that secret entrance. Is it by the cemetery?" He stared at me like he was trying to pull the information from my brain. "No? The lake? Aha!" he said, pointing at my face like I'd just given it away, which maybe I had. "It's by the lake. Hmm, there's a boathouse . . ." He pointed at me again. "It's in the boathouse, I can tell. Thanks, Runt. Let's go check it out."

Schnauzers, the kid was annoying.

"I'm not going anywhere with you," I said. "You'll just get me into trouble."

"Aw, lighten up." He looked at me. "I can help you carry the brains."

"Fine." I strode past him and headed for the lake, followed by fifteen zombies and one really annoying kid.

The boathouse was dark inside, just a few streams of light edging through the dust on the windows. Canoes hung along one wall, and a couple of trunks filled with life vests sat on the floor. Over in the corner was a box that could be pushed aside to reveal the secret entrance.

"Zombies, wait here. I'll bring you brains," I whined. Surprisingly, they all sat down. One of them pulled out a deck of cards and began dealing.

Pismo followed me down a ladder built into one side of a long circular tube. It felt like climbing down a well. Our steps echoed in the enclosed space as we clanged down the metal rungs. A cool, fresh, earthy smell breezed up from below.

At the bottom I pulled out my DPS, because I wasn't too familiar with this end of the dungeon. We were close to the cemetery, and I just didn't know what we'd run into in this unused section. I checked for the fastest route to the lab, put the DPS back into my pocket, and led the way. We walked down an unfinished corridor, the dirt floor lumpy with rocks.

Motion detector lights switched on when we walked past the sensors, then shut off after we'd gone by. We traveled in our own little moving tunnel of light. These automatic lights were so much better than the torches that used to line the dungeon's corridors.

The torches filled the hallways with smoke and creepy shadows. Plus they went out at very inconvenient times.

"Can I look at your DPS?" Pismo asked, pointing to my pocket.

"No. Just follow me."

"C'mon, let me have a look," he said. "It's so unfair that first-years don't get their own."

"You have to learn the rules first," I said. "Which means you'll probably get yours in six or seven years."

"I hate this school," he said. "The Pravus Academy gives each new student a DPS, a pet, and your very own minilab. I bet the students are a lot nicer too."

"Oh, fine," I said, handing over my DPS. "But you don't know what you're talking about. This is a great school."

We walked on. Pismo flashed through different screen shots as we went. "Cool, there's an underground grotto here."

"You do *not* want to go there," I said.

"Why not?"

"Two words: flesh-eating fish monster."

"That's four words."

"Yeah, but the first two are the only ones that matter."

He shrugged. "Why do you love this school so much?"

"Why do I love this school?" I repeated. "Where to start? I love everything about it. I love the teachers and the subjects we get to learn. Have you had your Battlefield Implements class yet?"

"No."

"It's amazing. Professor Portry lets you reenact famous minion battles, using the actual weapons! Plus I love the way the castle looks, so old and Gothic. How it's filled with secret passages and mysterious rooms. I love the sports teams, the extracurricular stuff, and the dorms." I went on and on and on, and Pismo listened quietly.

Too quietly.

I turned around and he was gone.

"Pismo?"

I ran back the way we'd come, looking down side passages, but he had disappeared. I felt a moment of panic—what if he got lost down here?

Then I remembered that he had my DPS and I felt better.

Until I realized that he'd stolen my DPS and ditched me.

Aw, shih tzu puppies.


I made it to Dr. Frankenhammer's lab, but it was locked. I rang the buzzer and soon heard the click of the door unlocking.

"Dr. Frankenhammer?" I said after stepping inside. "Why is your door locked?"

"Professor Vodum was just here," he said from across the room. He was studying something through his microscope and didn't look up. "The worm. He thinkssss I had something to do with the explosion in the cemetery." Frankenhammer shook his head. "Thinkssss I have it in for him, because he's a Critchlore by marriage. Please. I don't need to sabotage his work to prove he's uselessss. He does an excellent job on his own."

"Oh," I said. "Um. I was wondering if I could get some brains."

"Help yourself," he said, looking up briefly to point to the refrigerator. "I may be running low, though. Vodum ruined some in a fit of petulance."

"He farted?"

"Not flatulence, Higginsssss," Dr. Frankenhammer said. "Petulance. He's a big baby."

I walked over to the stainless steel refrigerator and opened it. There were four good brains left, and a few Tupperware containers labeled "Brain Bits."

"Should I take a brain, or the bits?"

"Leave the bitssss," he said. "They're for something I'm working on. Which reminds me—" He stood up and came toward me, scalpel in hand. "I need some fingernails for something I'm working on. Would you mind?"

I looked at his hand. One of his fingers was wrapped in a bandage, blood leaking from the sides. I quickly grabbed a brain and wrapped it in a paper towel, but as I turned to leave, Dr. Frankenhammer's hand clamped on my wrist. He smiled. "It only hurts for a minute."

And then the alarm sounded.

# CHAPTER 22

*An investment in minions is an investment in security.*
—DR. CRITCHLORE'S SCHOOL FOR MINIONS BROCHURE

A mechanical voice came on over the loudspeaker. "Unidentified chemical detected in the Research Zone. Commencing lockdown. Repeat. Unidentified chemical detected in the Research Zone. Commencing lockdown."

I heard steel doors slam shut, sealing off this quadrant of the dungeon. Dr. Frankenhammer was the picture of panic—he raced around the lab, locking things into airtight stainless steel containers. I reached for my medallion, but my hand only clasped empty space.

"Higginssss!" Dr. Frankenhammer yelled over the sound of the bell. "Those specimens need to be secured from contamination! Help me."

I raced over to his workbench, where petri dishes were arranged in three long rows. Dr. Frankenhammer was slapping lids on top of them, so I did the same.

They were filled with a brownish-gray goop, the color you get when you mix too many paints together. As I lowered one lid, tiny hands reached out of the goop and pushed the top off. I pushed it back on, struggling against those strong hands, and managed to turn the top closed.

"What are these?"

"Top ssssecret," Dr. Frankenhammer said. "I'm going to need to erase your memory when we're done."

An explosion shook the floor. "Stay here, Higginssss! Guard those petri dishes. I have to save another experiment next door."

He raced out. Just as I finished putting lids on the dishes, I heard a thump in the wall. I turned and saw the ventilation grate burst open, pushed by a huge mass of swarming insects. They looked like giant cockroaches, each one as big as a rat.

I don't like bugs. They give me the creeps. I once promised to do Frankie's dragon cleanup duty if he'd get rid of an earwig for me.

A waterfall of cockroaches plunged into the room and I stood there, frozen. Maybe if I had run for the door as soon as they came through the vent, I might have made it out safely, but once the insects hit the floor, they quickly swarmed the room, blocking my way to the exit. I was an island in a sea of cockroaches. I jumped up on the nearest table and looked for a weapon.

"Dr. Frankenhammer!" I screamed.

The cockroaches zipped past me, making a strange clicking noise. They weren't coming after me. They were going for the petri dishes.

"Dr. Frankenhammer!"

They climbed up the legs of the table and headed for the dishes.

I watched as they shattered the glass containers and slurped up the contents. They were eating Dr. Frankenhammer's top-secret project.

I ran to the opposite side of the table and grabbed a couple of petri dishes, trying not to look down because they creeped me out. I searched for a safe place to put them and decided on the stainless steel freezer, because it was close. I ran back to the table and made a stack of five more. The cockroaches continued to crack through the glass tops. They slurped and chewed and seemed to grow with each gulp.

I grabbed another stack, working as fast as I could. The cockroaches headed for me, coming from the other end. I stacked, ran to the freezer, unloaded, and ran back. I felt a hot pinch on my foot. A cockroach had eaten through my shoe and was going after my big toe like it was a T-bone steak. I kicked my foot, but it held on tight. I screamed and tugged it off with my fingers and flung it across the room. I practically convulsed with shivers.

I managed to save about twenty dishes before the bugs destroyed the rest. And then I grabbed a microscope and squashed the bugs with the heavy end. They were slow and fat from gorging on Dr. Frankenhammer's experiment, and they burst when I crushed them, spraying bug guts and digested experiment everywhere. I was freaking out, it was so disgusting, but I had to save the lab. I squashed with a fury I'd never known. I was a beast.

And then everything was quiet. No more clicking bugs, just me, breathing hard, standing in a soup of guts. Where was Dr. Frankenhammer?

I ran into the hallway. Heavy pounding echoed through the passageway, coming from the other lab. I heard Dr. Frankenhammer yelling for help. His door had been sealed from the outside.

"Dr. Frankenhammer? Are you okay?"

"Higginssss, open the door," he said. "The code is 4-5-6-2-7-9-3-8-7-1-0-0-9-5-4-2-8-1-3."

I entered the code after he recited it back a few times, but nothing happened.

"Drat! You need to find Bloggo, the dungeon superintendent."

"I can't," I said. "This section is still locked down."

"Use your DPS to call him."

I reached for my pocket, and then I remembered. "I haven't got it."

"Higginssss! You are always supposed to have it."

"I lent it to a first-year," I said. "Oh no, what if he's trapped in here with the gas?"

"My sensorssss are not detecting any gassss," Dr. Frankenhammer said. "I have to get out of here. Higginssss, go back to my lab. Use my computer to notify Dungeon Base that we're clear of gas and need help. Tell them to send Ssssecurity."

I ran back to the lab and over to Dr. Frankenhammer's computer, which was password protected, so I had to run back to get the password, which was "monstermaker457."

"Remind me to erase your memory," Dr. Frankenhammer mumbled through the door. (But I forgot to remind him and he forgot to erase my memory, which was a good thing, because if he had, I'd never have known why my foot was bleeding and I was covered in cockroach splat . . . Okay, maybe that wasn't something I needed to remember. To this day I still can't look at a cockroach without feeling nauseated.)

Dungeon Security finally arrived and released Dr. Frankenhammer. I told them everything as we followed him into his lab. The pain of his loss bent him over and seemed to crush him.

"Carnivorous cockroachessss," he said, stepping around the goop. "We haven't had an infestation in years. How did they get in?"

I pointed to the ventilation grate. Then I opened the freezer and saw that some of the petri dish experiments were shivering with cold. I pulled them out.

"I didn't know where else to put them," I said. "Those bugs were so fast."

Dr. Frankenhammer walked over with his arms outstretched, a blank expression on his face. He looked like a zombie. "Higginssss," he whispered. He took the dishes from me. "Oh, Higginssss, why the freezer? There's a storage locker right there." He pointed under the table at a very secure-looking row of lockers with metal handles. "They're destroyed," he said. "All my work. Destroyed."

"I'm so sorry," I said.

His expression turned fierce as he placed a dish down on the table. "Vodum," he said. "I saw the way he looked at me when I joked about him losing his minions—it was the look of a man bent on revenge. I should know; I invented that look! And now I've lost my minions. Coincidence? I don't think so."

"But why would he do something that hurts the school?" I asked.

"Oh, Higginssss, don't be naive," he said. "The man is pure ambition. He'll destroy anything to get his revenge." He paused, then added, "And you know what? So will I."

"Oh no," I said. I couldn't believe it.

"Oh yesssss," Dr. Frankenhammer said. He picked up his dish

and took off the lid, prodding the little thing inside with a finger. "I was going to name her Francine."

I tiptoed back toward the door, feeling terrible. I'd killed Francine.

As I neared the door, Mrs. Gomes strode into the room, followed by two of her security detail, black-clad men with stern faces. Margaret, her harried assistant, followed, carrying two bulging satchels and a notepad. Mrs. Gomes took one look at the scene and motioned for Margaret to take pictures.

Mrs. Gomes had been hired last year after the previous head of security, Mr. Rupplehowzer, retired. The school Employee Selection Committee had narrowed the replacement options down to two candidates: Mrs. Gomes and Captain Yardley. Mrs. Gomes was a petite woman, the mother of six, with a degree in investigative journalism. Captain Yardley was a retired military commander with a long résumé of leadership and private investigative work.

Dr. Critchlore hadn't hesitated. "I want Mrs. Gomes," he'd said. When asked why, he'd answered, "Because she's a mother. When I was growing up, my mother could imagine the most horrendously wicked things happening to me in any situation. If I wanted to go to the store, she'd say, 'You could be hit by a car, or kidnapped, or a tile could fall off the building and strike you in the head—don't forget to look up occasionally. Or there could be a stampede of animals, or the shop workers may go on strike and attack anyone who crosses their picket line. And it might be chilly, so put on a sweater.'

"If I wanted to play in my backyard, she'd say, 'Don't eat any plants, they could be poisonous. Watch out for wild animals, they

145

may smell you and jump over our fence to get you, or mole people may dig up a hole next to your sandbox and abduct you. And it might be chilly, so put on a sweater.'

"The things she could imagine, it was incredible. And that's the kind of thinking I want in my head of security. Someone who can imagine every possible disaster. I need a mom."

Mrs. Gomes wore a crisp blue suit with a cream-colored shirt. A badge that granted her access everywhere hung from a chain around her neck. She had poufed, highlighted brown hair that never moved, like a helmet. And she had the no-nonsense demeanor of a drill sergeant. She strode right up to Dr. Frankenhammer.

"Frankenhammer, what happened?" she asked, getting right to the point.

"We had an alarm for a chemical leak, the section was locked down, and I secured the petri dishes here and went to my other lab, leaving Higginssss behind to guard my work." He glared at me. Apparently, I'd failed.

"Higgins?" Mrs. Gomes asked.

I told her my story.

"Carnivorous cockroaches," Mrs. Gomes muttered as she checked out the vent.

Without turning around, she began barking out orders to her men. "Walthrop, I want you to make sure all dungeon vents are properly sealed. Iron bar reinforcements should do the trick. Adams, Tootles has experience with bug infestations, see if he can root out their nest. And let's add extra-strength bug spray to our safety stations."

She pointed to the wall where some canisters were mounted below Mrs. Gomes's very own safety symbol—two intertwined, giant blue *S*s on a yellow diamond trimmed with a green border. Dr. Frankenhammer's safety station already held a fire extinguisher, a first aid kit, a disposable respirator, a flashlight, and fluorescent green tape to mark accidents. Mrs. Gomes had installed the safety stations all over the school. The ones outside had sunscreen dispensers and an emergency sweater supply.

Dr. Frankenhammer pinched the bridge of his nose with his eyes closed. "Aren't you overlooking the obvioussss?"

"And what's that, Dr. Frankenhammer?" Mrs. Gomes didn't look up as she continued to scribble notes into her notebook.

"Intentional sabotage."

"That will be considered during our investigation, of course. First, I have to make sure we are safe. Then, we need to make sure this doesn't happen again. Safety first, prevention second, investigation third. Now, then, Higgins," she said. "You said you were bitten on your toe?"

"Yes, ma'am," I replied.

"Tell me, when was your last tetanus shot?"

Dr. Frankenhammer threw up his arms and stormed out of the room. "Vodum's not getting away with this."

# CHAPTER 23

*In the future, any student caught riding a dragon*
*without a helmet will get detention.*
—ALL-POINTS SAFETY BULLETIN NO. 47, FROM MRS. GOMES

Because of the lockdown, the investigation, and having to go to the infirmary for a tetanus shot, I was late for my next class, which meant I got my third tardy, which meant I got detention for the second day in a row.

"Hi, Mr. Griphold," I said, taking my seat. He shook his head sadly. Hector was back, sitting next to Melissa, a seventh-year shape-shifter.

"What'd you do?" I asked her.

"Uniform violation," she said.

Hector leaned over. "She went to class in her old Girl Explorers uniform, just to mess with the ogre-men. It was hilarious."

She smiled. "So worth it."

"They looked like they wanted to rip you apart," Hector said.

"Let 'em try," she said, and then she shifted into an eagle.

"Hey, Runt," Pismo said, sneaking up behind me. "You're some kind of misbehaving delinquent, aren't you?"

Surprise, surprise. Pismo was back. I ignored him.

"What'cha in for?" he asked.

"Three tardies," I said.

"Borrrring," he said.

"You?"

"That Tootles guy caught me cutting a hole in his hedge maze. I was trying to make a secret exit. You know, just in case some upperclassmen chased me in there. What kind of a name is 'Tootles'?"

"It's short for Tootlevexlinovous."

"Dang."

"Can I have my DPS back?" I asked.

"Yeah, about that . . ." He smiled a fake smile. A guilty smile. A smile that said, "Don't be mad at me, but—"

"What?"

"I ran into one of those Festering Boil Spitters, so I threw the DPS at it and ran away. Sorry." He shrugged. "But you can get another one, right?"

"No!"

"Well, you don't need it anyway; you said so yourself yesterday."

"I could have used it today, when the dungeon was locked down because of a chemical spill. I could have called for help."

"Bummer."

"All right, boys," Mr. Griphold said as he followed the last detainee in. It was Drangulus, the fourth-year lizard-boy, again. "Assignment time. I need two of you—"

"We'll take it," Pismo said, raising my hand with his. He smiled smugly at the other detainees, like he'd just won a giant stuffed animal at the fair.

"Great," Griphold said. "Report to Professor Vodum"—the upperclassmen laughed—"to help sort body parts from the cemetery explosion." Then the upperclassmen high-fived each other.

I scowled at Pismo. "Really?"

He shrugged. "Might be fun."

"Hector, you and Melissa can help Coach Foley set up for tomorrow's junior henchman test."

"Sweet," Hector said, smiling.

"And Drangulus, why don't you report back to Mistress Moira. She still needs help taste-testing her experimental ESP chocolates."

"I knew you were going to say that," Drangulus said. "'Cause I ate so many chocolates yesterday, see?" He looked at Pismo, then tightened his grip on his DPS. "Don't even think about it, short stuff." Pismo shrugged.

"Get going, boys," Mr. Griphold said.

I felt like smacking Pismo. Both of those jobs would have been great. But no, I got stuck with Obnoxious Boy, doing hard manual labor. That stunk (both the situation and, I imagined, the job of sorting body parts).

Argh!

"Incoming femur!" Pismo yelled as he threw a bone at my head.

"Ouch!"

"I said 'incoming.'"

"Just stack them, okay?" I placed the femur in one of my neatly stacked piles. We were working in the crater of the explosion. Dirt and body parts were loosely packed all around us. I had decided on a methodical approach: grabbing a handful of parts, some of them just bones, others with bits of flesh still attached, and climbing up out of the crater to put them in my piles. I looked over at Pismo's work. He'd made a village of bone teepees in the crater.

"Pismo! We're supposed to stack them."

"This is more fun. Hey, look at this bone, Runt." He waved a humerus in the air. "Look at the bone," he said again, his voice high, like he was talking to a baby. "C'mon, you wanna fetch? Sure ya do, boy. Here ya go, fetch the bone." He threw the bone as far as he could.

"That's not funny," I said. But a part of me really wanted to fetch it.

"Hey, Runt, aren't you gonna morph?" he asked.

"No."

"Have you ever morphed?"

"Once," I said. "When I was seven."

"Really?" he asked.

I nodded.

"Here's another one," Pismo said. He lifted a gigantic bone. "Ooh, heavy."

"Hey, I think I know who that is," I said. I ran over to him to get a better look. It was! Harold the Giant. Died 1657. He was buried in a massive grave right about where we were working. I used to visit this spot on Minion Remembrance Day.

Just as I was reaching reverently to touch the bone of the most famous minion in history, Pismo threw it.

My fist pulled back without my telling it to. I was overcome with an urge to slug Pismo right in the face. I'd never felt such powerful hatred toward another person. How could he be so disrespectful?

But I was a minion, and minions followed the rules. You can't hit another student, even if he really, really deserved it.

"Stop it, Pismo!" I screamed. "That's Harold the Giant. We have to keep his bones together."

Pismo shrugged. "They're mostly together," he said, pointing to one of his teepees.

"Bulldogs, Pismo! This isn't funny. These are respected warriors, and you're treating them like . . . like playthings!"

"Sorry," he said, all of a sudden looking humble and sad.

"Oh!" I was so mad. I stomped off to get the bone. "And another thing . . ." I turned around, but he was gone. I looked up and saw him standing at the top of the crater next to Professor Vodum. Pismo spread one arm out above my neatly stacked piles, like he'd done all that work.

"Well done, Pismo," Professor Vodum said. "You're dismissed." He looked down at me, and then at the teepee village. "Higgins! You just earned yourself another detention. That's incredibly disrespectful!"

I slumped. Pismo saluted me and ran off.

I headed for the cafeteria, a jumble of emotions swirling in my gut. I was furious because of Pismo. I was sad for Dr. Frankenhammer. I was worried about my school. And I was scared about not becoming a junior henchman and finding my family.

All that emotion made me feel weak. Or was it hunger? I slid my tray down the line and saw that the main course was something called "organic meat chunks." That didn't sound too appetizing, and it looked even worse. I think I saw little bits of hair and tiny white quills in it.

Cook was helping to serve. She took one look at me and shook her head. "Runt, honey, what happened this time?"

I looked down at my uniform, covered with cockroach guts and mud from the cemetery. "Do you really want to know?"

She shook her head again. "Get a new uniform after eating. You did wash your hands?"

I nodded. Then I asked her what the "meat chunks" were.

"Do you really want to know?" she mimicked back at me. "It's tough and stringy, and tastes a bit like, um . . ."

"Chicken?" I offered.

"No . . ."

"Beef?"

"No. I'd say it tastes like gym locker. But if you put some ketchup on it, it should be fine."

I sniffed. *Ew.* "Did you get this from the dungeon?"

"I'd rather not say. It *is* organic, though."

"I'll pass."

I headed for my table, surprised to see Eloni and Boris back with Darthin and Frankie. Eloni and Boris were devouring the meat chunks like they were prime rib—until Boris took a bite and hollered. "Ouch! My meat chunk just poked me." He spit out a little white barb.

Like me, Darthin had filled his tray with rolls, a heap of carrots, and a cup of ice cream. Frankie stirred a bowl of stew like he was looking for something edible.

"Why are you guys back?" I asked Eloni. Boris didn't look up.

Eloni nudged Boris on the shoulder. Boris shrugged.

"Boris got trapped by imps this morning, between classes," Eloni said.

"Really? Me too," I said, hoping to make him feel better. Boris still didn't look up.

"Yeah, well, they strung him up near Tootles's tree house. He was just hanging there, like a piñata. And instead of cutting him loose, the ogre-men got out their slingshots and took turns firing loquats at him."

Boris did look a little messy, and he smelled like overripe fruit.

"Big jerks," Darthin said.

"Yeah, when I came up, they told me to take a swing at him with Little Eloni," Eloni said.

"What did you do?" I asked.

"Oh, I swung Little Eloni, all right," he said, smiling. "Right into the loquat tree they were standing under. Those ogre-dorks got a nice shower of fruit."

I noticed Boris smile into his meat chunks.

"Hey," Darthin said to me, "I heard you got detention again."

"It's that Pismo. He's always getting me in trouble. I hate that kid."

"Do you want me to introduce him to Little Eloni?" Eloni asked, raising his club.

"You can't hit another student, Eloni. You know that," I said. "But thanks. He's just a pest."

"Did you hear about the dungeon?" Darthin asked.

"*Hear* about it?" I said. "I was there, getting brains for the zombies. I was next to the vent when the cockroaches swarmed into Dr. Frankenhammer's lab. They went straight for his new experiment."

"That's awful," Darthin said. "He's worked on those for months."

I nodded. "Dr. Frankenhammer thinks Professor Vodum set them off, in retaliation for the cemetery explosion."

"Why would Vodum do that?" Frankie said. "He's a stockholder. Everyone in his family owns stock in the school. If the school suffers, they lose money."

"People bent on revenge aren't always rational," Darthin said. "Normally, I wouldn't worry because Dr. Critchlore would take care of this. But what's up with him? He still hasn't done anything about that video."

"Syke said he's having a midlife crisis," I said. "He's got to get it together and put a stop to this interdepartmental sabotage. And find new minions."

I couldn't eat after all. I reached for my necklace, like I always do when I'm worried, but it was still gone. I had to get it back.

"I gotta go," I told the guys.

I left the noise of the cafeteria and walked down the hallway to the foyer. I looked up to the second floor, where Dr. Critchlore's office door stood open. Voices drifted down to me. Mumbles at first, but then louder as voices were raised in anger.

"How much more proof do you want?" That sounded like Dr. Frankenhammer. "It's not enough that Vodum's incompetent, but he planted those cockroachesssss, I'm sure it was him." Definitely Dr. Frankenhammer.

I sprinted over and stood by the elevator, straining my ears to hear more. Dr. Critchlore was barely audible. All I heard was ". . . circumstantial . . . you just don't like him . . . I can't . . . he's family."

"Oh, that's how it is, is it?" Dr. Frankenhammer said.

I couldn't hear anything after that, because more students exited the cafeteria in a cloud of chatter. But I'd heard enough to know that Dr. Frankenhammer was furious, and Dr. Critchlore wasn't going to do anything about it. I don't think I'd ever want to make someone like Dr. Frankenhammer angry; there was just no guessing what he might do.

# CHAPTER 24

*Like a good friend, a minion is there when you need him.*
—DR. CRITCHLORE, TO A FRIENDLESS EVIL OVERLORD

I headed to the Dormitory for Minions of Diminutive Size. They have their own building, where everything is properly sized for them. Apparently, it is very disheartening to have to use a step stool to reach the sink when you're a teenager.

Other than the size, the dormitory was arranged like all the others. There was a large common room that separated two wings of dorm rooms, one for the girls and one for the boys.

I stood in front of the door, bent down, and knocked. Nobody answered. I stood there for five minutes, knocking at intervals, until finally I just opened the door and walked in. I'd never been inside. It felt like I was trespassing.

Still, it had to be done.

The common room was packed with diminutive minions. Most were sitting on couches, watching a movie on TV. I watched a goblin grab a fried tarantula from a bowl and munch off each leg in turn. *Ew.*

I have to say, one diminutive minion alone is not at all scary, but seeing a big bunch of them is a totally different story, especially because most diminutive minion species are not known for their pleasant personalities. They're mean and vicious and sometimes say really hurtful things.

"What'cha doing here, big head?" Spanky said. He jumped up from the couch and charged over to me as I stood in the foyer. I guessed that he was mad at me for taking back the gum he'd stolen from my pocket yesterday. I should have let him keep it.

"Hi, Spanky," I said. "Um, I'm looking for Fingers. Do you know where he is?"

"What's it to ya?"

"I think he has my necklace," I said. "I lost it after he climbed on my back."

"What makes you think Fingers has it?"

"Um." How to put this diplomatically? "Because he's Fingers."

Most of the imps sitting around murmured their agreement, but Spanky looked furious. Because of their green skin, imps don't turn red when angry; they turn a brownish color. He bunched his fists like he wanted to punch me.

"Listen, you," he said, poking me in the leg, "we don't take kindly to big folks coming in here like you own the place! Accusin' us of theft. Just because we're smaller doesn't mean—"

"Now, hold on," I interrupted. "First of all, I didn't come in here like I own the place, I knocked. For five minutes. But nobody answered."

More murmurings. "Can't be bothered." "I'd lose my spot." "Who knocks anyway?"

"And secondly," I said, "in case you've forgotten, my name is Runt."

The imps looked at one another. "We thought that was one of them ironical names," Spanky said. "You know, like calling Eloni 'Tiny.' Or Boris 'Smarts.' On account of you're big."

"I just want my necklace back," I said. "It's the only thing I have from my family."

"Maybe you should have watched it better, then," Spanky said. "I'm not really in the mood to be nice to you."

"Why?"

"Because I thought we'd get bonus points for trapping you in the Strawberry Snare. You're a third-year! But when we reported the catch to Janet, our scorekeeper, she said, 'Higgins only counts for regular points.'"

"Why?" I asked.

He looked at me and raised his eyebrows. "Really? You don't know?"

I shook my head.

Spanky rubbed his arms. "*Brrr.* You must have let in a draft. Could you hand me a sweater from the safety station? We put it in the closet over there," he said, nodding to a door on my left.

I shrugged and went to the closet, and even though it was small, I managed to stick my head in and look around for the safety station. I was thinking that putting it in the closet wasn't such a good idea when I felt a kick on my butt and the door slammed behind me.

"That's why you only count for regular points," Spanky called through the door. "It's harder to trap a dead slug. Honestly."

"Oh." I was scrunched over and uncomfortable in the dark. "Can I come out now?"

"Nah, I'm still mad."

"But don't you get another point for trapping me again? That should make you happy, right?"

"Hey, you're right." He opened the door. "Now scram."

"Look," I said. I strode right past him to the middle of the room. I decided to do my best Coach Foley impersonation. Nobody messed with Coach Foley. I widened my stance and lowered my gaze. Using my pointer finger as a weapon, I aimed it at each of the imps in turn. "I'm not leaving until I get my necklace. Either you guys help me, or I'll search every room here. And I won't clean up afterward."

Silence filled the room as they all looked at me.

And then they jumped me.

"Hey, what's going on?" a voice called out. It cut through the air like a lullaby; it was so beautiful. I couldn't see her because I was covered in imps. I didn't need to see, though, to know who it was.

The imps jumped off me in a flash. I watched as they smoothed their hair and straightened their clothes, like it was photo day or something. I turned to the door and saw her. Janet Desmarais stood in the open doorway, her perfect face the picture of kind curiosity.

"Higgins?"

I sat up. My face felt hot and I wished I was back in the closet. Bullied by imps. How embarrassing.

"Are you okay?" she asked me.

"Oh, sure," I said, running a hand through my hair. "I'm fine. We were just—"

"Playing," Spanky said. "Yeah, that's right. We were just having a little fun."

"Hmm." She didn't look convinced.

Spanky scurried over and took her hand, kissing it gently. "What can we do for you, sweet lady?"

She smiled at him. It was a smile that lit up her eyes and made me want to buy her a candy bar. *No, that's not good enough.* A new bike, or . . . a castle! It had the same effect on all the imps and they rushed toward her, offering her anything they could think of.

"Do you want a drink?" "Come sit down, be comfortable." "How about a scone?"

"Tell them to give me my necklace," I muttered into the commotion.

Janet gasped, and the whole room fell silent. "You guys have Runt's necklace?" she asked. "Oh, you have to give it back. It's the only connection he has with his past."

"We don't have it." "Never seen it." "Gotta go."

The imps scurried away, bumping into one another in their eagerness to get out of the room. They ran up the staircase and disappeared.

I sighed and stood up. "Thanks for trying, Janet," I said. "I'll probably never get it back."

She smiled at me like I was the dumb kid who was standing at the board unable to solve the math problem. "Wait," she said.

I shrugged. Nothing better to do, so I might as well stand here and look at Janet. That got me thinking. "What are you doing here?"

"I'm the junior henchman assistant in Professor Votyakovsky's

Stealth Techniques and Strategies for Diminutive Minions class. I came to get today's scores."

"The Trap Other Students game? That's you?"

"Yes. Isn't it hilarious?" She smiled. It was such a great smile that I thought, *Yes! Yes it is hilarious*, before I remembered my day and thought, *Wait, no. It's really not.*

"I got them to trap Bianca in the hedge maze at lunch," she said. "That'll teach her to flirt with Rufus."

We heard thumping above us. The thumping got closer as the imps tumbled down the stairs in a giant scrum, carrying a reluctant Fingers in their midst. Fingers thrashed and swore and looked like he wanted to tear each of them apart. They pushed him forward, and he saw Janet.

"Oh," he said. His demeanor immediately changed from crazy aggression to rapt adoration. His eyes widened and took on that dreamy look all the other imps had. Janet was one powerful minion.

"Go on," Spanky said. "Give it back."

"Right," Fingers said. "It's just a piece of junk anyway." He reached into his coat and handed me the necklace. Relief poured through me. I felt like hugging the whole rotten bunch of them.

"Thank you," I said to Fingers. "You don't know how much this means to me." I turned to Janet. "Thanks." She smiled.

"Miss Janet, I have a little something for you too," Fingers said. He rooted around in his coat and pulled out a bracelet. It looked expensive, ringed with sparkling diamonds set in gold.

"Oh, aren't you sweet," she said, holding out her wrist. He fastened it on, beaming at her. "It's beautiful."

"It's been in my family for generations," Fingers said. He lowered his voice to a whisper. "I was told to give it to a beautiful lady and she would be mine forever."

"Yeah, right," Spanky said. "That looks an awful lot like Vodum's secretary's bracelet. Here's today's scores, Janet." He handed her a piece of paper.

"Thank you, Spanky, and you too, Fingers," Janet said. "But now I have to go." She spun around and left, and I hustled after her.

Once we were outside, I thanked her again.

"You're welcome," she said. "I couldn't bear to see you lose that necklace. I mean, how else are you going to prove who you are when your family finds you?"

"Huh?"

"It's been so long, they won't recognize you. It's like that story— about the prince who gets kidnapped and kept prisoner for years? At last he escapes, but when he returns to the castle, he's so changed from his difficult ordeal that nobody recognizes him, not even his beloved! But then she sees that he's wearing the royal ring, and she realizes he's the missing prince. It's such a romantic story!"

She did a little twirl and smiled at me. "Maybe you're a secret prince too," she said. "And when you're back on your throne, you'll remember the people who were nice to you when you were nothing but a pathetic excuse for a minion warrior."

Hearing Janet say out loud how she felt about me really hit me hard. Then a smile slowly spread across my face. Janet thought I was a secret prince! Chew toys, that was awesome!

Of course, I knew I wasn't a secret prince. I was a werewolf. But I was okay with Janet thinking I was a secret prince.

I noticed Rufus walking down the path toward the dorms. He saw me with Janet, and I could tell by his expression that if he had a rock, he'd throw it at me.

Janet put an arm around me and squeezed my shoulder. "Isn't Rufus cute when he's jealous?" she whispered in my ear.

*No.* I gulped. *He's really not.*

# CHAPTER 25

*People who use explosives often blow themselves up.*
—FIRST LESSON IN INTRODUCTION TO EXPLOSIVES, A CLASS
TAUGHT BY PROFESSOR "TWO FINGERS" FLICKSTONE

The next morning I snuck out of my room, not wanting to wake my roommates. I stopped by the kitchen to grab a muffin and get a good-luck hug from Cook, and then I jogged out to Mount Curiosity. Syke must have seen me from her room, because she swung down to join me.

"Hey, Higgins," she said. "I thought you'd be out here early."

"Hi, Syke," I said. We walked together toward the junior hench-man meeting spot.

"I wanted to warn you about Rufus," she said. "I overheard him talking to his friends. He wants to take you out during the test today."

"Me? Why?"

"Said he's sick of seeing you trying to steal his girlfriend."

"What?"

"Yeah, Princess Janet I'm-So-Amazing Desmarais," Syke said, putting her finger down her throat and pretending to gag. "You don't like her, do you?"

"What?" I felt my face get hot. "Of course not. I mean . . . sure I do, she's nice and pretty and—"

"'Nice'? Root rot, Higgins, she's the most egotistical, stuck-up, catty girl in the whole school! And she can't even sing. What kind of siren can't sing?"

"She got my medallion back from the imps," I said, showing it to her.

"Sure, she's nice to guys," Syke said, rolling her eyes. "She wants you all to worship her. Just be careful, okay?"

"I will. Thanks for the warning." As if I needed anything else to go wrong, now I had a pack of werewolves after me.

The other contestants trickled over, looking as nervous as I felt.

I had to do well on this test. I just had to. Since I'd completely blown the first task, I had a lot of ground to make up on these last two tests. Anything could happen, so I wasn't giving up. But labradoodles, I was nervous.

Rufus whispered to his friends, and they all looked over at me with eyes so squinty you'd think they were looking straight at the sun. I trotted closer to Professor Murphy.

"Okay, students, listen up," Professor Murphy said. "Coach Foley is going to explain the second task."

Coach Foley stepped in front of Professor Murphy. "This task will test your physical strength, your ability to perform under pressure, and your bravery."

"How is that different from the last test?" someone asked.

Coach Foley scowled. "Because this test has explosives."

Everyone went "*Ahhhh*."

"I call this test 'Steal the Secret Formula,' because, as you know, espionage is an important skill for a junior henchman. For this test, the enemy compound will be the old caretaker's house on the other side of the river."

I smiled, clutching my medallion. I'd just gotten it back and already my luck had improved. I knew every cobwebby corner, every broken stair, and every hidden nook of that old building. The house had been abandoned ever since Tootles became the caretaker forty years ago. He preferred his tree house. Syke and I spent the past summer pretending it was our secret compound.

Standing with the other junior henchman trainees at the base of Mount Curiosity, I could just see the front of the lonely and forgotten building. No glass remained in the windows, and a lot of the stucco had flaked off, revealing the concrete structure beneath. Weeds and vines crept up the walls.

"You will go in threes, each of you given a map to the general location of where your specific secret formula is hidden. You are not to look for the others. Secure your secret formula and return without being detected by any of our defensive measures. You may have to disarm a booby trap, you may have to open a safe using only the tools given, and if you set off any explosive devices, you will be disqualified."

"Real explosives?" Rufus asked. "If so, Runt should go first."

"No. The bomb traps will explode with flour. They're harmless. But hopefully you all remember what you learned last year in Professor Flickstone's Explosive Types and How to Defuse Them class. As for crossing the river, you may use anything you find next to the bridge: a pole-vaulting pole, the grappling hook, the trampoline, or the reverse bungee. You are not to use the bridge; it's missing a few slats, and that could be dangerous."

And pole-vaulting across a raging river wasn't? Jeez.

"You will be timed," Foley added. "Professor Murphy?"

Professor Murphy strode forward. "First up"—he looked at his tablet—"Rufus, Lapso, and Frieda. Line up, please."

They strode forward, pushing past me. "Good luck, guys," I said. Rufus snapped at my face.

They took off, and soon we heard the thunderous roar of an avalanche. Frieda had probably found her own way across the river by making a bridge of boulders. It was ridiculous, really, to think that an ogre could sneak in anywhere. Still, she'd probably do better than me.

I was excited, but since they'd started with the three top finishers from the first test, I knew I would probably be going last. Rufus was gone, so I felt safe wandering up the slope to sit on a boulder and wait.

I gazed out at the lake. A small island seemed to float in the middle, cut off from land by a mile of water. Just as I was wondering if islands got lonely and missed their families, a hand clamped over my mouth and I felt myself dragged backward.

I couldn't twist around to see who had grabbed me, but whoever it was, he was extremely strong. He dragged me up the mountain until we were behind some trees. Then he sat on me and morphed into a wolf.

I stared up into a set of drooling jaws inches from my neck. Long fangs glinted in the early morning sunlight. The beast was huge.

"Jud, get off," I said. Rufus's giant friend had me pinned.

Jud shook his furry head.

"Jud, what's the point? I'm not going to win this thing," I said. "Why are you picking on me?"

A line of drool dripped from one side of his jaws. He licked it away just as it neared my face. Then another line of drool made the same journey.

"Are you just going to sit on me, so I miss my turn?" I said.

He didn't answer.

"That means you miss your turn too. Are you doing this because Rufus asked you to mess me up? Of course you are. So, basically, by sacrificing your own chance of being in the program, you are saying to the world that you think Rufus is better than you."

He grunted at that.

"Why else would you let him beat you so easily? You didn't even put up a fight. At least I have enough self-respect to try my best."

I didn't think I was getting through to him, and I knew I couldn't push him off me. I gave up and looked back at the school. It was so beautiful. And I wasn't the only one who thought so. Someone had set up an easel and was painting a picture of the castle. I squinted and looked closer. Flea bites—it was Dr. Critchlore.

"He shouldn't be painting," I said. "He should be trying to save this school from interdepartmental rivalries. He should be finding new minions!"

Jud followed my gaze and grunted.

"Just so you know, Jud," I said, "I think you're a ten-times-better minion than Rufus. And you'd make a way better junior henchman too. You're smart and strong, and you have a way of seeing things that other people don't. Like that time we had Outdoor Ed? You were the one who got us out of the Caves of Doom by scaring the bats and telling us to follow them out. That was brilliant."

"He's afraid you'll beat him," Jud said, reverting to human form and sitting next to me. He ran a hand through his long hair. "He knows there's another component to the junior henchman evaluation. A likability component. It says on the form: 'A junior henchman needs to possess qualities that endear him to his master.' The teachers are going to be asked to rank each applicant on their likability, and that's a test Rufus knows he can't win. Apparently, niceness counts. Who knew?"

Nice people knew, I wanted to say, but I kept my mouth shut.

Jud shrugged, and then he re-wolfed and bounded down the hill.

I was about to follow, when the alarm sounded.

# CHAPTER 26

*Minions work best when they work together.*
—DR. CRITCHLORE'S SIXTH COMMANDMENT OF MINIONSHIP

We had fire drills all the time, but we'd never had one before school hours. I didn't see smoke rising from anywhere on the castle, but I had a feeling this was no drill.

Dr. Critchlore kept painting. Pizza the dog spun in circles around his stool, yapping. A few humans and monsters ran out of the castle, going to their assigned spots. Not many, though, because it was so early that most students were still in their dorms.

I thought I should probably get back to my test, but then a splotch on the side of the castle caught my eye—and the reason it caught my eye was that it was moving. A moving shadow, right below Dr. Critchlore's window. I squinted and watched it edge up the side of the wall.

I climbed down the hill to get a better look and was startled when a bit of tree fell down beside me. Only, it wasn't a bit of tree; it was Syke.

"You okay?" she asked. "I saw Jud tackle you, and I was coming to help."

"I'm fine, thanks. But look at that." I pointed to the splotch, which looked like it was growing.

Syke squinted. The splotch was about a meter off the ground when we saw a piece detach and fall. The little splotch exploded on impact, a quiet little explosion with a small puff of smoke.

"Oh no!" I said. "That splotch is one of Dr. Frankenhammer's explosive minions!"

"I remember those," Syke said. "I thought they'd all blown."

"Apparently not. If that big one reaches Dr. Critchlore's office and something startles it, the whole side of the building will go."

"They're attracted to the smell of death," Syke said. "Do you think someone died up there?"

I pointed to Dr. Critchlore, still painting as if an alarm wasn't blaring.

"Is that Critchlore?" Syke said. I nodded. "He's painting? The only paintings he's ever shown interest in are ones of himself."

"Not true," I said. "He loves that one outside the ballroom— *Massacre at Diporvy*."

"He does love a good massacre," Syke said, nodding. "Wait a sec, is he smelling a flower? That can't be Critchlore."

"It's him," I said. "I've got to warn him about the explosives." And knock some sense into him.

"I know something that might help," Syke said, taking off before explaining what it was. She moved quickly through the trees, like a monkey. It almost looked like the trees were gently tossing her to each other.

The alarm stopped blaring as I sprinted down the slope. I was out of breath when I reached him. "Dr. . . . . Critchlore," I panted.

"Oh, hello there . . . you," he said. Pizza was still running in circles, barking. "What do you think?" He pointed to his painting.

"There's . . . a . . . bomb." I didn't have enough breath for "escaped explosive minion."

"What? You think it's a bomb?" he said, giving his painting a critical eye. "I admit it's not done in the Realist style, but I rather thought I'd captured the essence of the building."

"No . . . Dr. Critchlore . . . something . . . beneath . . . your window."

"I agree. Adding people would give it that sense of scale," he said, looking thoughtfully at his painting.

"Splotch!" I pointed.

"No, that's a tree." He frowned at me. "It doesn't look like a splotch. Really, how insulting. You can go now."

I spotted the zombies huddled together under the giant oak tree near the base of the mountain. All at once a thought flashed in my head.

The zombies were already dead. They must smell like death. Maybe if they stood near the building, the explosive minion would go to them. Then I could have the zombies carry it to the lake, where the water would neutralize it.

I ran over to them.

"Zom-*beeeeeees*," I whined. "Follow *meeeeeee*."

They followed.

Slowly.

So slowly.

And they didn't really smell like death. More like a combination of freshly turned earth and morning breath. Maybe their death smell had been used up?

The explosive minion had split again. As I got nearer I saw that it was a pile of explosive minions, not one big one. They looked like little black porcupines with long claws. They inched up the side of the castle, chipping off bits of stone as they climbed.

I tried to remember what I knew about the explosive minions. They were highly unstable, blowing up at the slightest provocation, like they were filled with nitroglycerin. Once one blew, it triggered the others. They could creep along slowly, silently, sneaking into enemy fortifications and blowing them up. They were also attracted to the smell of rotting meat, so that after a battle, a bunch of explosive minions could be sent in to clear the field of mines.

We reached the wall, but the explosive minions had crawled out of reach. They had short legs but powerful hands and claws. I was about to tell Zombie Twelve to get up on Zombie Five's shoulders—he had the most intact shoulders—when Syke returned with an armful of flowers.

"Syke, I really don't think flowers are the way to go here," I said.

"Smell." She held out one of the flowers, which looked like a large purple leaf with a skinny finger jutting out of the middle. It smelled putrid, like a freshly rotting carcass.

"*Ew*," I said. "That's nauseating."

"*Dracunculus vulgaris*," she explained.

"Say what?"

"It's the voodoo lily."

"Still means nothing."

"The black dragon? The dragon arum? The stink lily?" she said. Finally she shook her head and explained. "It smells like rotten meat to attract flies. Then the flies pollinate it."

"Oh," I said, and then I got an idea. "Oh! We can give them to the zombies. Zom-*beees*, take a flower from Sy-*keeeee*."

The zombies each took a flower. My eyes were watering from the smell. It was awful. "Where did you get those?" I asked Syke.

She put a finger to her lips. "Tootles has a secret greenhouse for his unusual-plant collection. Don't tell."

It seemed like everyone at this school had a secret something.

"Zom-*beeees*," I whined. "Hold the flowers up to those splotches. Wave them in the air."

The explosive minions must have caught the scent, because they stopped climbing. They clung in place, like they were confused.

"More *waaaayyy*-ving," I said.

The splotches came down.

"Catch a splotch," I said. "Carefully. Carefully, Zombie Six! Be gentle. We're going to take them to the lake."

Each zombie held an explosive minion and a flower. The explosive minions seemed to snuggle up to their zombies, like affectionate toddlers. It made a very tender picture. We walked to the lake at zombie speed, which is slow. Actually, Syke and I walked a safe distance behind the zombies.

We talked about school, how conceited the ogre-men were, and what Professor Chowding had living in her hair this semester. And then Syke dropped *this* bomb on the conversation:

"Did you hear about the new Girl Explorer video?" Syke asked.

"Another one?"

"It was up for a day before someone deleted it, but Trish saw it. Apparently, the girls were perched on a rocky ledge in a meadow, when a cow walked by. Then there was a lot of camera shaking, and the most frightening high-pitched squealing Trish ever heard. When the camera settled, there was nothing left of the cow but a completely intact skeleton."

"That's got to be a joke," I said.

"Nope. They stripped it clean to the bone with their bare hands and teeth. That's what Trish said."

I gulped. "Who deleted the video? And why?"

"Probably the Girl Explorer Organization," Syke said. "That sort of behavior is bound to hurt their cookie sales."

That couldn't be true.

We were nearing the lake, and I noticed movement in the bushes. Spooked by Syke's story, I froze, grabbing her arm.

There was more rustling, and then Pismo jumped out onto the path. He ran in front of the zombies, waving his hands in the air.

"Whoa, fellows," he said to the zombies. "Back to the castle. Go on."

"Pismo, what are you doing?" I yelled.

Pismo spotted me and put his hands down. He looked at the zombies, then back at me. "What are *you* doing?" he asked. "Aren't you supposed to be at your henchman test?"

"I'm waiting my turn. We're taking these explosive minions to the lake, so they don't blow up the castle. Why are you shooing them back?"

"Um . . . They look like something that belongs in the dungeon?"

"They're too dangerous. Once one of them blows, they all will," I said. Pismo seemed really squirrelly, so I asked again, "What are you doing out here?"

He frowned. For a second, I thought he wasn't going to answer, but then he said, "I can't believe you would risk my classmate's life like that."

"Your classmate?"

"Yes, uh"—he turned to look at the back of a zombie's shirt—"Fifteen. I can't believe you would put my friend Fifteen in danger. Why does he have to carry an explosive minion? What if he blows up?" Pismo put his fist to his mouth, like he was about to cry. "I don't know what I'd do if something happened to Zombie Fifteen."

"He's full of it," Syke said.

"Mind your own business, tree girl." And with that, he ran off.

"He's up to something," Syke said.

"He's obnoxious," I said, watching him jog away. "Didn't I tell you?"

Syke shrugged, and then she pointed to the dock. "The zombies are ready."

They stood by a small dock that jutted out into the water like a long, floating T. I sent the zombies to the end, and we watched as they made their way along the dock.

"I feel kinda bad," I said. The zombies looked so tender with their explosive minion babies. "I don't think I can do it."

Syke rolled her eyes. "Zom-*beees*!" she whined. "Put the explosive minions in the water!"

The zombies gently lowered the little black porcupines into the water.

"Will it kill them?" I asked.

"I don't think so," Syke said. "It just deactivates them. Look."

One of the explosive minions was floating, its claws slapping the surface. It seemed to be gulping down water. I ran down the dock toward it; I couldn't let it drown. It wasn't its fault it was an explosive minion. I leaned over and pulled it out of the lake. A stream of yellow water leaked out its backside, landing on the dock and burning a hole right through it. I held the minion out over the lake as the toxic pee continued to stream out of it. It wriggled and wriggled in my grasp until it got free, climbed over my back, and jumped off me.

Syke and I immediately ducked down, expecting to be blown to bits, but it didn't explode. It burped.

The rest of the explosive minions swam around and then headed for shore. We went to meet them. All of us except Zombie Fifteen. His explosive minion swam to the middle of the dock. I watched him pull it out of the water, but it didn't leak yellow fluid like the others.

It started wriggling, like the rest had done.

"Throw it back in the water!" I screamed, momentarily forgetting to whine. "*Throwwww* it *baaack*, Zom-*beee* Fifteen."

It squirmed over his shoulder.

"Get *awaaaaay!*"

We covered our heads.

I'm not sure if Zombie Fifteen tried to throw it or not. We heard a bang, and when I looked up, the end of the dock was gone. Zombie Fifteen lay on the shattered edge, not moving.

Oh no!

If something happened to him, it was my fault. How could I have so carelessly risked their lives? Well, their second lives?

I ran out and knelt down next to him. "Oh, Fifteen, you were so brave to carry that explosive minion," I said. "You saved the castle."

I hated it that I didn't know his real name. Calling him "Fifteen" seemed so impersonal.

His mouth was slack and he didn't move. The other zombies crowded behind me. I put a hand on his shoulder. He felt clammy and cold, like usual. Then he raised his hand and clamped it on my wrist.

"Higginsbrains," he said.

I nearly cried. "Yes. Yes, Fifteen. You get brains." I hugged him tight, but then felt a bit of skin on his shoulder come off, so I let him go and tried to put it back on.

# CHAPTER 27

*I curse thee! Your firstborn child shall die*
*before he reaches his sixteenth year.*
—A WITCH, REALLY UPSET ABOUT SOMETHING

I asked Syke to get the zombies some brains, and then I raced back to my test. My heart sank when I saw everybody at the base of the mountain. The test was over. I stopped running and walked the rest of the way.

Coach Foley was covered in white dust, and his expression told me he was ready to lead the charge against an army of trolls that had insulted his mother. I approached him warily.

"There you are, Higgins," Professor Murphy said. "What happened to you?"

"I saw a bunch of explosive minions crawling up the side of the castle. I had the zombies take them to the lake. But one of them blew. Didn't you hear that explosion?"

"There were quite a few explosions," Professor Murphy said, nodding to the junior henchman applicants, half of whom were covered in white dust. "Do you realize what you've done?"

"Um." I wanted to say that I had just saved the castle from some expensive damage, but that sounded a little braggy, especially since it was the zombies who had done the dangerous work.

"You abandoned the test," Professor Murphy said. "Coach Foley went to check on you, and he triggered three bombs trying to find you." He turned to Coach Foley. "Again, I'm sorry, Gunner, I should have told you where they were."

Coach Foley stood with his arms crossed, looking stern.

"Disqualified," Professor Murphy said, marking something on the tablet.

"Mistress Moira? Do you think Dr. Frankenhammer would hurt the school, out of spite?" I asked during my first-period class. The fountain burbled and a cool breeze drifted through her wide windows. I sat on the couch in her airy room while she watered her carpet.

"Why do you ask?"

"Because I just stopped some of his explosive minions from crawling into Dr. Critchlore's office and destroying it. Frankenhammer was convinced that Vodum sabotaged his minions, and then he seemed furious that Dr. Critchlore would do nothing about it. Plus Darthin told me that Dr. Critchlore takes credit for Frankenhammer's work. Maybe he's had enough of that." I noticed a pile of sweats in the corner. "Hey, are you making some Critchlore Shape-Shifter Snap-Free Sweatpants™? 'Cause I could use a pair. I'm an adult small."

"Excuse me?"

"All right, youth large."

"Did you say *Critchlore* Shape-Shifter Snap-Free Sweatpants?"

"Yes," I said. "Isn't that what they're called?"

"No. They are Moira's Morphing Pants. I invented them."

"I thought it was Critchlore," I said.

"Why?"

"Because they say 'Critchlore's Snap-Frees' on the tag."

"Higgins, Dr. Frankenhammer would never do anything to harm Dr. Critchlore, but I certainly will." She lifted both arms in the air and chanted something I couldn't understand. It sounded like "Fingleton Yaw Yaw Finglemore Bep."

I reminded myself never to make Mistress Moira mad. She looked fierce. But then she smiled and sat down. "See how he likes his own Snap-Frees," she said. Then she giggled.

"Where were we?" she continued. "Oh, right. Frankenhammer. Fifteen years ago, when Dr. Frankenhammer was just Cyril Frankenhammer, janitor, he met Dr. Critchlore at a lecture. Dr. Critchlore was so impressed with Cyril that he made him give up his janitorial dreams and go back to school. Dr. Critchlore paid for everything: his tuition, his room and board, his books and supplies. Dr. Frankenhammer owes everything he has to Dr. Critchlore."

"Wow," I said, giggling. "His name is Cyril?"

"Yes," she answered. "Runt."

I stopped giggling.

"But if it wasn't Dr. Frankenhammer, then who? It's hard to believe that all these catastrophes are just accidents. Or bad luck. Oh," I gasped as another option entered my brain. Maybe it wasn't me that was cursed; maybe it was the school. "Do you think we've been cursed?"

"I don't think so," Moira said. She stood up, spread her arms, and chanted again: "Blakuvia Wangton Felp," or something. She repeated it three times, then looked out the window with the most intense stare I'd ever seen. It made my skin bumpy.

She sat back down. "Nothing new," she said. "Just the same old curses."

"What?"

"I can detect curses," she said. "I can't do anything about them, but I know when they're present."

"There are curses present?"

"Yes, indeed," she said. "Six at the moment. There used to be a seventh, but the witch who cast it probably died. That one was a doozy. Dr. Critchlore neglected to pay the subcontractor who built the bathroom in one of the back rooms in the East Wing. The subcontractor hired a witch, and she cursed the toilet to flush outward every fourth flush." She shook her head. "Very nasty."

"And the other six?"

"Mostly minor stuff. Cursed objects and protected places—the dragon hex, the billy goat curse, and the book curse. There's one biggie, which is a timed-death curse. You know the type: A certain someone will die on their sixteenth birthday, or twentieth, or thirtieth."

"Who?"

"That I cannot say."

"So no curse is causing all these incidents?"

Moira shook her head.

I slouched. Something sinister was afoot, as my classical literature novels always said. And if it wasn't Dr. Frankenhammer or a curse, what else could it be? Who could be causing it?

Dr. Critchlore had enemies. It came with the job. There was

Dr. Pravus, our rival school's headmaster. There was Dark Wendix, the overlord who'd lost a good chunk of land during the "Epic Minion Fail" debacle. There might be other disgruntled customers, for all I knew.

But how could any of them attack our school? We had every security measure imaginable. High walls with towers surrounded the school grounds. Nobody—nothing—got in or out without being scanned, photographed, and questioned. The perimeter was patrolled night and day by minions practicing their perimeter patrol skills.

I thought out loud. "Who is sabotaging the school? The cemetery, the lab, and now Dr. Critchlore's office. And every time an attack happens, there's nobody around. No witnesses. In the cemetery, the explosion happened at the same time that Vodum called a meeting of the necromancers in the castle, and they are the only ones who work in that area. And then in the dungeon, there was the gas leak, which turned out to be a harmless chemical, but it cleared out the place before the carnivorous cockroaches were released. And this morning, the fire alarm before the explosive minions."

"Interesting," Moira said. She placed her pointer finger on her temple and closed her eyes. After a moment she said, "I see three possibilities. One, a saboteur, if indeed these are acts of sabotage, wanted to create a distraction before attacking, so he or she wouldn't get caught. Or, two, our saboteur didn't want anyone to get hurt."

"What's the third possibility?"

"Coincidence," she said. "Never rule out coincidence. We are always looking for connections between events, and most of the time there is no connection. Trust me, I know connections."

I sat and thought again about all these events being unrelated instances of "bad luck." Was it possible?

"On the other hand," Moira said, "sometimes when we search for connections, that leads us to our answer."

I sighed. Moira was sort of the opposite of helpful.

I tried to see what these tragedies had in common. Cause and effect. First, I looked at the causes:

Minion fail: Caused by badly trained minions. Or a video trick of some sort.

Cemetery explosion: Caused by a bomb?

Dr. Frankenhammer's lab: Caused by a bug infestation.

Dr. Critchlore's office: Escaped explosive minions.

Not much connected the events. What about the results?

"Epic Minion Fail" hurt our reputation. We'd lost some new recruits when they'd opted to go to other minion schools.

Destroying the cemetery meant no new "dead" minions.

Destroying Dr. Frankenhammer's work meant no new "invented" minions.

I was beginning to see a pattern, but then I reached the explosive minions outside Dr. Critchlore's office. Why would someone place a bomb there when Dr. Critchlore was outside? He was in plain view.

If not to kill him, then what was the saboteur trying to accomplish?

Destroying Dr. Critchlore's office would throw him deeper into depression. It would ruin his office, his files, his collection of shrunken heads, and his books.

I gasped.

185

His books.

The *Top Secret Book of Minions*! The saboteur could have been trying to destroy it. Another potential source of minions!

But who?

If we didn't have any new minions, the school would close. There was only one person I could think of who could benefit from putting the school out of business, and that was Dr. Pravus. What if he had planted a mole right here in our school? It wouldn't be the first time a minion school has planted a spy at a rival school. It could be anybody: a guard, a groundskeeper, anybody.

Or it could be a student—someone who didn't quite fit in, but could inflict a huge amount of damage.

A student with a bad attitude.

Pismo had taken off for the cemetery right before it blew.

Pismo had tried to steal the *Top Secret Book of Minions*.

Pismo had ditched me in the dungeon right before the carnivorous cockroaches were released.

Pismo had tried to shoo the explosive minions back to the castle. It had to be him.

# CHAPTER 28

*Critchlore minions: For when you get the urge to
conquer large parts of the world!*
—AN ADVERTISEMENT IN THE *EVIL OVERLORD DAILY NEWS*

During my junior henchman class, I had trouble paying attention to Professor Murphy as he lectured about how a henchman never abandons his task. Once again, he said this while glaring at me.

Third period I had Study Hall, but instead of going to the library, I headed straight for Dr. Critchlore's private elevator. I had to tell him about Pismo.

Miss Merrybench wasn't at her desk. Dr. Critchlore wasn't in his office. *Where could they be?* I thought about leaving a note, but I didn't know what to write. No, I'd have to come back later.

I noticed a package on her desk for Professor Vodum, and that reminded me of something else I'd meant to do. I didn't like calling the zombies by their numbers. I wanted to know their real names. Professor Vodum could tell me what they were. And since I was going there anyway, I could save Miss Merrybench the trip and deliver the package for her. I picked it up and headed out.

I nearly ran into Miss Merrybench at the door.

"Oh," I said. "I was looking for Dr. Critchlore."

"He had to return to his quarters, due to a clothing mishap," she said. She smiled briefly, looking into his office. I followed her gaze and saw a pile of ripped-off clothes on the floor. Was that what Mistress Moira meant by "See how he likes his own Snap-Frees"?

Miss Merrybench looked at the package in my hand and raised her eyebrows. I hoped she didn't think I was stealing it.

"Oh! This package is for Professor Vodum, and since I'm going to his office anyway, I thought I'd save you the trip because I know how busy you are, you are probably the hardest-working person in the whole school, I'm always thinking, 'What can I do to make life easier for Miss Merrybench?' and this seemed like a good thing to do."

Her eyebrows didn't budge from their raised suspicion, and she didn't say anything for a few seconds.

"Well, don't just stand there looking stupid," she said. "Go already."

I raced out of there.


The Necromancy Building was quiet. Marcia, the secretary, wasn't in the little anteroom, and the offices behind her desk were empty. Maybe they'd closed down the whole department, now that the cemetery had been destroyed.

I walked over to Professor Vodum's door and peeked in. "Professor Vodum?" I called, thinking he might be somewhere out of sight. Nope, empty.

Rats.

Marcia's phone rang. I waited, but nobody came to answer. The machine picked up.

"Vodum, Dr. Evans here. Got your message about moving up the meeting regarding Critchlore. The board of directors is very concerned, given the stock price plunge this year. I'm backing Critchlore, as you know, but if there's another incident at the school, the other board members want his head. Not literally, of course. That business with Headmaster Colving was a special circumstance. But nine A.M., then."

Oh no! Things weren't looking good for Dr. Critchlore. The board of directors was losing patience. "Another incident?" It suddenly struck me that if we did have a saboteur (Pismo) in our midst, he could be planning another attack right now. I was going to have to find Mrs. Gomes at lunch and warn her.

I turned to leave, but as I opened the door, I bumped into Professor Vodum, who had his head down, reading something he held in his hands.

I couldn't help it: I yelped.

"Higgins. For goodness' sake, what do you want now?" he asked.

"Package for you, sir," I said. "And I have a question."

"Package?" He grabbed it out of my hand, reading the label as he stomped over to his desk. "Reliable Potions Corporation?"

He opened it and examined the packaging list.

"Twenty-five cc of Suggesterol." He looked confused. This was not unusual; most professors were constantly forgetting little things like names and birthdays and office supply orders because their minds were so focused on their studies.

He put the package down and pulled out his *Necromancers Desk*

*Reference.* "Suggesterol, Suggesterol," he muttered as he looked it up. "Here it is: 'Suggesterol is the strongest potion available for making a victim susceptible to suggestion. Eighty-seven percent success rate. Do not take with alcohol, other drugs, or puff pastries. Side effects include dizziness, nausea, and involuntary leg spasms. Do not exceed recommended dosage. Discontinue use after three days to avoid permanent brain damage.'"

That seemed like a pretty dangerous drug to me. Professor Vodum noticed me staring at him and said, "I didn't order this."

"Do you want me to take it back?"

"No, no," he said quickly, stashing the box under his desk. "I'll take care of it. Not to worry, Higgins. Now, then, what was your question?"

"I wanted to know the real names of your zombies. I don't like calling them numbers."

"Right, sure." He swiveled around and opened his file. "I have the names, of course," he said. He thumbed through the file until he found what he was looking for. "Here we go." He turned back around and handed me a paper. There were fifteen names beneath the title "Zombies—Vodum."

It was just a list of names. There was no reference to the numbers they wore. "How do I know which one is which?" I asked.

"How should I know?" he whined. "They all look alike to me."

I read the names. "You didn't keep track of their numbers?" I asked.

"Why would I? Now, if you don't mind, I'm very busy trying to save the school. The board of directors will not stand for another accident around here, and Dr. Critchlore seems more interested in recreational activities than in running things."

"Do you mind if I work with the zombies during detention?" I asked.

"Detention?"

"Yes, you gave me detention. In the graveyard. Because of the bones. Remember?" Why was I reminding him?

"Of course, right. Yes. That would be fine. Work with the zombies for detention. Now run along, I'm a busy man."

I had a plan. I'd warn Mrs. Gomes about Pismo at lunch, after Literature. Once that was done, I'd be free to work with the zombies after school. As I headed back to the castle, a part of me wondered what Professor Vodum was going to do with that Suggesterol, but I didn't have time to worry about that.

# CHAPTER 29

*True genius lies in identifying a minion's strength
and enhancing it for maximum effect.*

—FROM THE TEXTBOOK *MINION SPECIES*, BY DR. D. CRITCHLORE

At lunch I found Mrs. Gomes supervising the construction of a giant wall near the lake. She was nibbling on one of her manicured fingernails. Actually, all her fingernails had been chewed down.

"Mrs. Gomes? I have some new information for you."

"Higgins," she said, "I'm very busy right now." She pointed to one of the workers. "Hubert, that's not high enough. Darrell, I told you to check the expiration dates on the safety stations. Revis, when you finish here, you need to talk to Cook about having all potential choking hazard foods removed from the cafeteria menu."

"But this is important," I said, jumping in front of her so she had to look at me. "Um, what's the wall for?" I couldn't help it, I was curious.

"To protect us from tsunamis."

"Tsunamis? Don't they usually happen to cities that are, you know, near the ocean?" Stull was completely landlocked.

"That lake is as big as an ocean," she said. "It has tides! And we had three minor earthquakes last year, and then the temblor that triggered the explosion in the cemetery. It could be a precursor to a bigger quake. A big earthquake, centered under the lake, could be disastrous."

"But aren't you investigating the bomb? The leak in the dungeon? The explosive minions? Dr. Frankenhammer's work was destroyed, and Dr. Critchlore's office nearly was too."

"Yes, those investigations are ongoing. Don't worry, we have everything under control."

"Mrs. Gomes, I think someone is trying to destroy our supply of minions," I said. "And I think I know who it is."

"Really?" she said.

I told her about my suspicions. I laid it all out. The bad attitude, the curious way he was always near the sabotage. "It's obvious he's a plant by Dr. Pravus!"

"Higgins, that's all very interesting, but it's impossible."
"Why?"

"Every student's background is checked," she said. "By me. Are you suggesting that someone could get by me?" She glared at me.

"No," I said. "But don't you think it's suspicious?"

"Actually, I don't," she said. "Each of our students is a unique individual, Higgins. You can't judge someone by a few instances of bad behavior."

"But—"

"If it makes you feel better, I'll have a talk with the boy."

"Please don't tell him I said anything."

"Of course not. Now, please, go to class so I can do my job. There are dangers everywhere, and it's my job to protect us!"

I felt better having shared my suspicions. So after school I asked Frankie to help me with my zombie project, because he has a photographic memory. I sat him down at a computer in the library and showed him the cemetery database, which had information on everyone buried there, including a picture or description of physical characteristics. Frankie quickly memorized everything about each name on my list.

We found the zombies out by the Necromancy Building, swaying and chanting for brains. I darted inside and asked Professor Vodum if he had any brains, because the zombies were going crazy, but he said no, and could I please leave him alone so he could get some work done.

The zombies really didn't want to leave, but we managed to pull them back to the Memorial Courtyard and line them up by number. Frankie carefully looked at each zombie. Then, without hesitation, he walked down the line, naming each one as he pointed to it.

"Frankie, you're amazing!" I said. He seemed to blush a little, and I worried about how embarrassment might affect him. Would he pop an arm? A leg?

"Thanks," he said.

I studied my new list, now with numbers next to the names. I recited the names as I looked at each zombie. "Hilary, Harold, Eunice—"

But then I heard Frankie sniff. I turned and saw him blinking away tears.

"Frankie, what's the matter?" I asked.

"Is it true?" he asked. "Is it true that Darthin is Dr. Frankenhammer's assistant?"

"Not officially. He's just been helping him out with some stuff," I said. The tears Frankie had been battling broke free and dripped down his cheeks. "Oh, Frankie, I'm sorry."

He wailed. Somehow, between sobs, he managed to say, "Why does he hate me?"

"He doesn't hate you, Frankie," I said, putting a hand on his shoulder. I wished Dr. Frankenhammer could see the effect his careless words had on his creation. "He's just really, really self-absorbed. He doesn't think about other people. Or their feelings."

Frankie's whole body shook with sobs. He plopped down on the grass, and I sat next to him. He covered his face with his hands and said, "I just wish I knew what was wrong with me. Maybe I could fix it, and he'd love me."

"Frankie, there is nothing wrong with you. It's just your bad luck that you had to be created by a perfectionist. Don't you see? You can never make him happy, and that's *his* problem, not yours. I know it hurts, and I'm really sorry."

Just then a group of fifth-years came down the path from the lake. They were humans, laughing at something the biggest one said. At once, Frankie clamped down on his sobbing and wiped his eyes. He forced out a fake laugh and said, "That's so funny, Higgins."

The fifth-years stopped talking and looked at Frankie, which made him even more self-conscious. He swallowed hard and looked from me to them.

I nodded at them. "Hey," I said.

"Hey," the big one, Jeremy, said. "Everything okay?"

"Sure," I said. Then I looked at Frankie, and it was obvious that everything wasn't. He was trying so hard not to cry. I recognized the signs of imminent head popping: the blinking eyes, the biting of his lower lip, the rapid breathing. "Frankie," I whispered, "it's okay to cry, just let it out."

He shook his head. "I'm . . . fine."

The fifth-years weren't helping by standing and staring at him. But I couldn't really blame them. How often did they get to see a head pop?

"Is he gonna blow?" another fifth-year asked. I tried to answer him with an angry stare that said "Shut up, you idiot," but my mouth said, "He's fine. You guys can keep going." I tilted my head in the direction they'd been walking, hoping they'd get the hint.

"Oh no!" Frankie said, right before his head popped off. I caught it in the air, placed it on the ground, and reached for Frankie's body.

"A little help, please?" I said. Jeremy ran over and the others followed. I guided them through the steps, and we put the head back in place. I asked them to leave before I turned the blood flow on again.

"Frankie?" I said.

He blinked a few times and sat up, noticing the blood on my shirt. "Again? You've got to be kidding me."

"It's okay, Frankie," I said. "I know why your head pops off."

"Really?"

"Yes! Don't you see? You were fine until you tried to stop yourself from crying. You have to let your emotions out. When you clamp down on them, the pressure inside you must build up until . . ."

". . . my head pops off," he finished. "Higgins, you're right!"

I smiled.

"But I can't let people see me cry."

"Why not?"

"Because Frankenminions don't cry," he said. "Daddy said that when he saw me crying. He wanted me to jump over to the roof of the castle, but I could only make it to the third-floor windows."

"That's stupid. Everyone cries."

"Try telling *him* that," Frankie said. "I just can't look at him without being scared."

"Hmm," I said. "Did you know his first name is Cyril?"

Frankie looked at me, his face blank. Then a laugh burst out from behind a huge smile. "Cyril? Really?"

I nodded. For some reason, it was hard to be frightened of a Cyril.


At dinner Pismo charged up to me and stabbed my chest with his pointer finger. "You filthy little squealer!" he yelled, loud enough for the whole cafeteria to hear.

It's not often someone confronts me like that, and I froze. I don't like confrontation. I probably looked so feeble, standing there blinking in confusion, my mouth hanging open. My face grew hot when I noticed everyone looking at us.

"I thought you were my friend! Ha! Everyone says how nice you are, and you go and accuse me of stuff I didn't do. What's your problem, huh?"

He thought I was his friend? He'd only stolen my exploding gum, gotten me detention—twice!—lost my DPS, taken credit for my work, and left me to be killed by the muscle Thing. I wondered how he treated his enemies.

"I . . . you . . . who told you I . . ." I stammered. I couldn't form a complete sentence if my life depended on it.

He mocked me. "I . . . you . . . what . . . Do you know what you've done? If I'm expelled, who knows where my father will send me? Do you even care?"

"Maybe you'll go to the Pravus Minion Academy," I said. "Since you love it so much."

"I was already expelled from there! This is my third flipping minion school, and I'm still a stupid first-year!"

Whoa.

"You were at Pravus's?" My voice must have been shocked too, because it came out as a whisper.

"Shut up," he said. "Just shut up for once in your life!"

I could tell he hadn't meant to say he'd been at Pravus's. It had come out in anger. And you know what? That made me even more sure he was the saboteur.

My friends—Darthin, Frankie, Eloni, Boris, and Syke—came over and stood behind me for support.

"You and your loser friends," Pismo went on. "You're nothing but a bunch of misfits."

Once again, whoa.

I don't have a problem with someone attacking me. I have thick skin. Because I'm a werewolf. But nobody attacks my friends.

"Misfits?" I said, stepping forward. "I don't think so. Darthin knows more about biology and chemistry than half of the professors here. Frankie is a physical marvel with a photographic memory. Eloni and Boris are the most loyal friends a person can have. And Syke is tougher than most of the monsters I know. They are the kind of students that make this school great. You, on the other hand, are selfish, mean, and conceited. You'll never be a minion."

"At least I know what I'm not," he said. I heard everyone in the room gasp.

"What do you mean?"

"You're not a werewolf, Runt," he said. "Everybody knows that but you."

I stood there, shocked. I think I stopped breathing. How do you answer something like that? It was ridiculous. I forced out some laughter. Then I looked around the room. As soon as I caught anybody's eye, he or she quickly looked away.

"Don't listen to him, Higgins," Darthin said.

"Yeah, he's just mad," Frankie added.

"He's just trying to hurt you," Syke said.

Pismo shook his head. "You're such an idiot," he said. Then he turned around and left.

# CHAPTER 30

*A friend in need needs minions.*

—A PROMOTIONAL GIFT CARD,

REDEEMABLE FOR A GIFT OF MINIONS

I had a rough night. My friends had assured me that Pismo was crazy, angry, vengeful, and wrong, but I couldn't get his voice out of my head: "You're not a werewolf, Runt. Everybody knows that but you."

Me? Not a werewolf? Impossible.

Wasn't it?

I had grown up with wolves. I remembered that. I had a medallion with a wolf on it. I had morphed when I was seven.

My fist wrapped around my necklace, but I couldn't sleep. At last I stopped trying and got up. I had no junior henchman test that morning. Coach Foley needed an extra day to think up the final one, so my morning wasn't going to start as early as it usually did. I didn't want to go to breakfast and face Pismo again. That left me with too much free time before my first period with Mistress Moira.

I decided to find out for myself, once and for all. I had to know if what Pismo said was true.

I grabbed my slingshot and headed for the stables.

The stables were a series of buildings and pens located behind the castle, past the boulderball field and far enough away that the smell wore off by the time it drifted to us. On my way there I passed the road that led to the aviary, also located behind the castle but closer to Mount Curiosity. I heard the crows cawing, the owls hooting, and the harpies complaining about the food. I thought about making a detour because I loved helping Master Ping feed the birds. No, I didn't have time for that. I was on a mission.

I continued on my path, heading farther away from the castle. As I neared the stables, the odor got stronger: the smell of animals and hay and dung. There were three stables: one for horses, another one for the cows and goats and smaller animals, and one for the dragons. I entered the dragon stable.

The stalls were nice, each as big as a classroom. The dragons sat on piles of fake treasure: gold bars and coins, diamonds and rubies. Dragons like treasure.

I put a coin into the treasure dispenser, turned the knob, and a handful of mini-goblets and plastic gems tumbled into my hand. The dispenser was for guests, just like the one in the barn that gave out little food pellets so visitors could feed the goats and sheep. I tossed the dragons handfuls of loot as I passed. In return, they didn't breathe fire at me.

I wasn't there for the dragons. The creature I was looking for lay curled up asleep in the rafters.

I pulled out my slingshot, loaded a pebble, and shot. I hit the beast in the rump, and she sprang up hissing.

Killer, the mountain lion. The dragons seemed to like the giant cat, so the stable master let them keep her. She had a horrible disposition, always hissing and spitting at anyone who came near.

I shot again.

Killer jumped down from the rafters in one smooth leap. I stepped back, my breath coming in shallow gasps as I realized that maybe this had been a stupid idea. Slowly, she stalked closer, keeping her head low. *Wow, she has really big teeth*. I kissed my medallion for luck.

*Morph*, I told myself.

I had to morph. I was facing certain death. If ever there was a time to morph, it was now.

*Morph!*

The cat neared me, her eyes as cold and lifeless as the dungeon's darkest corners. I was so scared I started shaking.

*Morph!*

I stretched my neck, checking for thickening hairs on the back, but it was smooth. I howled as loud as I could. "*Ahhh-wooooooooo!*"

*MORPH!*

But my feet remained feet, my hands remained hands, and no fangs grew in my mouth. The massive, angry cat lunged at the puny human boy that I remained and knocked me backward. My head clanked onto some treasure, and everything ended.

Until I woke up.

My head throbbed and I felt tiny prickles all over my body. I was lying in a haystack. I looked over and saw Jake, the stable master.

"Hey there," he said.

"Hi, Jake. What happened?"

"Killer pounced on you," he said. "But I chased her off. Good thing I'd just had her declawed. Stupid cat keeps scratching up my furniture."

"Ouch," I said, feeling the lump on the back of my head.

"What were you doing, Higgins?" He held out an ice pack and gently placed it behind my head. The cold was shocking, but I let him hold it there. I deserved to be in pain. I was such a loser.

"I was trying to make myself morph."

"Into what? A chew toy?"

"No, into a werewolf," I said. "Jake, do you think I'm not a werewolf?"

Jake sat back and sighed. "Yes, Higgins," he said. "I think you are not a werewolf. Don't tell Cook I told you. She said if anyone told you, she'd make him miserable for the rest of his life."

"But I remember being with wolves," I said. "I remember a momma wolf and a daddy wolf and brothers and sisters."

Jake shrugged. "I'm sorry, Higgins. You're the nicest kid here, but you're not a werewolf. And that's a good thing. If you were a werewolf, you wouldn't be you."

"Huh?"

He shrugged again.

I closed my eyes. How could my not being a werewolf be a good thing? All my life I'd had a certain confidence that came from believing I was a powerful beast. But I wasn't. I was nothing but a scrawny human.

But that wasn't the worst of it. If I hadn't been left by the pack, then who left me here? Who hadn't wanted me?

I felt small. And weak. And hopeless and depressed.

"You need to get to the infirmary," Jake said. "You've got a concussion. Mrs. Gomes has new rules regarding concussions, you know." He looked off into the distance. I think he'd had his share of concussions himself. He scratched his head with a burn-scarred hand. "What was I saying?"

"That I'd better run along, or I'll be late for class," I said.

He smiled at me and helped me up. I handed him the ice pack.

"You need to get to the infirmary," he said. "You've got a concussion. Mrs. Gomes has new rules regarding concussions."

"I know," I said. "Thanks, Jake."

I left.

My head hurt, but I decided to put off going to the infirmary. I was due at my first-period assignment with Mistress Moira, but I decided to skip that too. What did it matter? Did anything matter anymore? Being a great minion? Being a junior henchman? There was no werewolf family to be proud of me. I wasn't a litter runt lovingly left where someone would take care of me. I was just another unwanted human. I was nothing, and nobody would want me. Ever.

I trudged back toward the castle. When I passed the aviary, I detoured inside.

# CHAPTER 31

*An untrained minion is as useful as a pet rock.*
*The nonexplosive kind.*
—DR. CRITCHLORE

The aviary consisted of a hatchery building nestled inside a net-covered area as big as a small village. The net stretched to one side of Mount Curiosity. Hundred-meter-tall supports held the net up on the other side. When you were inside it didn't feel "inside" at all.

There was a pond for the waterfowl, lots of trees for nests, and a "practice swarm" arena for drills. I liked to climb partway up the side of Mount Curiosity and sit on a boulder that looked out over the entire space. It was a good thinking spot. I hoped it would be a good sulking spot. My dreams had been crushed; the world as I knew it had just disappeared, like it was swallowed up by a sinkhole.

I sat down and crossed my weak little human legs, resting my stupid human head on spindly little human hands.

What could I do now that my very reason to live was gone?

Sure, I could still be a minion—a human minion. There were always a few humans in every graduating class, but they were pitied because they were so lame. Not one evil overlord had shown interest in my foster brother, Pierre, which was why he worked in the kitchen. I guess that was my future.

"'Sup, Higgins." I turned and saw a gray parrot sitting on the rock beside me.

"Hi, Kibwe," I said. "I'm not a werewolf."

Kibwe stretched out a wing and patted me on the back. He had always been my favorite. Master Ping told me it was Kibwe who'd found me when I'd been left outside the school's south entrance.

"Two princes," Kibwe said. He always said that when he saw me.

"Yeah, two princes. That's us."

"*Squawk.* Two princes. You don't need two princes."

The Critchlore parrots were funny. Sometimes they spoke like they understood you; other times it just seemed like they repeated random phrases they'd heard.

"Want a cookie?" I reached into my pocket and pulled out a half-broken one. Kibwe gobbled it up.

"Werewolves overrated," Kibwe squawked. Then he flew off.

A flock of white doves flew in formation, heading right for me. They swirled around me. I wondered if this was a new attack formation. I stood up and they continued to swirl, round and round. Then they all landed on my rock, and when they did, I saw Mistress Moira, her robe as white as the doves, walking up the path to where I was.

"I thought you might be here," she said. "Thank you for finding him, my friends," she added, to the birds.

She motioned for me to sit back down, then joined me. "What's happened? Your aura has had a major disruption."

"I'm not a werewolf," I said. And then I started crying. Moira held out her arms and wrapped me in a hug.

"There, there, child. You can't get upset about what you're not." She rubbed my back. "I always wanted to be a nightclub singer, but, alas, I'm tone-deaf."

I pulled back and looked at her.

"You have to love the you that you are," she said. "Now, tell me what happened."

"Yesterday, at dinner, Pismo told me I'm not a werewolf, and that everybody knew it but me."

"What a beast," Moira said, shaking her head.

"At first I thought he was just trying to hurt me, because I'd ratted him out to Mrs. Gomes."

"Ratted him out?" She reached into a pocket, pulled out a handful of seeds, and threw them to the doves.

"He's done a lot of suspicious things since he came here, almost all of them at the same time as the sabotage. He ran for the cemetery just before it exploded. He ditched me in the dungeon right before the carnivorous cockroaches got loose. I think he had something to do with the explosive minions, because he was shooing them back to the castle. And then I found out he'd been expelled from the Pravus Academy. But what if he hadn't been expelled? What if he's an undercover double agent?"

"I see."

"Well, I told Mrs. Gomes about him, and she must've told him I told, because he was really angry. I figured that's why he said that mean thing to me. But I just had to know, so this morning I tried to make myself change, and I couldn't. I'm not a werewolf. I know that now. I'm nothing but a weak little runty human boy."

"Hold on, now," she said. "Just because you are not a werewolf, that doesn't mean you're weak. Strength doesn't come from size, or mystical animal powers."

"Where does it come from?"

"Muscles," she said. Then she laughed. I must have looked miserable because she added, "I'm just joking, Higgins. Never lose your sense of humor, no matter how low you feel."

She tapped my chest. "Strength comes from in there. And you are the same in there that you've always been. The only thing that's changed is up here." She tapped my head.

"I don't belong here," I said. It was weird saying out loud something I hadn't even dared to admit to myself. If I didn't belong here, where did I belong? Where did you go when nobody wanted you? "I'll never be a junior henchman, who was I kidding?"

"Why did you want to be a junior henchman?"

"I thought it would help me find my family," I said.

"You wanted to be a junior henchman to find your family," Moira repeated. "But your family is right here."

"What?"

"Family isn't always based on biology," she said. "You have Cook, who loves you like a son. As does the rest of the kitchen staff. You have Tootles and Riga and Syke. And you have me."

A little piece of my puny human heart melted, and I hugged her.

"And you belong here as much as anybody. Why, look what

you've done these past few days. You saved Dr. Critchlore on the mountain; you saved the castle from the explosive minions."

"You know about that?"

"I know a lot more about what's going on than most people. And besides, you told me."

"Oh, yeah."

"And now I'm telling you—go on doing the best that you can do, and everything will work out fine."

I stood, buoyed up by the frustration I was feeling. "But I don't know what to do!" I started pacing. "I'm pretty sure there's going to be more sabotage, but Mrs. Gomes doesn't believe me. She doesn't even think there's a saboteur. On my way here I saw her arguing with Tootles about the danger of high magnetic fields caused by the power lines. Normally, I wouldn't worry, because Dr. Critchlore controls her crazier notions. But he's not in control right now. He's completely out of it. If only I could find some hard evidence—"

"So find out," Mistress Moira said, tossing more seeds. "You're smart, you can do it."

"But I'm only human."

"And I'm just a crazy old lady," she said. "But that didn't stop me from winning this year's motocross competition. Over-forty division."

I thought about that. Maybe I could do this. I just needed proof that I could take to Mrs. Gomes, so she would refocus her troops on something other than the small possibility of magnetic radiation leaking into the atmosphere.

"Is it true you've made some ESP chocolates?" I asked.

"Oh yes," she said. "But they have a nasty side effect. Have you seen Drangulus?"

"Yes. You mean the boils on his face?"

"That's just acne, poor fellow. No, the side effect is incontinence."

"Incontinence?"

"No control of your bladder."

"That's not good."

I really wanted to read Pismo's mind. I could find out his next target, and then I could stop him—I knew I could. I would just have to forget about the fact that I wasn't a werewolf.

Of course, I didn't want to pee on myself, but it was a small price to pay if it meant I could save the school. That would be a pretty good accomplishment for a runty human.

"Could I try some anyway?" I asked.

# CHAPTER 32

*In times of peace, minions make good sandwiches.*
—AN ADVERTISEMENT FOR DR. CRITCHLORE'S MINIONS

Mistress Moira said not to eat the chocolate on an empty stomach, so I put them on my tray as I went through the lunch line. I spotted Darthin already at our table. He looked pale and the new bumpy hump he'd added had fallen down to the middle of his back, making him look like a turtle. I must have been distracted, wondering what had happened to him, because when I looked down at my tray, the chocolates were gone.

*Dog whistles!* It was the imps, probably. Those chocolates were my only hope. How was I going to find out what Pismo was up to?

I trudged over to the table, feeling terrible, but Darthin looked worse.

"Darthin," I asked, "what's wrong?"

"I . . . I think I overheard something I wasn't supposed to."

"What?"

"I went to Frankenhammer's lab." He sat up straighter, shifting his hump back up. "When I got there, he wasn't alone. I didn't want to intrude, so I waited outside."

"Who was with him?"

212

"I don't know!" Darthin threw up his hands. He wasn't used to not knowing things. "When the stranger came out of the room, I pretended like I was just arriving. He scowled at me, but I'm sure I've never seen him here before."

"What were they talking about?"

"PX-993."

"PX-993?"

Darthin leaned forward, his chin almost touching the top of the table. He whispered, "Dr. Frankenhammer's secret experiment."

"I thought they were destroyed."

Darthin shook his head. "He was able to thaw a few of them," he whispered. "And I'm pretty sure he gave a prototype to that man. He said, 'Nobody must know where you got this. Take it to your boss. Tell him about me.' I think he's finally had it with Critchlore stealing his ideas."

"Wow. What did the guy look like?"

"Tall, muscular, pale complexion, short brown hair neatly parted on the side, brown eyes, goatee, scar through one eyelid, expensive-looking suit, pinkie ring with a green stone," he said. "That's all I've got."

Three bells chimed, alerting us to an incoming announcement. The screen at the end of the room lit up, but instead of Dr. Critchlore's face, we saw Professor Vodum, wearing a business suit, not a lab coat.

"Good day, students and faculty," he said. "I'm speaking to you on behalf of Dr. Critchlore, who is unable to perform his duties as headmaster at this time. The board of directors has given me leave to direct today's festivities."

The teachers came out of their soundproof room. They wore various expressions of surprise on their faces. A wave of murmuring washed through the cafeteria. Everyone quieted when Professor Vodum spoke again. "School spirit has hit a new low, much like our stock price." He smiled at his joke. "Well, I'm going to change that. Today, I am directing everyone to Mount Curiosity, where we shall enjoy a feast while watching the final test that will determine which of our fine third-year students shall enter our prestigious Junior Henchman Training Program. There will be a raffle for some incredible prizes, including a grand prize of unprecedented wonderfulness—unlimited use of Puddles the dragon for all home visits for a year! Imagine how impressed your friends and family will be!"

A huge cheer exploded in the room. That was unprecedented, all right. Having Puddles meant total freedom. You could go anywhere, do anything. You might get burned to a crisp, but still. What an incredible prize.

"See you this afternoon!" he concluded.

Once again, the image faded before the microphone was turned off, and we heard Professor Vodum say, "That was very leaderly, wouldn't you say? I knew I had a knack for this. It's not fair I haven't been allowed to lead. I'm a leader. I *aaaammmmm*."

Everyone started talking excitedly. The only people who didn't look happy were the other junior henchman trainees like me, the ones who knew they had no chance to win a spot in the Junior Henchman Training Program. Now we would be missing out on the fun and prizes while we competed.

Actually, most of the teachers looked concerned. "Outrageous." "Who in their right mind would pick Vodum to take over?" And "This is it, then."

Someone else didn't look happy. Pismo. I saw him across the room. He stood still, looking from one face to another. Confusion, hurt, and anger all played out on his face.

The ESP chocolates! He must have eaten them. And now he was getting some unfiltered audio of what people were thinking about him. Oh, that couldn't be good.

# CHAPTER 33

*One should never, ever eat a minion.*

—DR. CRITCHLORE IN A PUBLIC SERVICE ANNOUNCEMENT,

EXPLAINING HOW HIS LAST ADVERTISEMENT

MIGHT HAVE BEEN MISINTERPRETED

I had to do something. I rushed over to Pismo, thinking, *You idiot, you took my ESP chocolates.*

His gaze shot over to me. "They hate me," he said. "Everyone hates me."

I put a hand on his shoulder and tried not to think, *Well, you are obnoxious.*

"I'm obnoxious?" he said. "No I'm not! I'm cute and funny."

"Laughing at other people doesn't make you funny. It's mean, Pismo. Your pranks are mean. People won't like you unless you treat them nice."

He pushed me aside. "You can all just go down with your stupid school!"

I stood there watching his back as he ran out of the cafeteria. What did he mean we could go down with our school? Was the school going down? Was his next sabotage going to be something huge?

I went back to my table, hoping my friends could help me figure out what he was planning.

"Hey, guys. Suppose that all the accidents we've had here—from the 'Epic Minion Fail' to the attempt to destroy the *Top Secret Book of Minions*—were deliberate acts of sabotage. What do you think would be the next target?" I asked.

"The Dormitory for Minions of Impressive Size," Eloni said, flexing a bicep. "They're the only minions that really count." Boris nodded.

I shook my head. How could they be so biased?

"No, that's not the pattern," Darthin said.

"Darthin's right," I said. "The accidents all hit one of the school's minion supplies, not the minions who are already here. The cemetery, the labs, the book," I recounted. "That leaves just one type of minion generator that hasn't been targeted."

"The aviary," Darthin, Frankie, and I said at the same time that Eloni said, "The ogre village."

"Or the aviary," Eloni added.

"And there's always been a distraction before the destruction," I said.

"That party seems like it would be a pretty big distraction," Darthin said.

"Everyone will be there," Frankie added.

"That's right," I said. "Pismo is going to strike while everyone is on top of Mount Curiosity after school today."

"I think you're right," Darthin said. "What should we do?"

The bell rang for next period and everyone stood to leave.

"I'll talk to Critchlore," I said. "I can probably find him be-

217

fore Dance class." Maybe Professor Vodum's announcement had knocked some sense into him.

It wasn't hard to find Dr. Critchlore. As I ran into the castle foyer, there he was, his face purple, screaming at Professor Vodum, who was looking more cowardly than leaderly. Professor Vodum had his hands up, like a cornered animal expecting an attack. I couldn't blame him—Dr. Critchlore looked like he was about to hit him.

"Who gave you the right?" Dr. Critchlore screamed. "I'm in charge here. You can't make decisions without me!"

"I cleared it with the board of directors," Professor Vodum said. "They agreed with me."

"You went over my head?"

"It wasn't hard, seeing how your head has been buried in the sand!" At that Professor Vodum stood up straight, looking Dr. Critchlore right in the eye.

Dr. Critchlore broke eye contact first, grabbing his skull in both hands. "*Arrrr!*" he screamed. "My head feels like a thousand fire ants are scrambling inside it!"

"Derek," Professor Vodum said, putting a hand on Dr. Critchlore's shoulder, "the stress of the job has gotten to you. Clearly, you need a break. Temporary. I'll take over until you feel better."

Dr. Critchlore shrugged off Professor Vodum's hand. "Over my dead body," he said.

He raced to the elevator. Professor Vodum ran after him, using the stairs. I followed.

I caught up as they continued their argument in Miss Merry-

218

bench's outer office. I hid just outside and heard Dr. Critchlore's voice: ". . . for decades. Your side of the family will not take control. This is my school!"

"It's the family's land. The family's castle. The family's school. It's not fair that you act like it's all yours. It's not *faaaiiiir*."

"It would have been sold off to pay taxes if I hadn't taken over when I did."

"Nobody is saying that you haven't done brilliant work, Derek," Professor Vodum said. "But times change. You might have been the best Critchlore to run the school before, but now it's time for some new blood."

"I'm not stepping down," Dr. Critchlore said.

"The board of directors won't give you a choice. One more 'incident' and they will force you out. Dead or alive."

I peeked in and saw Dr. Critchlore, his face twisted with pain and anger. "I have to do something." Then, suddenly, his facial expression changed to worry. "But I need to find out if Tina's going to leave Greg for Stephen on *All Our Lives*." He shook his head violently. "No! That's ridiculous. I have to act!" He threw himself against the wall. "But Tina can't leave Greg. He loves her! Stephen's just after her money."

It was like watching an intense battle between two strong foes who happened to be in the same body. My chest felt tight, like a giant had just snatched me up a little too roughly. What was happening to Dr. Critchlore?

"Derek, let's sit down," Professor Vodum said, his voice calming. "We'll watch your show, I'll make you some tea. We'll discuss this—"

The bell rang. I startled, realizing I was late for Dance class. I'd have to warn Dr. Critchlore later.

Two lines of minions stretched down the ballroom, with girls on one side and boys facing them on the other. There were two girls without partners: Bianca, a pretty girl minion, and Frieda, the ogre. I smiled at Bianca and she smiled back. Finally something was going my way. I was about to head over to take my place opposite her when I felt a hand on my shoulder. I turned and saw I wasn't the only tardy.

"Please, dude," Eloni said. "She doesn't try to kiss scrawny guys."

I hesitated. I didn't want to dance with Frieda. She was twice my size and not very nice.

"Please," he begged, smiling his blindingly white, toothy, infectious smile.

"Oh, fine," I said.

"I owe you, bud," he said, and then he ran to stand opposite Bianca.

Scanning the rest of the line, I saw Rufus with Janet. Even though I knew there was no way she'd ever like a guy like me, it felt like a little bit of my heart fell into my stomach, landing with a queasy splash.

They made a cute couple too. He was tall and good-looking. She was Janet Desmarais. She was such a good dancer—if she danced the tango, it would only take one.

Fiona and Frankie, Jud and Syke, Darthin and Grace—the whole room was filled with properly sized couples. The music started up and the boys approached the girls, bowing as we reached them.

"Good evening, Frieda," I said. "May I have this dance?" I had to say that. It was part of the protocol.

She curtsied, which was painful to watch. "Charmed," she said in her low, scratchy voice. She looked far less than charmed, but she knew the protocol as well as I did.

"You look lovely this evening," I said. Yes, I had to say that.

"Okay, cut the crap, Runt-boy. Let's just get this over with."

I took her catcher's mitt hand in mine, and we turned to promenade. Once around the circle I faced her again. I was supposed to twirl her, but that wasn't going to happen without a ladder, so she turned while I held my arm in the air. I noticed that the other dancers seemed to be enjoying themselves, dancing and talking and laughing. I bet it wasn't even from protocol either.

We began a bit where we stepped away from each other, then approached with a spin. As I neared her I asked, "How'd you do on the last junior henchman test?"

On the next approach, she said, "I got third. It was pretty easy. Rufus won again. Jud was second."

Step back, step back, spin. Step forward, step forward, spin.

"Congratulations," I said.

"It doesn't matter," she said. "This school won't be around long enough for me to graduate as a junior henchman."

My heart fell even further hearing this, but I had to admit it was probably true. We wouldn't be getting any more minion recruits. Customers were already going elsewhere for their minion supply.

On the final approach I put my arm around her back and took her hand in mine in the classic dancing position. We twirled together, walked a few steps, twirled again, and walked. I don't think she meant to crush my shoulder with her heavy hand, but I felt like I was dancing on a tilt.

"Frieda," I said, "what will you do if the school closes?"

"I have an offer from the Pravus Academy. I guess I'll go there."

"They offered you a spot?"

"With a scholarship. They want me for their boulderball team."

We parted and went back to our lines. Then the whole thing started again with the approach. It was difficult, but we managed to have a conversation.

"I told them over the summer that I wasn't going to transfer," she said during one approach. On the next she added, "But I just saw Miss Merrybench throwing their recruiter out of the castle. They were probably talking about me."

"A Pravus recruiter was on our campus? How?"

"Security's a mess right now, what with all the investigations going on. Mrs. Gomes seems really distracted. He probably just walked in."

"What'd he look like?"

"Scrawny," she said.

Hmm, that didn't help. "Did he have brown hair? A goatee?"

"Yeah. Did you see him too? Boy, they want me real bad. You know, I was first-team all-conference last year. That's never happened for a second-year."

"I know," I said, mostly because she said this every time I talked to her. "I saw the game against Vilnix Academy. You were brilliant. That move you put on their center. Wow." I hadn't seen the game, but she always talked about that play so it felt like I had.

She seemed to blush, something I'd never seen in an ogre. It made me wonder. Maybe ogres brag so much because nobody compliments them. They have to do it themselves.

The music was coming to an end. "You're not so bad at tackle three-ball, Runt," she said. "Even if it *is* a sissy sport."

"Thank you."

So Dr. Frankenhammer had met with a Pravus recruiter. He'd given him a sample of his work. I knew Frieda thought he was here for her, but Frieda was conceited and probably wrong.

I had a feeling that the recruiter was here to steal something other than a gifted athlete. He was after our best scientific mind. We had an intruder, and this was the proof I needed to get Mrs. Gomes focused on the very real danger of more sabotage.

# CHAPTER 34

*Don't count your minions before they're trained.*
—THE MORAL OF THE FABLE *GRANDOR'S MINIONS*

I ran to find Mrs. Gomes, expecting her to be near her tsunami wall. She wasn't. She'd gone back to her office to check the website trackingkillerbees.EOCapproved.evl to see if they were heading our way. The workers told me that she had left muttering, "If only the Center for Disease Disbursement would set up trackers for swine flu, dragon pox, and the green plague, my life would be so much easier!" (One of the workers did a spot-on imitation of Mrs. Gomes.)

I didn't have much time. I had to convince her to guard the aviary no matter what. She could stop the sabotage and catch Pismo, I was sure of it.

I reached the crossroad. The dormitories were in one direction; the security building was in the other, at the end of the road, near the perimeter wall. I had to run past the maintenance building and worker housing to get there.

I could do this. I could warn her and make it back in time for my test.

And then I heard someone cry for help.

I couldn't help but think of the old fairy tale, about the boy who yelled tiger. We studied fairy tales as children because they taught important lessons. Sometimes the lessons weren't obvious. You had to really think about the story. Take, for instance, the story the "Three Little Sheep." Lots of kids thought it was a lesson about laziness, because the two sheep who built shoddy houses were eaten by the dragon. But if you ask me, it taught us that family should stick together.

"The Boy Who Yelled Tiger" taught me that, even if someone pretends to be in danger two times, it doesn't mean he's lying if he yells for help a third time. I just thought it was sad that a boy had to die in order for the villagers to learn that lesson.

When I heard that cry for help coming from the forest, of course I thought it was the imps again. Then I realized that maybe this was my third time. Maybe this time the imp really *was* in trouble. Maybe this time he would die if I didn't come to his aid.

But another part of me thought that running into that forest would bite me in the butt, like a Veluvian butt-biting cat.

I froze for a moment, unsure what to do.

"Help me!" the small voice cried.

"I'm coming!" I yelled as I charged around the maintenance building.

And then I found myself trapped in a net, being dragged away by a team of giggling imps. They dumped me into a little trailer hooked onto the back of an electric golf cart. The maintenance workers used these carts to zip around the grounds. The trailer was usually filled with tools—and, by the smell of it, manure.

They drove on a dirt service road that wound around the grounds, away from the buildings and people who could save me. Four imps held me down in the attached trailer. Six more packed into the cart. One of the imps held his stinky little hand over my mouth so I couldn't yell. Not that there was anyone to hear me if I did. Everyone had gone to the party.

The path briefly wound behind the Monster Minion Dormitory, and I saw Rufus hiding behind a tree, smoking a cigarette.

I squirmed, trying to get my mouth free so I could scream. Imps aren't particularly strong, but unfortunately neither was I. I did have something they didn't, though. Desperation. And in my desperation I managed to free my mouth for a few seconds. Long enough to yell something important before we passed him.

"Rufus! Don't smoke! It's so bad for you! And addictive!"

Rufus raised an eyebrow. "Gee, Higgins, you're going to be late for the last test. Pity."

Hands clamped down on my mouth again and we zipped away. I watched Rufus stomp out his cigarette and turn to leave. I struggled some more, but it was too late.

Maybe I should have screamed for help instead of warning him of the dangers of smoking.

Stupid imps.


They took me to the edge of the lake. I kicked and thrashed, but they strung me up just like they'd done to Boris. I tried to get free, but nothing worked. Not pleading, or bribing, or threatening. They just laughed at me.

I could see across the lake to Mount Curiosity, where bright flags waved in the breeze and the people looked like colorful dots. Except for the giants. From this far, they looked like tiny people.

I pictured the junior henchman trainees lining up, listening to Coach Foley describe the final test. I bet it had something to do with strength and performance under pressure and bravery. And meanwhile, the birds were in danger. I couldn't bear to think about something happening to Kibwe, or the doves, or any of the other birds. Even the blue jays. They were incredibly annoying, but they didn't deserve to die.

I covered my head with my hands.

The imps sat under the tree, arguing about who was winning their "trapping other students" competition. Was that why they were doing this to me? For a measly point?

I heard the crunch of gravel through the forest. It sounded like another golf cart was heading our way. *Oh, please let it be Eloni,* I prayed. Eloni could walk right through these imps, and they couldn't do a thing to stop him. The imps stopped arguing and looked over.

But it wasn't Eloni. It was Pismo. The imps relaxed.

"I'm tellin' ya, Spanky, they have twenty-seven points," one said.

"Yer daft. Twenty-two, max."

"Runt!" Pismo yelled. "I heard Rufus laughing in his head about you being trapped."

"Pismo?" I said. "Don't you have some sabotage to get to?"

"I'm not the saboteur. I've come to free you so you can make it to your test."

Oh, so now he wanted to free me? "Pismo, the test doesn't matter. You were right; I'm nothing but a runty little human. I'll never be a powerful minion."

"Probably not," Pismo said. "You're extremely gullible and naive."

"Gee, thanks. Did you come all this way just to insult me?"

"Just being honest, bro. Listen, Runt, the school needs you. Dr. Critchlore needs you. It doesn't matter if you're only a human; you have a passion for this school. Passionate people do great things. My dad is constantly telling me that. 'Pismo, you have got to find your passion. You won't succeed until you find it.' Watching you, I totally see what he means."

I sighed. It sounded nice, but I wasn't sure I believed him. I kept expecting him to say "Gotcha!" and then laugh at me.

"Runt, I'm sorry for everything I did to you," he said. He jumped out of the cart. "You were right, I was a jerk. I guess I feel the need to tease people before they tease me. At least, that's what Mistress Moira was thinking about me when I passed her in the hall. I can see why you thought I was sabotaging the school. I've been acting strangely, and for some reason I always ended up where the sabotage took place. But that was just coincidence, I swear. I would never do something to hurt this school. Or you. You're the only friend I've ever had."

"You don't treat me like a friend, Pismo," I said. "Stealing my stuff, getting me detention, taking credit for my work—"

"I know," he interrupted. "I thought I had good reasons for all that stuff. You'd understand if you knew my secret. I just . . . I just haven't been able to tell anyone."

"What?"

He shook his head. "It's not important right now. I came to find you because I overheard something when I was in the teachers' bathroom—"

"You were where?" The teachers' lounge was completely off-limits to students.

"They have a nicer bathroom and I really had to go," he said. "But I didn't make it." He glanced down at his pants, which looked a little damp. "Anyway, I got stuck there when all the teachers arrived at the lounge for a pre-party meeting. All their thoughts came through the door. Runt, one of them is planning more sabotage."

"Who?"

"I don't know. But during the test, something big is going to happen. The test is just a distraction."

"I knew it!" I said. "But who could it be?" Dr. Frankenhammer? One last blast before he defects? Or maybe Professor Vodum; then he'd get Dr. Critchlore's job for sure. Or maybe some other person planted by Dr. Pravus? I was back to square one.

"It could be anyone. There were so many thoughts coming out of there, they were all scrambled up. Oh, there's going to be a pop quiz in your Literature class tomorrow."

"I have to warn Dr. Critchlore, Mrs. Gomes, everyone!" I said.

"They're all at the party," Pismo said, pointing across the lake.

"Pismo, can you go get Eloni so I can get out of here?"

"Who needs Eloni?" he said. He reached into the back of the cart and pulled out Little Eloni, Eloni's giant club. The imps stopped arguing among themselves and stood up.

"Did you steal Little Eloni?"

"Kinda. I thought I might need it." He strode right for the imps. One look at his face and I could tell he meant business. The imps just laughed at him.

"He wouldn't dare," Spanky said, still laughing.

"Pismo, you can't hit another student," I said.

"Oh, I'm pretty sure I can," Pismo said. He walked right up to an imp and swung the club. The imp crumpled sideways, clutching his arm. "Anyone else wanna try and stop me?"

The imps scattered, and Pismo got me down. I looked across the lake. Banners flew on the ledge where I'd freed Puddles. We could hear the trumpets announcing the start.

The electric carts couldn't do more than twenty miles per hour. We wouldn't be able to make it in time.

But then the trumpets abruptly stopped. I could hear Coach Foley talking through the music speaker system. His voice carried across the lake on the still air.

"Dr. Critchlore!" he yelled. "Don't jump! Dr. Critchlore!"

I squinted and looked across the lake. There he was, on top of a ledge on Dead Man's Peak.

Dr. Critchlore was going to jump.

# CHAPTER 35

*Minions are power.*

—DR. CRITCHLORE, TO THE EVIL OVERLORD COUNCIL

D r. Critchlore stood on top of the cliff. The drop was sheer
granite, broken up by a few trees. The shore of the lake was
rocky.

"We've got to save him," I said. The rest of the school couldn't
get to him, because of the river between Mount Curiosity and
Dead Man's Peak. But if we circled back and went around the far
side of the lake? No, that would take hours. "If only we had a boat!"

"Follow me," Pismo said. He ran into the lake and dived in. I
chased after him. He popped up and turned to me. "Swim in and
grab my shoulders," he told me.

I did as he said, because a good minion always obeys orders.
When I grabbed his shoulders, he dived underwater. He pulled
away so quickly I almost lost my grip. I couldn't believe how fast
we were going. I looked back and saw that he had a tail, like a
dolphin.

When we rose for air, I said, "You're a mer—" and then we were
under again. Once above I said, "Merperson?"

"Yes, I'm a flipping merman," he said. For some reason, I could hear him speak, even when we were underwater. We were moving so fast! Diving down and bursting into the air.

"Do you get it now?" Pismo asked.

I did. He was embarrassed about being a mermaid, er, merman.

"Why didn't—" I said on an upswing, and then we were under; once up again, I finished, "—you tell me?"

"I didn't want anyone to know, obviously. And you don't have to talk with your mouth. I can read your thoughts when we're underwater. And you can read mine."

This last bit didn't sink in right away, because the next thing I thought was, *Mermaids, mermaids, what do I know about them? Let's see, they are incredibly stupid.*

*We are not!* Pismo's voice exploded inside my head.

Oops. They were half fish. All the time.

*We can use a spell to become human,* Pismo said. *But I have to submerge myself in water every eight to ten hours.*

*Of course!* That explained why Pismo ran off before the first explosion—he wasn't running to the cemetery to plant a bomb, he was running to the lake! And in the dungeon—he wanted to find the grotto!

*And I was shooing the zombies away from the lake because I didn't want anyone following them out there and seeing me,* he said in his mind.

We were going as fast as a speedboat. Pismo kept leaping out of the water so I could breathe, and when he did, it felt like we were flying.

"Pismo—" I said as we surfaced for air, but then he dived back down, so I thought the rest in my head. *None of us would have cared that you're a mermaid.* "I think it's cool," I yelled as we surfaced.

"Yeah, right," he said. "I've heard all the jokes. And they put me with the Class 5 minions—bodies, no brains. Everyone thinks merpeople are dumb."

*I'm really sorry.*

*It's not your fault. It's the sirens. They're so jealous of us, since they're stuck on shore and we can breathe underwater. They're the ones that made up that stupid creation myth, and all the dumb mermaid jokes. The Siren Syndicate is so powerful, they can say whatever they want, and people believe them.*

Growing up in landlocked Stull, I had no idea of this rivalry.

*Will we make it in time?* I thought.

*I don't know.*

*How much farther?* I asked, because I couldn't see anything through the spray of water.

*We're almost there. I stashed my merman battle gear at the bottom of the lake. I need my slingshot.*

Slingshot? I didn't even pause to figure out what he meant by that. My brainpower was focused on Dr. Critchlore. I knew I could talk him down from the cliff. I had just the thing to tell him. I'd been thinking about it since the first day of school, when I'd found him crying because he doesn't have any children.

*I'm going deep,* Pismo thought at me.

We went down, down, down. My ears hurt from the pressure, but still we went down. I held my nose closed with one hand and blew out to equalize the pressure. I had no idea the lake was so deep.

I was surprised to realize that my lungs weren't burning. In fact,

I felt like I could stay underwater forever. It was so cool. Mermaids really were magical creatures. I might have actually thought that in my head, because Pismo's next thought exploded in my brain:

*You don't know the half of it!*

We reached the bottom. *Don't let go of me*, Pismo thought. I kept my grip on his shoulders. He grabbed one hand and spun me around to face him while he attached something to his back.

*We use these to attack things on land.* The harness nearly reached the bottom of his tail, and at the top was a bow that lay across his shoulders, stretching far beyond them. It was a giant crossbow, and he was wearing it on his back.

*We call them slingshot crossbows*, he thought at me. *Pull the pocket down until it clicks into the lock.*

I did. The pocket was big enough to hold a cannonball.

*Grab my shoulders and put your feet in the pocket.*

It just dawned on me what Pismo planned to do, but we were swimming up before I could organize my thoughts into a scream of *NO!*

*When I breach, I'm going to launch you. You'll fly right to Dr. Critchlore!*

I could picture what Pismo meant, and I wasn't sure I wanted to fly through the air at a wall of jagged granite. And how did he know I'd hit the ledge? Did he have some special mer-power that enabled him to hit a target like that?

I had to believe that he did have that kind of power. I felt Pismo working his tail furiously. We were going so fast. At last we broke the surface, and Pismo and I flew into the air like a missile.

We were more than twenty feet high when Pismo yelled, "Firing!"

I was flung from his back so fast I couldn't breathe. I felt like the human cannonball from the circus.

I soared upward. I could hear screams coming from the crowd across the river. They'd seen me too.

The wall of granite got closer. I could see the ledge. I held my arms out straight in front of me, like Superminion, the caped superhero. I could see Dr. Critchlore's eyes widen at the sight of his minion flying right at him. Maybe he would catch me in his arms and all would be well.

He didn't.

He stepped back as I impacted on the side of the ledge. My arms scrambled to find something to hold on to, but it was too gravelly, and I fell backward. And down. I tumbled down the face of the cliff that Dr. Critchlore had been about to jump from.

I hit a rock with my side and heard the crowd moan, "*Ooooh.*" Then I ricocheted off a tree, and I heard an "*Owwww.*" A bush, "*Ooooh*"; another thump into a tree, "*Owwww.*" I was a human pinball.

My feet and hands tried to slow my fall, but still I fell. Down, down I went, the rocks and bushes slicing up my arms and legs. At last I thumped down on a boulder and lost my breath.

I looked up and saw Dr. Critchlore leaning over the ledge. "Hinklebert! Are you okay?"

I couldn't speak. I couldn't move. I blinked a few times. I raised one hand and made the "okay" symbol with my fingers.

"There! Look!" Dr. Critchlore shouted at the crowd. "He's giving us the 'okay' sign! He's okay!"

The crowd cheered. I smiled as I lay there in incredible pain. They liked me. They really liked me.

Dr. Critchlore turned around and climbed down to me, finding toeholds I'd missed. My lungs relaxed and I breathed in deeply, but I was afraid to move. Afraid that I'd be hit with a wave of pain that meant I was seriously injured.

"There, now," he said when he reached me. He put a hand on my chest. "You'll be fine." A pinecone hit him in the head. "Stupid trees," he muttered. Then he shouted, "How many times do I have to say I'm sorry?"

I sat up. It hurt. Everywhere.

"Dr. Critchlore," I said, "were you going to jump?"

"I was," he said. "But after seeing you fall down the slope, I realized it would be a very painful way to go. I'll think of something a little easier. A stampede of animals, maybe. Or jumping into the Pit of Fire. Oh! Cook has threatened to poison anyone who tells that little cursed orphan boy he's not a werewolf."

"Dr. Critchlore, don't kill yourself," I said before that last part sunk in. "Wait, what did you say?"

"Hmm?" He looked down at me, and then his eyes widened. "Um, nothing."

I had to stay focused, so I took a deep breath and said the words I'd wanted to tell him ever since I found him crying in his office. "I think I know what's been getting you down. I noticed it the first day of school—how sad you were when watching that commercial with the father and daughter on TV. You're depressed because you don't have children of your own. And you're hoping that all these new hobbies will hide the pain of not having children. But Dr. Critchlore, you do have children!"

He raised an eyebrow. "Do you know something I don't?"

I took another breath. My side hurt like crazy, but I put it out of my mind. This was too important. "All of us," I waved a hand at the minions across the river. "We're your children, Dr. Critchlore. All five hundred and twenty-six of us. The school is our home, and you've raised us with your lessons. But someone is trying to destroy our home. It's your job to protect it, to protect us. We're all counting on you."

I had him convinced, I knew I did. Now he was going to see the truth and get back to work.

"The students are my children," he repeated, looking out over the lake. Then he laughed. "What a ridiculous notion! As if I would send my child to a school for minions. The very idea. Oh, Hagforth, you slay me."

He turned serious. "My family is filled with backstabbing, traitorous megalomaniacs. The last thing I want is more family."

"Really?" How could I have been so wrong? How could anyone think family was a bad thing? If a loving family wouldn't keep Dr. Critchlore from jumping, I wasn't sure what would. "Dr. Critchlore, we need you. Please don't kill yourself."

"I'm afraid I have to kill myself," Dr. Critchlore said.

"What?" I wanted to strangle the man. "Why?"

"I was given a choice," he said. "I can't remember the exact words, but I had to do something completely repulsive, or I had to kill myself. I can't remember . . ." He left the thought unfinished.

239

"Who told you that?"

"A voice in my head. I'm not sure. I'm feeling very confused and a little dizzy, and I have a craving for a cream puff." His legs started twitching.

Suggesterol!

"Did Professor Vodum give you something to drink?" I asked.

"Yes. He chased me to my office and told me to calm down so we could discuss things. He made me a cup of tea," he said. "But I can't remember anything he said. Honestly, if he weren't family, I'd fire him. He's an insufferable bore." He shook his head. "I sent him down to the dungeon with my trapdoor, ha! Third time, that was. You'd think he'd learn."

"Was it after you drank the tea that the voice told you about the choice?"

"I think so."

"Dr. Critchlore," I said, standing up. "You've been given a potion. Suggesterol. I think Professor Vodum is trying to get rid of you."

"Get rid of me? Why?"

"So he can take your place. That's why he met with the board. He thinks he can do a better job than you."

I grabbed Dr. Critchlore by the shoulders and looked him right in the eye. Maybe I could make a suggestion of my own. "You do not have to kill yourself. We are going to climb down and get in that boat." I could see Miss Merrybench at the front of the pontoon boat coming to save us. Pismo stood next to her, in human form. He looked worried, so I gave him a thumbs-up. Tootles stood at the helm, beneath the sunshade roof, with Syke next to him. She was smiling and shaking her head.

"We are going to climb down to the boat," Dr. Critchlore repeated. "I do not have to kill myself."

"That's right," I said. "Let's go."

It took us a little while to climb down. I know it wasn't very minion-like, but Dr. Critchlore was obviously still under the power of the Suggesterol, so I decided to make a few more suggestions.

Tootles angled the boat sideways to shore so we could climb on. Miss Merrybench helped Dr. Critchlore aboard and then found a blanket to drape around his shoulders. I was pretty sure Dr. Critchlore was fine. I, on the other hand, was bleeding from five or ten or sixty open wounds. I climbed on and sat next to Syke as Tootles steered us back toward the dock.

"Oh, Derek," Miss Merrybench said. "I ran to the dock as soon as I saw you on the other side of the waterfall. I insisted that Tootles take me to come save you, but he made me wait for these . . . children." She sneered at Pismo and Syke.

"They looked like they needed help too," Tootles said. "The boy was soaking wet, and Syke thinks there's something wrong up at the party."

Syke gazed up at the mountain, and a look of confusion, or sadness, replaced her smile. "I can't hear the trees up there."

"Huh?"

"There's something wrong with the trees. It's like they've gone to sleep. Or they're dead." I'd never seen Syke look so nervous, so scared.

"There's definitely something wrong up there," Tootles said. "It's too quiet. I'll check it out as soon as I drop you all off."

"I think Dr. Critchlore needs to go to the infirmary," I said. "He's been drugged with Suggesterol."

"Nobody cares what a stupid little third-year thinks," Miss Merrybench whisper-hissed at me. Louder, she said, "I'm going to take care of him."

"The boy's right," Tootles said. "The man needs to be looked at."

Miss Merrybench scowled, but agreed.

We reached the dock, and I was surprised to see Darthin, Frankie, Eloni, and Boris standing there, waiting for us.

I jumped off the boat, followed by everyone else, and rushed over to them. Every muscle ached and protested, but I felt good.

"Why aren't you at the party?" I asked.

"We were looking for you," Darthin said.

Even though I was bleeding and sore and cold, hearing those words made my whole body fill up with warmth.

"I have to find Mrs. Gomes and tell her to arrest Professor Vodum. He just tried to kill Dr. Critchlore. And he's going to sabotage the aviary."

"Mr. Higgins." I turned and saw Miss Merrybench standing with Dr. Critchlore. Tootles and Syke stood behind them. "I forgot to tell you something important. Before all the excitement, I was looking for you myself." She smiled down at me. "To tell you that your parents are here."

# CHAPTER 36

*A man is known by the minions he keeps.*
—THE MORAL OF THE FABLE *MAX AND HIS MINIONS*

I felt like I'd just tumbled down the mountain again. "What?"

"Yes. They're back. They've come back for you," she said. "Tell him, Dr. Critchlore. Tell Higgins that his parents are waiting in your office to see him."

Dr. Critchlore looked from Miss Merrybench to me. "Higgins, your parents are waiting in my office to see you." He looked toward the building. All was quiet as this information sunk in.

My parents had come back?

"Come with me, Mr. Higgins," Miss Merrybench said. "Tootles, why don't you take Dr. Critchlore to the infirmary. The rest of you children go and join the party. Go on. There's cake and punch."

I turned to my friends. They were all smiling at me. "Go on, Higgins," Darthin said. "We'll find Mrs. Gomes."

"Yeah, we got it covered," Eloni said.

"I'm so happy for you," Syke added. "You idiot."

Boris, Frankie, and Pismo waved me off too. I had to jog a little to keep up with Miss Merrybench's rapid speed walking. I still couldn't believe it. My parents had come back for me! And not only that, but the school was safe now. Mrs. Gomes would arrest Professor Vodum, Dr. Critchlore would get fixed up in the infirmary, and the school could get back to normal.

I was going to miss my junior henchman test, but I didn't care. I'd found my parents, which was the only reason I wanted to be a junior henchman in the first place.

I followed Miss Merrybench into Dr. Critchlore's private elevator. She kept her gaze forward. I wanted to ask her a million questions, but they all jumbled up in my brain and none of them could make it out of the bottleneck in my mouth.

The doors opened, and Miss Merrybench strode out. It took all my self-control not to race past her with my arms wide. I followed her into Dr. Critchlore's office, where she turned around and scowled at me with a terrifying look of anger on her face.

I looked around. The office was empty.

"Where are they?" I asked.

Miss Merrybench glared at me, her lips pursed together tightly. "Your parents are not here, Higgins," she said. "They were never here. Not today, not eight years ago."

"Then—"

"You've gotten in my way for the last time."

She nodded at something behind me. I turned and saw that the whole pack of imps had silently crept into the room. My head did that swivel thing—I looked at the imps, then back at Miss Merrybench, then back at the imps. And even with all that, I couldn't figure out what was going on.

"Tie him up," she ordered.

"They work for you?" I asked. My brain finally caught on.

"Yes," she said. "Though not for long, if they keep MESSING THINGS UP!"

The imps muttered to themselves as they tied my hands behind my back. I didn't put up a fight. What could I do?

"Simple orders, imps," she went on. "'Trap Runt Higgins.' How hard can it be? But no, he gets away in the Strawberry Snare. He gets away on the tower. You trap the wrong kid. He gets away from the net."

"Mumble, mumble . . . not our fault . . . mumble, mumble . . . hit on the arm . . . mumble, mumble . . . kid has too many friends."

"Well, you better make sure nobody finds him," Miss Merrybench said. "At least for the next hour or so."

"Why?" I asked. "Why did you want them to trap me?"

Her lip curled up in a sneer. She walked right up to me and grabbed my chin. "You little pest," she said. "You ruin EVERYTHING!" She screamed

right in my face. I tried to edge away from her, but her grip on my chin was really tight.

"What'd I do?"

"I was supposed to save Dr. Critchlore on the cliff after I sabotaged his climbing gear. I was supposed to get credit for the puppy, and I was supposed to diffuse the explosive minions under his window! But no, you had to go and take all the credit for yourself, you little . . . credit-stealing brat!"

"I didn't know," I said. "If you'd told me, maybe I could have helped you."

"Oh, don't give me that 'I'm so nice' routine," she said. She released my chin and started pacing in front of me. "We all know it's an act."

She stopped in front of Dr. Critchlore's huge window, her gaze on Mount Curiosity. I looked out and saw my friends. They hadn't gone to the party. They were at the foot of the trail. Syke was pointing at something up on the mountain.

"I was the one who gave him the paint set," Miss Merrybench went on. "So I could pose for him, au naturel."

*Ew.*

"Nothing I do works!" She threw up her hands and resumed pacing. It was like she was talking to herself, not me. "I give him a love potion—and he falls in love with the dog. The Suggesterol. I followed directions to the letter: Give with milk, wait five minutes, suggest something to your subject. 'Dr. Critchlore,' I say. 'You have to marry Miss Merrybench. You have to do it or you'll die.' And what does he do? He goes off to kill himself!"

All ten imps seemed to burst out laughing, but quickly turned their laughs into coughing fits. "Dusty in here." "I've had a cold for weeks." "Frog in my throat."

"I was supposed to save his school by finding the saboteur." She turned to me and looked like she wanted to crush me with her stare. "Not you. Not you, not you, NOT YOU!"

"Vodum isn't the saboteur, is he?" I asked.

"That clod? Good grief, no."

"You set up everything."

"Of course I did. I blew up the cemetery as soon as I heard that Vodum had called a meeting of his stupid Necromancers Club, so it would look like he knew about it. I sent him to Frankenhammer's to get a brain before I set off the carnivorous cockroaches. I ordered the Suggesterol in his name. But then you had to go and deliver it to him. I had to sneak into his office after school, and you almost caught me too, when those annoying zombies showed up chanting for brains."

"It was your perfume they smelled."

"Yes. That was close," she said. "And I was going to catch Vodum trying to destroy the castle after he drugged everyone with sleep-inducing pollen. And then Dr. Critchlore would love me. Because I saved his school."

"But if you love him, how could you destroy his school?" I asked. "The cemetery, Dr. Frankenhammer's work, Dr. Critchlore's office—you tried to destroy them all."

"Do you think I could afford potions on the pittance that man pays me? Do you know how expensive one dose of Suggesterol is? I could have retired to the Goyan Riviera with what I spent on love potions, midlife-crisis-inducing potions, impulsivity potions, sentimental potions, and the Suggesterol. Not to mention the explosives. And the spa treatments." She patted her hair, then looked at her nails. "Very expensive. No, I had to find someone willing to pay me for those little deeds. Killing three birds with one stone—I get rid of Vodum, I set myself up to be the hero, and I get paid extremely well to do it."

"Pravus," I said.

"That's right," she said. "That man is utterly obsessed with Dr. Critchlore. He'll pay anything to see him suffer. And he's fantastically rich. He gave me money and ideas. He supplied the carnivorous cockroaches that I planted outside Frankenhammer's lab. He gave me the vines that have knocked everyone out up on the mountain with their sleep-inducing pollen. I told him I hated this school, and once it was destroyed Derek and I could leave and never come back."

"The Girl Explorers in the video, that was Pravus too, wasn't it?"

Miss Merrybench took a step back and held up both hands, like she was terrified. "Those aren't girls. He calls them land piranhas. They can strip an animal to its bones in seconds. They're evil. And they do whatever Pravus tells them to do. He controls them!"

She shook all over, then turned to look out the window. She took in a big gulp of air and slowly exhaled. "I did everything right, but none of it worked. Because of you." She turned to look at me. "And you know what, Runt Higgins?"

"What?"

"You are not going to beat me." She stopped pacing and walked to the door. Then she turned and said, "Say good-bye to your beloved school, Mr. Higgins. It's going to collapse down upon Dr. Critchlore's beloved four pillars of business success."

My eyes went wide. We weren't safe. Something else was going to happen.

"Take him to the dungeon. Use Dr. Critchlore's secret stairs. Mr. Higgins is going to have a front-row seat at the show."

# CHAPTER 37

*Fortune favors those with minions.*

—FORTUNE COOKIE SAYING

M iss Merrybench strode over to the bookshelves and pulled out a book. A latch clicked and the wall of books opened up to reveal a dark doorway.

"You have one hour before those columns blow," she said.

"Aren't you coming?" one of the imps asked.

"No." She fluffed her hair and then laughed hysterically. "I'm off to the infirmary to pick up my future husband. One more potion and we're going to live happily ever after. Someplace far, far from here."

The imps pushed me through the door. I was smushed into the middle of the imp scrum, half of them in front, half behind. Stairs led downward in a tight circle.

"Sorry about your arm, Toady," I said to the imp with the sling. "I never thought Pismo would do that."

*Grumble.*

We reached the bottom of the stairs and entered a room lined with bookshelves. I noticed a liquor cart, a couple of leather wing-back chairs, and a pool table. *How cool,* I thought, *I've finally seen Dr. Critchlore's secret lair.*

"This ain't no fun," Spanky said. "Let's go. Merrybench can stuff it."

"Yeah, who needs her?" another imp said.

"Don't you guys work for her?" I asked.

"We don't work for nobody," Spanky said. "It just so happened that she asked us to do things that were in keeping with our nature, so we obliged, see?"

"So you feel no loyalty to her whatsoever?"

"Hardly."

"How's about we prank her back?" I said. If she could appeal to their mischievous nature, maybe I could too.

"What'cha got in mind?"

"Okay, this is going to be hilarious. First untie my hands, then we'll go get some grown-ups to come help."

"Everyone's out cold, up on the mountain," one of the imps said. "The professors, Mrs. Gomes, everyone."

*No, not everyone,* I thought. Syke and the guys were still at the base of the mountain. I'd seen them from Dr. Critchlore's office.

I tried to think about what to do. *Okay, prioritize,* I told myself. First, the bombs. I wasn't the best bomb defuser in my class; that was Darthin. Between us, maybe Darthin and I could defuse them before they went off in—yikes!—fifty-five minutes.

Miss Merrybench was on her way to abduct Dr. Critchlore, who was in the infirmary. I could send Eloni to block the doors with boulders, since the infirmary was right next to the boulderball supply shed.

But if Merrybench and Critchlore made it out of the infirmary, I'd need people to block the exits, including the lake.

"All right, I think I've got it," I said. "Spanky, I want you to find Darthin and get him back here, pronto. Tell Frankie to carry him to the Column of Duty as fast as he can. If we can stop Miss Merrybench's bombs, she'll totally flip—it'll be great.

"Quip, you get Eloni. Tell him to block the infirmary doors with boulders.

"Toady, you find Pismo. He's probably by the docks. He's got to watch for Miss Merrybench leaving by the lake.

"Uhoh, you look for the first-year zombies. Tell them to block the main exit and not let anyone out. But you have to tell them in a whiny voice. And tell them Higginsbrains sent you.

"Doink, Peanut, and Hackmatack, you three grab some gas masks from the safety stations and take one to Mrs. Gomes, up at the party. See if you can revive her and tell her what Miss Merrybench is planning to do."

They all hopped up and down, eager to get going. "And one last thing. If this works, I'll give you guys anything you want. Anything in my power to give you."

They hopped a little faster and dashed up the stairs. Dog biscuits, I hoped this worked.

The four pillars of business success: Discipline, Duty, Determination, and On-Time Delivery. The four pillars that both literally and figuratively held up the school. Miss Merrybench was planning to blow them up so the castle would collapse into the dungeon.

I had fifty minutes left. The first thing I did was run to the central-hub room and hit the alarm. I didn't think anybody was left in the dungeon, but just in case, I had to warn everyone to get out.

I waited for Darthin next to the Duty pillar. Etched in its side were the words "A Minion Knows His Duty, and His Duty Is to Obey."

Secured to the pillar by a chain was a briefcase. Okay, briefcase bombs. What did I know about them? I sat down and saw that it was one of those briefcases with a lock. A four-letter lock.

Just as I was thinking up words to try, Frankie rushed into the room, carrying Darthin, who had his bumpy hump back. He also had his bomb-defusing tool kit.

Forty-three minutes.

"Step aside, Higgins," he said. He spread out his kit. Frankie's head swiveled around as if he were expecting an organized assault—which, come to think of it, was one of the scenarios we'd trained for last year: a decoy bomb to scatter the enemy, followed by a surprise attack.

Darthin picked out a tool, and in two seconds he'd opened the briefcase.

Yikes, there were a lot of explosives in there.

"She planning on blowing us to the moon?" Darthin asked. "Oh, this is clever."

"What?"

"See these wires here? It makes it look like your standard Pipsly-Splocket bomb, with a delayed-fuse igniter. But it's a trap. If I'd defused this Pipsly-Splocket-style, it would have blown."

"How do you know?"

"Because of this little beauty here, the Wachtingblurg trip wire. See how thin it is? Oh, this is good work."

"Can you defuse it?"

253

"'Course I can." He straightened his hump and got to work.

"Oh no!" Frankie said. He was looking at his DPS.

"What?" I asked.

"Dr. Frankenhammer's still in his lab." He pushed a few buttons to call him. "He's not answering."

"He probably thinks it's another false alarm."

"I have to go get him before this blows," Frankie said. He looked at Darthin, then at me. "Not that I don't have confidence in you two."

"Go," I said. "He can help us."

Frankie zoomed off.

I watched Darthin work on the bomb. He was so focused. I checked my watch. Thirty-two minutes. It had taken him eleven minutes to defuse the bomb. There were three more bombs. Uh-oh.

"I'm going to have to defuse one of the bombs," I said. "You don't have time to do three more."

"Watch me again, on the next one," Darthin said. We ran to the next pillar, Discipline: "A Disciplined Minion Focuses on His Task and Only His Task."

I focused on my task of watching Darthin, memorizing every move he made. My hands moved in the air, mimicking his. He kept up a running commentary of what he was doing, and I tried to repeat it all in my head.

Open case . . . freeze-spray the Winkle-Snapper . . . twist the blue-green wire around the copper thingy . . . clip the Tangle Nublet . . .

"Do you have an extra can of freeze spray?"

"No. But you can come with me to the third pillar and then take it when I'm done. You'll have time to do the rest. But Higgins, if the clock hits three minutes, just get out. You're more important than this building. Okay?"

"Okay."

"Promise me."

I looked at my watch. Twenty-one minutes. Yikes.

"Just remember to stay clear of the trip wire. You can do it, Higgins."

We ran to the third pillar, Determination. "Nothing Can Stop a Determined Minion!"

I tried to let those words fill me up with confidence. I was determined. As soon as Darthin finished with the freeze spray, I grabbed it and the other tools I'd need and ran to On-Time Delivery: "You Never Have to Wait for a Critchlore Minion."

Twelve minutes. Where was Frankie? He should pass through here coming back from Dr. Frankenhammer's lab.

My hands shook crazily, but I opened the case. Okay, freeze-spray, done. Twist the wire, done.

Ten minutes.

What was next? The Tangle Nublet, or the Flip-Switch Button? I closed my eyes and tried to picture Darthin's quick hands flying through the steps. Nublet or Flip-Switch? I couldn't concentrate; panic raced through my body.

Nine minutes.

"Darthin!" I yelled. "Is it the Nublet, then the Flip-Switch?"

Silence.

Eight minutes.

I didn't want to die.

All of a sudden, it came to me. It was the Nublet. I knew it.

Clip the Nublet, press the Flip-Switch, gently remove the Zarnok Packet.

Five minutes.

I wiped my hands on my pants. I had about ten more steps.

Darthin appeared behind me. "We can't do it in time," he said. "Come on."

He grabbed my arm.

"No, we can do it," I said, yanking my arm back. "Together."

I sat down and began working on the Zarnok Packet. Darthin sat next to me. "Time?"

"Four minutes."

He shook his head, but his hands flew as he recited what he was doing. "Defusion fogger, Henly cog, argh, there's not enough time."

"Three minutes."

"We have to go, Higgins. Please!"

He got up and ran for the door, his hump bumping wildly on his back.

I looked at the bomb, and then I ran away from it as fast as a determined human could run.

# CHAPTER 38

*Great things are accomplished when minions
work together toward a common goal.*
—QUOTE FROM DR. CRITCHLORE'S
"GREAT EDUCATORS" TRADING CARD

The bomb exploded just as I caught up with Darthin in the castle's entrance hall. The floor shook beneath us and we could barely stay on our feet, but we managed to prop each other up as we raced out the front door, down the steps, and outside to safety.

"We made it!" I yelled, putting my arms in the air in the universal sign of victory.

And then a giant sinkhole opened up in the ground, and we tumbled back down into the dungeon.

Fortunately for me, Darthin broke my fall.

Fortunately for Darthin, he landed on his fake hump.

Unfortunately for both of us, we were stuck at the bottom of a sinkhole with rocks and debris falling all around us.

Fortunately for the school, the explosion didn't ignite the other bombs. Even though Darthin had defused them, they were still filled with live explosives.

"Are you okay?" I asked. Darthin sat up and nodded. "You were brave, Darthin. Real brave."

"Thanks."

And then I remembered that I hadn't seen Frankie or Dr. Frankenhammer outside. "Darthin, give me your DPS."

He handed it to me, and we both watched the screen as I typed in Frankie's name. The green blip showed up right next to where the bomb had exploded.

"Oh no! We have to get out of here. We have to go get Frankie!"

Darthin braced himself against the wall. I stood on his hump to reach the edge. I pulled myself up and then reached for Darthin. Once he was out of the hole, we turned back to the castle.

Smoke billowed out of the entrance, but I knew we had to go in. We had to find our friend. He couldn't be dead. Not Frankie.

I'd only taken one step forward when a dark shape appeared in the smoke. A shadow. Darthin put a hand on my arm, and we watched a figure emerge from the wreckage.

It was Frankie.

He carried an unconscious Dr. Frankenhammer in his arms. Tears were streaming down his face, but he kept walking. We ran to him, reaching him as he lowered Dr. Frankenhammer to the ground.

"Is he . . . ?" I asked.

"He passed out from the smoke," Frankie said. He wiped his face. "He wouldn't come with me, Runt. Told me to leave him alone. I started crying, I was so frustrated. I tried to stop, but I could feel what was happening. My head was going to pop—so I just let myself cry. Dr. Frankenhammer looked disgusted. I cried and cried, and then I remembered that I may not be twenty times as strong as a normal man, but I am ten times stronger than Dr. Frankenhammer, so I grabbed him and ran out."

"You saved his life, Frankie," I said.

As relieved as I was that Frankie was okay, my gut still twisted with worry. What if Miss Merrybench had gotten away with Dr. Critchlore? That would almost be worse than the school getting destroyed. We could rebuild the school, but we could never replace Dr. Critchlore.

What if the other imps hadn't done what I'd asked?

"Darthin?"

"Yeah?"

"Why did you come to the dungeon with the imp?"

"I didn't believe him at first," he said. "But then he said you needed me and that if I didn't go, the imps would never achieve their dream."

"What?"

"He told me you promised them they could be on the tackle three-ball team."

"Oh." So that's what they wanted.

I was about to run to the infirmary to see if Dr. Critchlore was okay, but after one step I collapsed to the ground.

I woke up in the infirmary, groggy, sore, and tired. There was a plate of cupcakes next to my bed—my favorites, the kind with the little chocolate sprinkles on top. A new uniform was draped over the back of a chair.

I tried to ask questions, but Nurse Rollo just kept hushing me.

I awoke again and my cupcakes were gone. I couldn't remember eating them, but maybe I had. Rollo still wouldn't answer any questions. He told me I needed to rest and not get too agitated.

"You know what's agitating me, Rollo?" I asked him. "You not answering my questions."

It could only be bad news.

I was sad and frustrated and not at all tired. Darthin snored on the bed next to me. I stared at the boring white wall with the boring picture of a village under siege by rampaging minions and felt sick with worry.

I heard a tap at the window. I got up and unlatched it and looked down. Pismo, Eloni, and Boris stood beneath it. Eloni lifted Pismo up to the window and he crawled in.

"Pismo. I'm so happy to see you. Nobody will tell me anything. Did they catch Miss Merrybench? Is Dr. Critchlore okay?"

"Relax, dude," he said. "Jeez, you'll hurt yourself."

I gave him my exasperated look.

"Fine. Get back in your bed, and I'll tell you the whole story."

"I like stories," Boris said from outside.

"You can listen too," Pismo said. He stood by the window so Eloni and Boris could hear. "Darthin, why don't you start."

Darthin, awake now that the room was noisy, sat up. "Okay. The test was about to start, and nobody knew where you were. While Boris, Eloni, Frankie, Syke, and I were looking for you, we heard everyone at the party scream, and we saw Dr. Critchlore on the cliff. We all watched you rescue him."

"Excuse me?" Pismo said. "That was a joint rescue operation."

"We didn't know you'd launched Runt up there, Pismo," Dar-thin said. "But fine, we watched you and Runt rescue him. Miss Merrybench screamed at Tootles to get the boat, and they picked you up."

"I got it from here," Pismo said. "By this time everyone at the party had passed out. Tree-Girl knew something was up and wouldn't let us go up there after you left with Miss Merrybench to see your parents. So we waited. And then we saw that pack of imps race out of the castle. We knew they were up to no good. I told Eloni to pound the living crap out of them, but he said, 'I can't hurt another student.' And I said—"

"'I'm pretty sure you can,'" I filled in for him.

"Right. But the imps started screaming about you being in trouble, and for some reason we believed them and did what they said. Darthin and Frankie ran to find you. Eloni and Boris ran to the infirmary. I went to the lake. Syke climbed the tallest tree to be a lookout.

"Well, it turned out that Miss Merrybench was in the infirmary with Dr. Critchlore. When Eloni started blocking the exits, they couldn't get out."

"Miss Merrybench was very angry with me," Eloni said. "She told me she was going to take my club. I told her it was already gone."

I glared at Pismo. He smiled and shrugged. "I'll give it back," he whispered to me.

"But they got out through a hatch in the roof," Pismo continued.

"I tried to wrestle her to the ground, but—" Boris couldn't fin-ish his sentence. We could all picture what had happened, though.

Miss Merrybench, tough Iron Woman competitor, could easily outmuscle little Boris.

"Syke screamed that they were heading for the lake," Pismo went on. "So I got into position. Dr. Critchlore was still under the power of the drug she'd given him, because he followed her like a lamb. But Miss Merrybench must have forgotten that I'm a merman. I waited for her to pick a boat, and then I disabled it, merman-style."

"What's that?"

"I rammed it with my battle helmet. I'd stashed my battle gear at the bottom of the lake when I first got here, so I was a fully armed merman machine! The boat sank just as she got back to the pier. Miss Merrybench decided to try for another exit. Syke yelled that she was heading for the front gate, but that's where you sent the zombies, and . . ." He paused.

"And what?" I asked.

"Well, the rest of this is sketchy, since none of us saw it. But it seems that Miss Merrybench bumped into the zombies, and apparently she wears too much perfume, because the zombies went crazy for her brain."

"Oh no."

"Oh yes." Pismo nodded and smiled. "The guards tried to pull them off, but there were too many of them. Miss Merrybench was quickly turned into Miss Missingbrain, if you know what I mean."

"Oh no."

"Oh yes."

"What about Dr. Critchlore?"

"They gave him the antidote to the Suggesterol. He's fine."

"Thank goodness."

"Except that now he's pining away for Miss Merrybench."

"What?"

"Yeah, Syke overheard him telling Vodum about her evil schemes. Apparently, he's smitten. 'A woman like that doesn't come around every day. If only I had known the depths of her scheming heart!'"

Cook came in next, shooing out the guys.

"You really scared me, sweetie," she said, giving me a hug. "Thank goodness you're okay."

"Thanks," I said. "And thanks for the cupcakes."

She sniffed and waved a hand at me, like it was nothing. "If anything ever happened to you . . ." She turned abruptly and sat in the chair.

"I love you too," I said. "But why didn't you tell me?" All these years she'd been assuring me that I would morph eventually—why lie?

She pulled her chair closer and grabbed my hand. "Do you remember when you were seven, how you used to follow the werewolves around?"

"Yes."

"You looked up to those werewolves, and that bothered Pierre. At one point, he couldn't take it anymore, so he told you that you're not a werewolf. You were depressed for days, wouldn't come out of your room, barely ate. I was so mad at Pierre. He was mad at himself too, so he tried to fix it."

"Fix it?"

"He made you think you morphed. He put a wood frame in place of your mirror and got a werewolf friend to stand behind it, mimicking every move you made. His friend Larry dressed up like a swamp creature. And you were drowsy; he'd woken you up at midnight. I'm not entirely sure he didn't slip you a suggestive potion of some kind. He denies it, but of course he would. The next day, you were elated. I was just so relieved to have you back to your normal happy self."

"Did he give me this medallion?" I asked, pulling it out from under my shirt. "Was that part of the plan?"

"No, honey," she said. "You were wearing that when we found you."

"I always thought it was from my werewolf family."

"Uncle Ludwig thinks it will help us find your real family. He made a copy of it and keeps it in the library. He's trying to decipher those symbols around the edge."

We sat in silence for a few seconds.

"You okay?" she asked.

I nodded. Then I shook my head. "Am I cursed?"

"What?" I'd expected Cook to be shocked, but instead, she looked angry. I'd seen her angry face enough to know the difference.

"Dr. Critchlore said you'd poison anyone who told that, quote, little cursed orphan boy he's not a werewolf, unquote."

"Runt," she said, squeezing my hand. "No more secrets." Then she sighed. "When you came to the school, Mistress Moira sensed a curse on you, yes. But we've been working on finding out who did it. I know if we find out who, and why, we'll be able to stop it."

"Stop the curse?" I said, and then I remembered Mistress Moira's list of curses at the school. "Am I cursed to bring bad luck to every-one around me?"

She didn't say anything, just looked at my face. My insides felt all hollow, because I knew which curse I was.

"I'm the timed-death curse, aren't I?"

Cook started crying.

"You never told me I'm not a werewolf because you knew I was going to die soon."

"No!" she said. "No. We're going to stop it. Uncle Ludwig's been researching. I know he's getting close. What do you think he's been working on all this time?"

I felt my eyes tear up. "How long do I have?"

"According to Uncle Ludwig, the standard for timed-death curses is the victim's thirtieth birthday. But there have been instances of twenty-five, twenty, even . . ."

"Even what?"

"Sixteen."

I had three or four years to live. Or, on the bright side, eighteen. "I don't even know how old I am."

"It's an old curse. Probably cast before you were even born. The witch could die before you reach the, er, deadline."

"Deadline," I repeated. How true.

# CHAPTER 39

*Without question, the most important beings on the planet are the dryads, without whom we would all perish, for without trees we would have no oxygen. Plus they're very beautiful. And intelligent.*

—DR. CRITCHLORE, TO REPORTERS FROM HIS
HOSPITAL BED AFTER SUFFERING MULTIPLE INJURIES
IN AN UNEXPECTED ACORN ATTACK

Darthin and I were released from the hospital to attend a special assembly. The auditorium was packed. Professors sat in the first two rows, students behind, and then the school's employees—the marketing department, the accounting department, maintenance crews, and others. Someone had saved us a couple of seats in the middle next to Dr. Frankenhammer . . . though maybe "saved" isn't the right word.

I noticed Syke over by the side, surrounded by tall, slim women with brown skin and hair tinted green. Hamadryads. They looked fierce as they glared at Dr. Critchlore.

On the stage, the members of the board of directors sat in a row of chairs. Dr. Critchlore sat on an elaborate throne in the middle. He was back, I could tell at a glance. He sat up straight, as if he had a spine of steel, with a determined look in his eye. To the side of the stage, Professor Vodum sat in the Chair of Shame, a small stool usually reserved for a student who had failed miserably in some way. The look on his face made me think he was about to say, "It's not *faaaiiir*."

"Why is Vodum up there?" I asked Dr. Frankenhammer.

"Dr. Critchlore was not pleased at how eagerly Vodum tried to take over while he was indisposed," he said, smiling. "Not pleased at all."

Dr. Critchlore rose and walked forward, his voice amplified by a wireless microphone. "Greetings, minions, school employees, my lovely ward, Syke, and your visiting relatives from the forest, who I wish were as forgiving as they are beautiful—"

"Why do the hamadryads hate him?" I asked Dr. Frankenhammer.

"He burned down a hamadryad-protected forest to make the boulderball field."

"The fire that killed Syke's mom?"

"Yes. He didn't know hamadryads were living there."

"I thought it burned down accidentally, and Dr. Critchlore saved Syke."

"He saved Syke from a fire he started," Dr. Frankenhammer said. "The hamadryads despise him, but Syke had no other place to go, so they made Critchlore keep her. You mustn't tell her." He put a finger to his lips.

Dr. Critchlore had killed Syke's parents? That couldn't be right. Still, maybe I wasn't the only one who didn't know the truth about my past.

". . . and esteemed members of our board of directors," Dr.

Critchlore said. "Greetings, all. I have called you here today to explain the unfortunate events that have taken place recently. Rest assured, the danger to the school is over. We can now continue with our mission to train the best minions in the world. Syke's relatives have expressed their displeasure at what they believe is a reckless method of child rearing, but I'm here to assure you all, no one was ever in any real danger."

I looked at Darthin—a bandage covered his head. Whenever I moved, something hurt. Yeah, I'd say there had been some danger.

"First, to explain what happened. As you all know, Dr. Pravus is determined to crush our school. He and I go way back, and he can't stand any successes I might have. I had thought I had prepared us for any kind of attack, but it is probably due to my humble nature that I didn't see the threat sitting right outside my office. How was I to suspect that someone would fall in love with me to such a degree that she would risk everything to have me? I should have known, of course. I'm very desirable.

"Fortunately, I was able to detect the signs that I had been poisoned with a variety of potions. I decided to play along, let Pravus think he was succeeding. The school was thrown into disrepair, customers fled, things seemed dire indeed. But rest assured, I had everything under control.

"I alerted Professor Vodum to evacuate the cemetery when I suspected that would be a target. Dr. Frankenhammer managed to place dummy minions in his lab before the carnivorous cockroaches attacked. The building was never in any danger from the explosive minions. I was keeping an eye on them over the top of my easel. All part of my ruse."

I blinked and shook my head. Clearly, none of that was true.

"I staged my little suicide attempt in order to clear the way for our saboteur to plant her bombs, intending to catch her in the act. The bombs were defused, except for the Column of On-Time Delivery, which I was planning to get rid of anyway, so no harm done. I've wanted to replace it for some time now. Maybe 'Diligence' or 'Dependable' or 'Dauntless.'"

"'Dingbat,'" Pismo whispered in my ear from behind. "Or 'Disposable.'"

"In addition," Dr. Critchlore continued, "my little ruse allowed us to stage some espionage of our own. Thinking we were crumbling under his attacks, Pravus sent his top spy here to steal our best scientist. Dr. Frankenhammer, on my direction, gave the man a sample of my latest idea, the Minion Saboteur—a minion that pops open in an enemy's lair and hatches a swarm of acid-spewing worms. An excellent job of following directions, Dr. Frankenhammer."

Dr. Frankenhammer remained ramrod-straight and didn't acknowledge the applause.

"Once again, I assure you all, the school is well and will soon be back on top. But I did want to mention some changes that we've implemented. Although I can't recall deciding on this, it appears I have ordered Jake to enhance our collection of creatures. This afternoon he is expecting a shipment of unicorn foals."

The girl minions went wild with happiness. "Baby unicorns!" they screeched. Dr. Critchlore looked surprised at the reaction, but then he smiled. "Well, that's all right, then."

I felt Syke glaring at me, and when I turned she mouthed, "You?"

and I nodded. She must have heard me whispering in Dr. Critchlore's ear when we'd gotten to the boat. She shook her head and rolled her eyes. I could hear her voice in my head, saying, *Higgins, you idiot*. I held out my hand in the "stop" position and mouthed, "Wait."

Dr. Critchlore went on. "And I'm happy to announce, with our honored guests sitting in attendance next to my beloved ward, Syke, that we are breaking ground on our forest expansion project. With input from both Syke and Tootles. And her relatives, if they wish to participate. Of course," he added, "if I do indeed become cursed with sudden oak death, as has been threatened, then the deal's off."

Syke smiled at me. "Thanks," she mouthed.

"Finally, I have selected the five students who will continue in our Junior Henchman Training Program, and I will announce them now: Rufus Spaniel, Janet Desmarais, Frieda Knockslammer, Jud Shepherd, and Runt Higgins."

I couldn't believe it.

Me? How? I'd been DQ'd from every test. I felt pats on my back, but I couldn't move. I was shocked.

What just happened?


A reception followed Dr. Critchlore's speech. Tables surrounded the fountain in the courtyard in front of the castle. I went over to my friends, who were standing in the buffet line. They smiled at me.

"How could I have passed the junior henchman test?" I asked.

"Well," Darthin said. "The first test was 'Save the Master,' which you did. The second test was 'Steal the Secret Formula,' and you saved the secret formula, by saving the *Top Secret Book of Minions*. And you'll never guess what the third test was."

"What?"

"'Defuse the Bomb,'" he said. "Which you did."

"No," I said. "You did."

"Under your direction," he said. "That's very henchman-y, don't you think?"

Maybe. I smiled.

Dr. Frankenhammer approached us and pulled me aside. "Congratulations, Mr. Higginssss."

"Thank you."

He pulled me away from my friends, toward the cypress trees that lined the road to the front gate. "You have learned an important henchman lesson, I think."

"What?"

"A henchman is rewarded handsomely for letting his boss take credit for his work. You and I both know that it was your quick thinking and decisive action that saved the school. And now you're a junior henchman. A position that suitsss you, I think."

"But he took credit for your work too."

"So he did." Dr. Frankenhammer stopped walking and pulled a thin whistle from his pocket. He blew into it, but I didn't hear anything. As he put on a pair of leather gloves, a sleek little red dragon swooped in and landed in front of us.

"Is that a new dragon?" I asked.

"Indeed. Like I said, a henchman is rewarded handsomely for letting his boss take credit for his work." He ran an appreciative

hand down the dragon's flank, smiling. "Come along, Frankie!" he yelled. "Let's go for a ride, son."

Frankie ran over, wearing a smile as wide as his creator's.

I knew I should be feeling bad, because I wasn't a werewolf and I was cursed, but I just couldn't help smiling at my incredible, big, happy family. Cook and Pierre were serving the buffet, Cook trying to heap more food on Uncle Ludwig's plate. Darthin, Eloni, and Boris were waving me over to join them in line. Tootles and Riga were happily talking to Syke's tree nymph relatives. Mistress Moira was passing out chocolates. I caught her eye, and she winked at me. The zombies swayed under the oak tree. I didn't have to hear them to know they were saying, "Higginsbrains." Pismo, standing with the skeletons, nodded at me with a smile, and I nodded back. He was going to be a good friend, I just knew it.

And standing on the top of the steps, overseeing everything with his steely gaze, was Dr. Critchlore. My school was safe again; everything was back to normal.

Dr. Critchlore seemed to be squinting at something behind me, so I turned around. Someone was walking up the gravel road toward the castle, dragging a heavily loaded red wagon.

"Is that a Girl Explorer?" I asked Dr. Frankenhammer.

# ACKNOWLEDGMENTS

Writing a book is a long journey, one I would never have completed alone. So many people helped make this book a reality. I'd like to thank my agent, Molly Ker Hawn, who is tireless and brilliant and funny, and my editor, Maggie Lehrman, whose wisdom and insight worked magic on the pages. And thanks to Erica Finkel, for taking over and guiding this book to completion.

I'm truly blessed that Joe Sutphin's beautiful illustrations grace the pages of this book, and that Chad W. Beckerman and Jessie Gang designed such a gorgeous layout. I appreciate all the work done by Jason Wells, Morgan Dubin, Jim Armstrong, Richard Slovak, Rob Sternitzky, and everyone else at Abrams. Thank you so much for your hard work. And thanks to Susan Van Metre and Michael Jacobs for making a dream come true.

I'm so grateful to my writing buddies—most of all to Ashley Shouse, whose writing prompt kicked-off this story. A huge thanks to my most devoted writing partner, my brother, Gordon Jack. Thanks to my critique partners Joy McCullough-Carranza, Ki-Wing Merlin, and Sage Collins, and to the many online critiquers who commented on the early parts. Thanks to Brooks Sherman for his insightful feedback, and to Allison Hunter Hill for her early enthusiasm and input.

And, finally, thanks to my family. To my husband, Juan, without whose unwavering support I never would have started writing. To my kids, Rachel, Ricky, Alex, and Daniel—thank you for inspiring me every day. Thanks to my parents, Joan and Bob Jack, and my siblings, Lisa Jack and Gordy Jack, for filling my childhood with laughter and adventure. Thank you, thank you, thank you, everyone.

Sheila Grau grew up in an old house that had a secret closet nestled behind the bookshelves in the library. She was able to tuck herself into that little nook to ponder life's mysteries, like how her mother knew she was dropping her broccoli to the dog at dinnertime. (Answer: The dog didn't like broccoli, either, and spit it out on the floor.) Through the years, one mystery in particular seemed to have no answer: Where do evil overlords get their minions? Unable to find an answer, she thought it would be fun to make one up. *Dr. Critchlore's School for Minions* is her first book.

Sheila currently lives in Northern California with her husband and four children and, sadly, no minions.